crafted story that will leave the reader longing to dig into the next Nightcreature book as soon as possible."

—*Night Owl Romance Reviews*

"Handeland is at the top of her game in this taut thriller. Part detective tale, part supernatural chiller, this is a full-on exciting read." —*Romantic Times BOOKreviews*

"Provocative, intense, and rife with creepy beings. The romance is sultry, solid, and very intense."

—*Romance Junkies*

"Handeland has a gift for creating and sustaining a mood throughout her stories that keeps the reader eagerly turning the pages." —*Fresh Fiction*

RISING MOON

"Eerie atmospherics and dark passion intertwine, making this a truly gripping and suspenseful read."

—*Romantic Times BOOKreviews*

"What makes the latest in her Nightcreature series stand out is how Handeland paints such a vivid portrait of the Big Easy and its inhabitants. The city itself is a character, not unlike its real-life counterpart . . . her gift to skillfully repel and attract commands the reader's attention to the very end and will lure genre readers enamored of paranormal romance or mysteries." —*Booklist*

"Phenomenal...the story, characters and dialogue, and descriptive setting are perfect."

—*Romance Reader at Heart*

"Keeps you guessing until the very end…I was awed."
—*Fallen Angel Reviews*

"A great plot, wonderful characters and a setting to die for. You gotta pick this one up."
—*Fresh Fiction*

"Mmm…mmm…mmm! Get ready for the ride of your life…an intriguing eye-opener…Twists and turns, secrets and shadows, captivating characters, a well-written, well-developed plot, and a romance."
—*Romance Reviews Today*

"*Rising Moon* is suspenseful, passionate, and edgy, but it's also a true feel-good read with a message of hope and redemption."
—*Eternal Night Reviews*

CRESCENT MOON

"Strong heroines are a hallmark of Handeland's enormously popular werewolf series, and Diana is no exception. *Crescent Moon* delivers plenty of creepy danger and sensual thrills, which makes it a most satisfying treat."
—*Romantic Times BOOKreviews*

"Handeland knows how to keep her novels fresh and scary, while keeping the heroes some of the best… pretty much perfect."
—*Romance Reader at Heart*

"An enchanting and romantic love story…compelling characters and a gripping plot…This captivating tale is wrought with mystery, mayhem, and an electrifying passion hot enough to singe your fingers."
—*Romance Junkies*

"Enticing, provocative, and danger-filled."

"Will appeal to readers on the most primal level. It effectively centers on the dark side of life, the forbidden temptations." —*Curled Up With a Good Book*

DARK MOON

"A riveting continuation to Handeland's werewolf series...Handeland displays a talent for creating characters that are original and identifiable to the reader... her styling and creativity ensure that *Dark Moon*, though third in the series, can be read as a stand-alone work...Handeland has once again delivered a remarkable werewolf tale that is a superb addition to the genre. Fans of this genre won't want to miss out on this paranormal treat." —*Fallen Angel*

"The end is a surprising, yet satisfying, conclusion to this series...another terrific story." —*Fresh Fiction*

"The characters are intriguing and the romance is sexy and fun while at times heart-wrenching. The action is well written and thrilling especially at the end...*Dark Moon* is another powerful tale with a strong heroine who is sure to please readers and a hero who is worth fighting for. Handeland has proven with this trilogy that she has a bright future in the paranormal genre." —*Romance Readers Connection*

"Elise is Handeland's most appealing heroine yet...this tense, banter-filled tale provides a few hours of solid entertainment." —*Publishers Weekly*

ST. MARTIN'S PAPERBACKS TITLES
BY LORI HANDELAND

THE NIGHTCREATURE NOVELS

Blue Moon

Hunter's Moon

Dark Moon

Crescent Moon

Midnight Moon

Rising Moon

Hidden Moon

Thunder Moon

Marked by the Moon

THE PHOENIX CHRONICLES

Any Given Doomsday

Doomsday Can Wait

Apocalypse Happens

Chaos Bites

ANTHOLOGIES

Stroke of Midnight

No Rest for the Witches

CRAVE
THE MOON

Lori Handeland

St. Martin's Paperbacks

This is a work of fiction. All of the characters, organizations, and events portrayed in this novel are either products of the author's imagination or are used fictitiously.

CRAVE THE MOON

Copyright © 2011 by Lori Handeland.

All rights reserved.

For information address St. Martin's Press, 175 Fifth Avenue, New York, NY 10010.

ISBN: 978-0-312-38936-9

Printed in the United States of America

St. Martin's Paperbacks edition / July 2011

St. Martin's Paperbacks are published by St. Martin's Press, 175 Fifth Avenue, New York, NY 10010.

10 9 8 7 6 5 4 3 2 1

ACKNOWLEDGMENTS

Thank you to Peggy Hendricks, whose wealth of information in many areas has been a constant help to me. This time, I appreciate her knowing the intricacies of loans, deeds, and foreclosures.

And a big thank you as well to Sharon Antoniewicz, my go-to girl on all things motorcycle.

Any mistakes are always my own.

In the first century, he lived for vengeance.
During the second, he hungered for blood.
By the third, he yearned for destruction.
But eventually . . .
All he craved was the moon.

CHAPTER 1

"You got another letter from moldy, old Dr. Mecate."

Gina O'Neil glanced up from grooming a horse to discover her best friend, Jase McCord, holding up a brilliantly white business-sized envelope. She knew exactly what business it contained. How could she not, considering the obstinate Dr. Mecate had sent her at least half a dozen others just like it?

It would behoove you to allow me to dig on your property.

What in hell was a behoove?

Proving my academic theory would increase the cachet of your establishment.

She had the same question about cachet.

I would be happy to advance remuneration.

Who *talked* like that?

"Helloo." Jase waved the envelope back and forth, his wide, high-cheekboned face softened by the chip in his front tooth that he'd gotten when he was bucked from a horse at the age of eight. His face, combined with his compact but well-honed body, made him look like a marauding Ute warrior, which was exactly what he would have been if born in a previous century. "What should I—?"

Gina snatched the envelope from his hand. "I'll take care of it." In the same way she'd taken care of all the others.

Direct deposit into the trash can.

Gina turned back to Lady Belle, and Jase, who was familiar with Gina's moods, left.

Nahua Springs Ranch was not only Gina's home but also her inheritance. Once one of the most respected quarter-horse ranches in Colorado, Nahua Springs had become, after the death of Gina's parents nearly ten years ago, one of far too many dude ranches in the area. Nevertheless, they'd done all right. Until recently.

Recently she'd begun to receive as many letters from bill collectors as she did from Dr. Mecate. Certainly his *remuneration* would be welcome, considering their financial difficulties. Unfortunately, what he wanted from her was something Gina couldn't give.

If she opened the letter she knew what she'd find. A request for her to let him search for Aztec ruins on her property.

She couldn't do that. What if he went there? What if he found . . . it?

Gina crossed to the open back doorway of the barn, drawing in a deep breath of spring air as she stared at the ebony roll of the distant mountains and the new grass tinged silver by the wisp of a moon.

Giiiiii-naaaa!

Sometimes the wind called her name. Sometimes the coyotes. Sometimes she even heard it in the howls of the wolves that were never, ever there.

The singsong trill haunted her, reminding her of all she had lost. She'd come to the conclusion that the call was her conscience, shouting out the last word her parents had ever uttered in an attempt to make sure she remembered, as if she could ever forget, that they had died because of her.

Everything had both started and ended in that cavern beneath the earth.

"Kids will be kids," she murmured, echoing her father's inevitable pronouncement whenever she and Jase had gotten into trouble.

Let them roam, Betsy. What good is having this place if she can't run free like we did?

Gina's parents had been childhood sweethearts. Boring, if you left out the star-crossed nature of their relationship—Betsy, the daughter of the ranch owner, and Pete, the son of the foreman. Everyone had considered them as close as brother and sister. When Betsy's father had found out they were closer, he'd threatened to send her to college on the East Coast, right after he used his bullwhip on Pete.

The reality of the coming grandchild had ended both the threat of a whipping and any hope of college. Not that Betsy had cared. She'd loved the ranch as much as Pete had, as much as Gina did now.

Gina and Jase *had* been kids that day, heading straight for the place Jase's granddad, Isaac, had warned them against.

At the end of Lonely Deer Trail the Tangwaci Cin-au'-ao sleeps. You must never, ever walk there.

According to Isaac, the Tangwaci Cin-au'-ao was an evil spirit of such power that whoever went anywhere near him died. Basically, he was the Ute Angel of Death, and he lived at their place. What fifteen-year-old could resist that?

Certainly not Gina.

She'd become obsessed with the end of Lonely Deer Trail. She'd crept closer and closer. She'd taken pictures of the flat plain that dropped into nowhere, yet a tree appeared to grow out of the sky. And when that sky filled with dawn or dusk the tree seemed to catch fire.

How could anyone not want to explore that?

Jase hadn't wanted to go, but she'd teased him unmercifully. In the end, he'd given in, as she'd known he would. To Jase's credit, he'd never once said, *I told you so.*

Not when the earth had crumpled beneath them.

Not when they'd tried to climb out and only succeeded in pulling an avalanche of summer-dried ground back in.

Not when they'd been buried alive, unable to move, barely able to breathe.

Not even when they'd both understood they would die there.

Because if Gina's sleep was disturbed by the ghostly, singsong trill, if on occasion the wind also called her name, if she felt every morning in that instant before she awoke the same thing she'd felt in that cavern—the stirring of something demonic, the reaching of its deformed hand in a mad game of Duck, Duck, Goose, pointing first at Gina, then at Jase, before settling its death claw on her parents, well . . .

That was probably *I told you so* enough.

Mateo Mecate stared at the hieroglyphics until they blurred in front of his overworked eyes. He might be one of the foremost scholars in Aztec studies, but the letters still sometimes read like gibberish. He shoved them aside, removing his glasses and rubbing a hand over his face.

According to the calendar, May meant spring. As usual, Tucson wasn't listening. The temperatures had been pushing ninety for a week.

The door to Matt's small, dusty, scalding office opened, and his boss, George Enright, stepped in. His gaze went to the papers on Matt's desk, and he frowned.

"Mateo." Enright's voice held so much disappointment, Matt expected him to cluck his tongue, then shake his head, or perhaps his finger, in admonishment. "This has to stop. I've put up with it thus far because of the respect I had for your mother. But the time has come to move on."

Enright was the head of the anthropology department at the University of Arizona, where Matt was a professor of archaeology—his specialty, like his mother's before him, the civilization of the Aztecs.

Nora Mecate had been a descendant of that great civilization. She'd been fascinated—some say obsessed—with proving a theory she'd gleaned from ancient writings passed down through her family for generations. She spent her life—no, she *gave* her life—trying to prove it.

"You could become the chair of this department when I retire. But you need to abandon your mother's ridiculous theory. You're becoming a laughingstock." Enright lowered his voice. "As she was."

Matt stiffened. Any academic who refused to face facts became an amusing anecdote at the staff water-cooler. Matt had noticed a lot of the graduate students staring and whispering lately.

Not that such behavior was anything new. For some reason the women around here liked to fashion him a

Hispanic Indiana Jones. He wasn't, but that didn't stop them from pointing and giggling and showing up during his office hours with foolish questions they already knew the answer to.

Matt wasn't interested. Not that he didn't occasionally date—if the willing women he took to dinner, then back to his bed, then never saw again could be considered dates—but his life was work, and he had little use for anything else.

"I have one more location on my mother's list of possibilities," Matt said.

Enright lifted his artificially darkened brows. Everything about Enright was artificial—his gelled, black toupee, his high-gloss manicure, even his right hip.

When Matt did not elaborate, Enright sighed. His breath smelled of the Jack Daniel's he kept filed under *W*.

"The semester is nearly done, Mateo. By fall, be ready to move on."

"Move on?" Matt echoed.

"Choose a different avenue for your research or choose another university." The door shut behind Enright with a decisive click.

Matt glanced at his mother's notes. As he shuffled them, searching for something he might have missed during the eight thousand other times he'd shuffled them, he could have sworn the scent of her—oranges, earth, and sunshine—lifted from the pages. Sometimes, when he touched them in the depths of the night, their whisper was her voice calling him in from childish explorations across every dig they'd ever shared.

He'd enjoyed a charmed childhood. What wasn't to love about living in a tent, searching for buried treasure, and never once—until he'd come here—stepping foot in a school?

Nora had been the only child of the very wealthy Mecate family. When she'd chosen to become an archaeologist more than a few inky black Mecate eyebrows had been raised. She didn't *need* to work for a living; she most definitely didn't need to dig in the dirt. That she wanted to had been beyond the comprehension of many, including her father.

However, only poor people were crazy. Rich people were eccentric, and the more eccentrics in a rich family the greater their prestige. The raised eyebrows had lowered before too long.

When Nora had turned up pregnant—not a boyfriend or a husband in sight—no one had bothered to exert their eyebrows at all. That Mateo would be a Mecate, and carry on that precious name, had gone a long way to bridging the gap between Nora and her father.

She'd dragged Matt with her all over Mexico and the Southwest. She'd taught him everything she knew about how to research and explore. Then she'd died on a dig the summer before he left for college.

"Hell," Matt muttered, tracing one finger over his mother's chicken scratch scrawl.

While still a young woman, Nora had translated the ancient Aztec writings she'd uncovered in the musty library of the family estate and discovered something amazing.

The reason the Aztecs never lost in battle was because they possessed a secret weapon, what Nora referred to as a superwarrior, a being of such incredible strength and power she believed him to be a sorcerer. That warrior had been buried somewhere in the American Southwest. All she had to do was find the tomb.

Scholars would have accepted her searching for remains north of the Rio Grande, even though most believed the Aztecs had not ventured farther than Central Mexico. But the tomb of a supernatural warrior? A sorcerer?

No one but Nora believed that.

Certainly when Matt was a child his mother's tales had captivated him. He'd accepted them completely. But as time went on, Matt's enthusiasm for a supernatural warrior waned.

However, Nora's research on the tomb itself was solid. There was something buried at an as-yet-undiscovered site north of the Rio Grande. Perhaps nothing more than a very large, freakishly strong, and more deadly than usual Aztec, but if Matt found that tomb and those remains, he could vindicate his mother's theory. Or at least those parts it was possible to vindicate. Then she would no longer be a laughingstock.

And neither would he.

His mother had translated a list of half a dozen possible sites from the hieroglyphics she'd found. They'd explored all of them—save one—and to date they'd found nothing but rocks.

Detractors pointed out that the Spanish had destroyed most, if not all, of the Aztec records—flat, accordion-like books known as codices, fashioned from deerskins or agave paper. Any texts that survived had been written under the strict supervision, and often with the help of, the Spanish clergy.

Therefore, the writings Nora Mecate had based her life's work upon—*Superwarrior? Sorcerer? Indeed!*— were nothing more than a hoax perpetrated by some laugh-a-minute priest in the fifteenth or sixteenth century.

"Because priests back then were known for being extremely 'ha-ha' kinds of guys," Matt muttered.

Matt had been studying the documents himself ever since Nora had died. He could find nothing wrong with her geographic translations. He had found no other viable sites.

Therefore, Matt had one last chance to prove her theory. If the final location yielded nothing new, he'd have little choice but to give up his mother's dream—which would be tantamount to admitting she was a crackpot—and move on. However, he'd encountered a problem with the remaining site.

Matt pulled a glossy three-fold brochure from the center drawer of his desk. The front panel revealed majestic mountains, four shots: spring, summer, winter, and fall—green, blue, gold, brown, white, purple, and orange abounded. Horses gamboled. He turned the brochure over to see if bunnies hopped and cattle roamed.

Instead, he found an artsy portrayal of a cowboy in silhouette, head tipped down, hat shading his face. However, the outline of the body was every ride-'em-cowboy-wannabe's dream.

Inside lay the propaganda—several gung-ho paragraphs superimposed over a sepia print of what Matt assumed was the main house, which, despite the "old-time" feel of the photograph had obviously been updated and well maintained. According to the text, gourmet food complemented an authentic western experience.

"Yee-haw," Matt murmured, rubbing the slick brochure between thumb and forefinger before removing another older, less slick, more crumpled paper from his desk.

He wasn't an expert on photography, but he was still fairly certain the person who'd taken the pictures for the brochure was the same person who had taken the image Matt had uncovered on the Internet about a year ago. The one that matched the final descriptive translation for the burial site of Nora Mecate's superwarrior.

Somewhere on this dude ranch lay his last chance to vindicate both his mother's and his own life's work. He'd had his assistant leave a dozen unanswered phone messages, followed by as many unanswered e-mails. Then Matt had taken over and begun to write letters, reiterating the request for permission to dig. He'd yet to receive a single response. It infuriated him.

Deep down he knew that his single-minded devotion to proving his mother's theory, or as much of it as *could* be proved, was based on guilt. He'd stopped believing in the superwarrior long ago. He'd started to wonder if his mother was the kook everyone thought her to be.

Grow up, Mom. I did.

Even now, Matt winced at the memory. She'd died still believing and he'd—

"Gone on," Matt murmured. He hadn't really known what else to do.

So, if Gina O' Neil, owner of Nahua Springs Ranch, thought her silence would make him go away . . .

Matt booted up his computer and clicked the tab for Expedia.com.

She'd soon find out how wrong she was.

CHAPTER 2

Jase had left to retrieve their guests from the La Plata County Airport. The group wasn't full again, and that worried Gina.

She moved through her room on the second floor of the ranch house, French-braiding her long, dark hair as she went. Sometimes Gina thought she should wear hers like Jase, who, despite his Native American roots, insisted on keeping his ebony locks Marine sergeant regulation length. Short hair would be a lot less trouble, especially on the overnight campouts that were part of every workweek.

She'd never be able to do it. One of Gina's fondest memories was of her mother brushing out the tangled strands before bed. Gina had the superstitious belief that if she cut her hair, and therefore stopped brushing it in just the same way every night, that memory of her mother would disappear as quickly as shorn locks in a winter wind.

The sounds of a car door opening, then closing, made Gina frown. Still a little early for Jase to be back.

Which could only mean trouble. Lately, anyone who arrived at Nahua Springs uninvited was.

She crossed to the window and glanced through, careful to stay out of sight as a man unfolded himself from the car. His back to her, the sun sprinkled mahogany highlights through dark brown hair, which spread across his broad shoulders like the tail fan of a pheasant.

Gina didn't recognize him, but judging from his well-worn jeans, faded white T-shirt, and lived-in boots he probably lived in the area. Most guests showed up in nearly the same attire, except everything was brand-new.

His forearms were taut and tanned; his biceps weren't bad, either. Gina's gaze slid up the long legs to another part that wasn't bad.

He turned and, startled, Gina straightened. That face belonged in a magazine, perhaps advertising the no-doubt expensive horn-rimmed glasses perched on his too-perfect nose.

Who was this guy?

As if he'd heard her question, or perhaps just seen her move, the man lifted his head. She couldn't distinguish the shade of his eyes from here, but considering his hair and skin, they were probably as dark as her own. He was exotic in a way she'd never encountered—the rugged body tamed by a face just short of pretty, the wildness of his hair tempered by those retro-geek glasses.

He started for the house, and Gina hurried to meet him, boot heels clattering down the staircase. The front door was open, allowing the spring breeze to blow in through the screen, allowing him to hear her steps, glance up, see her, and smile.

"Hello."

His voice was slightly rough, as if he'd spent the night in a bar that still allowed smoking, woken up after a bourbon bender, or called out someone's name in passion so long and so loudly he wound up hoarse.

Where had *that* thought come from?

"I wanted to discuss something with you. Could I come in?"

The contrast of that craggy voice with the overly polite words increased his exotic quotient by ten. He appeared Hispanic—at least part—so perhaps English wasn't his first language.

"I—uh—"

Hell. Since when did she get tongue-tied around men? She'd been raised by one, been raised with one, worked next to them, and worked for them. However, she'd never seen one quite like this.

Gina took a deep breath, which smelled oddly of oranges, and tried again: "Sure."

Opening the screen door, he stepped inside. He was a lot taller standing next to her than he'd looked from the upstairs window. For the first time in a long time Gina didn't experience the urge to slouch. She stood five ten in her stocking feet. Put on her boots and she was pushing six foot.

Here, in the land of itty-bitty women, Gina was a giantess. She didn't need anything else to make her feel like a freak. Being labeled an orphan had long been good enough.

Her gaze was caught by a single white envelope on the hall table. Dr. Mecate again.

She cursed beneath her breath, snatched up the letter, and tore it in half, then in half again. For good measure, she crumpled the parts into a teeny-tiny ball and tossed them into the trash.

The stranger cleared his throat. "Bad news?"

"Sorry." What had gotten into her to behave like that in front of a potential customer? Since he was still waiting for an explanation, she shrugged and told him the truth—or at least part of it. "Some professor . . ." Gina couldn't help it; her mouth twisted on the word. "Wants to dig up my land. Ain't happenin'. Not in this lifetime."

He blinked a few times. "Ah. I see."

"What can I do for you, Mr. . . . ?"

"I'm Teo." He held out his hand.

Gina took it, enjoying the scrape of his calluses against her own.

"I was—uh—" He looked around as if he could find what he wanted in her front hall.

"Were you interested in one of our packages?" Gina prompted.

Why else would he be here? Unless it was to try to collect on a bill.

"Sure," he blurted. "That's why I'm here."

"Our Trail and Spa package starts today. That's a three-day trail ride, followed by two days of spa services in the lodge and surrounding area; then we finish up with a slightly more difficult four-day trip. Does that sound like something you'd be interested in?"

"Definitely."

"Then if you'll just follow me to my office, Mr. Teo . . ." Gina realized they still held hands, but when she tried to retrieve hers he held on.

Confused, she lifted her gaze. His eyes weren't brown as she'd thought but hazel and, when surrounded by long, dark hair and a well-bronzed face, as striking as the face itself.

"Just Teo," he said, voice even rougher. "And you are?"

"Gina O'Neil." She pumped his hand once more, and this time when she pulled back he let her.

"The proprietor."

"Have we met?" Gina knew damn well they hadn't. Him she would remember.

"Your name was in here." He pulled their brochure from his back pocket. "Gina O'Neil, owner."

Gina was happy to see those brochures had been good for something. They'd cost a bundle she hadn't wanted to spend, but Jase had insisted self-promotion was the key to increasing their business. Maybe he was right.

"Let's get you registered, Mr.—" He cocked his head and his garnet-streaked hair slid over one sun-kissed cheek. "Teo," she corrected. "This way."

She led him down the hall toward her office at the back of the house. Since the last guests had left the day before and the newcomers hadn't yet arrived, the only scents drifting from the kitchen were those of coffee and toast. Most days the smell of eggs, bacon, pancakes, cinnamon rolls overlaid with the zest of salsa and the saccharine of syrup would draw everyone within sniffing distance to Fanny's domain.

Gina flicked the lights and sat at her desk. When she glanced up, Teo stood in the doorway seemingly trans-fixed by the photos on her wall. Most people didn't even notice them.

"I was going to ask who'd taken the pictures for your brochure. But I can see now it was . . ." His eyes met hers. "You?"

Gina shrugged. He was the first person who'd ever noticed that the pictures in the brochure had a similar style to the ones on her wall.

"You're very talented. Where did you study?"

"Study?" Gina laughed. "I picked up a camera, and I pointed it at stuff."

His eyebrows lifted, and he glanced at the photos once again. "Then you're even more talented than I thought."

She had to look down so he wouldn't see how much those words pleased her. She'd never told anyone, not even Jase, how much she loved photography. There was no point. She'd had the choice of selling this place and attending college or sucking it up and staying here.

So, in truth, she'd never really had any choice at all.

And that was all right. It wasn't like she couldn't still take pictures. She did so all the time. She'd just never be able to make a living at it.

Nahua Springs Ranch was her life. Unless, of course, she lost the place.

Gina cleared the uncommon thickness from her throat and reached for a registration form. "Fill this out, and we'll get you settled."

His fingers closed over the paper; he grabbed a pen. The chair creaked as he sat; then scratching noises followed as he complied. Outside, several car doors slammed.

Jase and the others were back.

Gina stood just as Teo signed his name to the bottom and held out the sheet to her.

She gave the document a cursory glance. Teo Jones. From some town in Arizona she'd never heard of—there were a lot of them. He was a teacher, which explained the glasses but not the body. Unless he was a phys-ed teacher, who perhaps coached track and basketball on the side and worked construction in the summer. She was more intrigued by the minute.

"Anything wrong?" he asked when she continued to stare at his registration.

"Uh, no." Her gaze flicked to the two most important items on the page. He could ride a horse. He'd been camping often. That was all she needed to know. "If I could just get your credit c—"

He dropped a handful of cash onto the desk. Gina's mouth hung open with the word *card* on the tip of her tongue.

"Cash is better, yes?"

Gina nodded. Who carried around that much money?

No one she'd ever met.

"About the pic—" he began.

"Gina!" Jase called from the front of the house. Usually she was waiting out front to greet the guests when they arrived.

"Coming!" she shouted, but his footsteps sounded in the hall an instant before he appeared at the door.

His gaze went from the pile of cash on the desk, to her startled face, to Teo Jones, who smiled his charming smile. It didn't work half as well on Jase as it had worked on Gina.

"Who the hell are you?" Jase demanded.

From the tone of his voice and the tension in his shoulders Jase had pegged Teo as a bill collector. Several of them *had* begun to demand cash up front.

"A walk-in," Gina said so brightly Jase's frown deepened. "Teo, meet Jase McCord, my partner."

Teo's welcoming smile faded a bit. Jase had never bothered with one in the first place. He wasn't much of a smiler, but then neither was Gina.

Still money was money and this was *cash*. Jase should

be clapping Teo on the back and claiming him as his new best friend. She wanted to.

The men stared at each other so long, Gina thought they might refuse to do the meet and greet altogether. If they'd been dogs, their ruffs would have been lifted along with their lips.

Gina cleared her throat, and Teo's hand shot out. "Pleased to meet you."

Jase blinked. Because the welcoming words did not match the level, challenging stare or because the drawing room vocabulary sounded so strange in that ruined Clint Eastwood voice?

Gina took a step forward. Why she had no idea. Did she plan to forcibly lift Jase's arm and *make* him shake Teo's hand?

At last Jase found his manners, placing his palm against Teo's and shaking once. From Teo's stifled wince, once had been enough.

Men.

"I'll just show Teo to his room," Gina began. "Then—"

"No." She glanced at Jase. He was still staring at Teo. "I'll show him the room." Jase jerked his chin toward the front of the house, where she could hear the others milling and murmuring. "You deal with them." He stalked into the hall.

Gina gave Teo an apologetic smile. "One of the new guests must be a . . ." She paused, not wanting to speak ill of one paying customer to another.

"Royal pain in the behind?" Teo finished, and Gina laughed.

"Yeah. Those Jase leaves to me."

"Hey, *buddy*!" Jase shouted from the hall.

What was *up* with him?

"I'd better go."

"Once everyone's settled," Gina said, "we'll meet at the barn and get you a horse that suits your riding ability."

Teo lowered his head, a mini-bow. "I'll look forward to it."

Gina watched him leave—she couldn't help it; the view was incredible. Still, there was something about the guy that made her twitchy.

She just wished she knew what it was.

Matt hadn't planned to give a false name and join the party. But the instant Gina had torn up his latest letter, then tightened her mouth and narrowed her eyes as she explained why, he'd known that she would throw him off the place as quickly as she'd destroyed not only that letter but also every one he'd sent before.

Luckily, he'd dressed and packed for the trail, as he'd naively believed he could explain what he wanted and Ms. O'Neil would take him to it.

Matt gave a mental eye roll as he left her office. Sometimes he was as clueless about human behavior as any absentminded professor.

He was also thankful that the need to grease local wheels, hire day laborers who weren't exactly legal, and buy things at places where only cash would suffice had ascertained he had enough money to pay for the package. He couldn't very well offer a credit card with his real name emblazoned on the front.

Matt found McCord at the bottom of the polished wood staircase, fingernails tapping on the newel post, boots scratching against the floor as he shifted his feet. The guy reminded Matt of several of his students.

After they'd gone off Ritalin.

He tried again to smile. Again, he earned a scowl

before the man stomped up the steps with a muttered: "Come on."

If this was how they ran their business, Matt was surprised they had *any* customers.

He cast a longing glance toward the office. He would have liked to study those photographs further and ask Gina about them. Though none of the images matched the one in his bag, the similar style made him even more certain that the place depicted in it was located here and Gina knew exactly where.

Matt's gaze was drawn to the screen door, through which half a dozen men and women were visible, hanging around his rental car, seemingly lost. Then a door slammed at the back of the house and Gina appeared.

She strode toward the newcomers, long legs encased in worn, loose jeans. Matt had never considered that loose jeans could be so enticing. Most of the women at the university wore jeans so tight he wasn't sure how they ever got them off. Or on.

But Gina's made him wonder things the others never had. Like the shape of her thighs as the wind blew the soft denim against them—there and then gone and then there again, a mere hint, just enough to arouse. And the tail of her flannel shirt—cinnamon, chocolate, and lime-green stripes—which barely reached the curve of her rear, fluttering in that wind, drawing his gaze and holding it there.

She greeted the others, the warmth of welcome in her voice. Everyone in the yard straightened and smiled, unconsciously leaning toward her like flowers long denied the sun. It appeared he wasn't the only one captivated.

Turning, Gina gestured at the house, and the movement of her arm drew that well-washed shirt taut against her breasts. They were very nice breasts. He wanted to—

"Buddy!"

Matt yanked his gaze from Gina. Unfortunately, his mind stayed right where it was, imagining the taste of those breasts, the weight of them in his palms, the sensation of them dragging across his chest, nipples hard and full.

How strange. As an adult, his imagination had been nil. He had little room for fantasy in a life devoted to pursuing facts. However, considering what had just meandered through his mind, and how alive it had made him feel, maybe he'd been wrong.

"You gonna eye-fuck her all day?"

Matt jolted at the vulgarity. Not that he hadn't heard similar words on every dig; he'd just never gotten used to them. When you spent your life immersed in a language composed of beautiful pictures, sometimes you lost track of the vocal crudities. But there was always someone there to remind you.

McCord stood at the top of the steps, and Matt started up, head down so the other man couldn't see the telltale flush in his cheeks. Because he had been doing exactly what Jase accused him of, and he would not be doing so again.

Matt would discover as much as he could about the ranch and surrounding area. If Nahua Springs contained the final location pinpointed in his mother's research— and with every minute he became more certain that it did—he needed to discover that location, then find a way to convince Gina to let him dig there.

He'd have to tread carefully. She was touchy about

her land. No reason to arouse her suspicions and get himself thrown off the place before he knew for certain that he was right.

If Nahua Springs Ranch was merely another misstep in a long line of them, why tell Gina the truth at all? He'd just go on the trip, then quietly fade away.

Before Matt reached the landing, McCord spun about and disappeared into the nearest room. A quick glance revealed that there were similar doors extending down both sides of the hallway.

Matt stepped inside. A large four-poster bed sat to the left, a matching oak dresser to the right. But what dominated the room was the wall of windows opposite the door. From it Matt could observe the entire valley.

"Exquisite," he murmured, and McCord blew a quick burst of air, somehow both amused and derisive, between his lips.

Matt started to ask what was so damn funny but didn't bother. He never understood jokes, wasn't up on current lingo. He'd spent his formative years with his mother and her colleagues. He'd never had playmates, not even imaginary ones. By the time he went off to college, people his own age . . . Well, they only confused him.

"Gina said you were her partner," Matt ventured.

McCord's dark brows lifted. "So?"

"The brochure lists her as the owner of the ranch."

"She is."

"Then your partnership is—"

"Physical," McCord interrupted. "Which is why you need to keep your eyes, and your hands, and any other part of you that might want to glom onto her off."

"Glom," Matt repeated. He wished he'd taken more linguistics. However, modern language patterns would be of no use to him while attempting to translate ancient Aztec.

McCord stepped close, crowding into Matt's personal space. The man had to lift his chin to meet Matt's eyes, since he was several inches shorter, but he did so with a challenge any alpha animal would recognize. Matt had never considered himself an alpha—he'd had his ass kicked as a kid too often by every bullying local in every town he and his mom had ever visited—nevertheless, he had to suppress an urge to bump chests and snarl.

"Touch her," McCord murmured, "and I will end you."

CHAPTER 3

Gina couldn't figure out which of their guests was the one who had sent Jase over the edge. They all seemed normal enough to her. Or as normal as most of the guests got.

If working with the public for over half her life had taught Gina one thing it was this: People were weird. Every day, in some small or large way, her theory was proved right.

For instance—the Hurlaheys, Mel and Melda, were nearly as interchangeable as their names. Short, round, with curly white hair that framed their always-flushed faces, they resembled a mini Mr. and Mrs. Claus. Gina would have thought they'd skipped the North Pole—leaving the elves, the reindeer, and Mr. Claus's beard behind—if the Hurlaheys hadn't cursed like rap singers and finished each other's sentences as if they were literally of one mind.

"We've always wanted to come here," Mel said. "Ride a goddamn—!"

"Horse," finished Melda. "Damn straight. Go west, young—"

"Dude. Shi-i-i-it," Mel said, then smiled with such beatific sweetness Gina was left thinking she couldn't have heard what she had.

Since neither Mel nor Melda had ever ridden a horse, Gina assigned them the oldest, gentlest beasts in her stable. She apologized mentally to Lily and Viola. Although Gina doubted the mares would be disturbed by cussing as long as the words were uttered in the same matter-of-fact tone as all the others. Since this appeared to be Mel and Melda's MO, Gina merely patted the mares on their noses and moved on.

Tim Gordon, newly divorced anesthesiologist, had brought his fourteen-year-old son to Colorado from Cleveland for a little bonding time. Unfortunately, all Derek cared about were his video games and that he'd had to leave them at home.

"The new Halo is coming out this week," the kid whined.

"It'll still be there next week," his father said with the absent tone of one who'd already said the same thing two dozen times before.

"By then everyone will have beaten it but me."

"Whatever," Tim muttered, earning a glare from his son.

Gina glanced at Derek's registration form. The kid had listed a fairly wide range of outdoor activities.

"Says here you're good with a bow and arrow, as well as a rifle. And . . ." What was that scrawl? "Swords?" He must mean fencing. Derek shrugged. "Great!"

His shoulders straightened at her praise, and Tim cast Gina a grateful glance. Poor guy. It couldn't be easy to share the kid with his mom. Gina had had plenty of divorced parents who brought their children here for some quality time together. The trip often got off to a rocky start, but once pulled away from cell-phone towers, cable TV, and video games both kids and their parents began to interact—usually for the better.

Gina eyed Derek, sizing him up for the perfect mount. The boy was too skinny, which went against everything she'd read about his generation—allergic to exercise, with a junk-food addiction. Sure, he could use some sun on his pasty white face, but that's why he was here.

"You've ridden before." She glanced at the paper again. "A lot."

"I kicked Red Dead Redemption. And I rule Assassin's Creed."

Gina paused. Was the kid speaking in tongues?

"I . . . uh . . ." She glanced at Tim. "Huh?"

"Games." Derek's dad rubbed his eyes. "Those are video games with horses."

Derek wandered off to stand at the fence, watching Mel and Melda ride Lily and Viola sedately around the paddock.

"He's never ridden?" Gina asked.

"An actual horse? No."

"And the archery, the rifle?"

"Turok and . . ." Tim's face creased. "SOCOM."

"I'm gonna go out on a limb here and guess that his experience with a sword wasn't in fencing club."

"Gods of War."

Now Gina rubbed her eyes. "I don't think our program is the best idea for your son." Gina glanced at Mel and Melda, wishing she could take at least one of those horses back, though even a gentle mare might not be gentle enough for a kid who'd ridden nothing but a couch his entire life. "He could get hurt."

Tim's gaze went to Derek. The boy still stood at the paddock fence, although he appeared to be either texting or playing a game on his phone instead of watching the live action, which, considering that action was old folks on old horses, Gina kind of understood.

"I just wanted him to do *something* outside this summer."

"But—" Gina pointed at the form. "He plays soccer."

"FIFA."

"I don't know what that means."

"The International Federation of Association Football."

Gina went over the acronym in her head. "That doesn't match."

"In French it does."

French. Right. Sometimes Gina felt as if the whole world had moved on while she'd remained right here, frozen in a long-lost decade.

"So all the things he's said he can do," Gina tapped a fingernail against the sheet, "he's only done them on a video game?"

"Why do you think we're here?"

Gina was beginning to understand the source of Jase's crankiness. She was even grinding her teeth.

Tim saw the movement and panicked. "Don't kick us out. I'll pay extra. Twice as much."

Gina couldn't charge the guy more, even if taking his kid into the mountains was probably going to be one of the dumbest things she'd ever done.

Tim interpreted her hesitation as denial and blurted, "Three times."

"That's okay," she began at the same time Jase said, "Will that be cash or charge?"

"We can't take his money," Gina insisted later that day and for the umpteenth time.

Jase, who was watching the guests groom their horses as he'd taught them, ignored her. He'd already taken it, and, as he'd informed her, she couldn't make him give it back. They needed the money too damn bad.

"If you want to send someone packing," Jase murmured, "get rid of that guy." He pointed at Teo.

"He's the only one who knows what he's doing!" Gina threw up her hands in exasperation.

"Shh." Jase put a finger to his lips.

Gina glanced at the guests, but they were occupied with their horses and didn't appear to have heard. Except for Teo. His gaze met hers, and Gina's stomach did a little shimmy. Must have been the Southwest burritos they'd had for lunch.

"No one knows what they're doing," Jase said. "Or at least not completely. That's why they call it a dude ranch. You do know the meaning of *dude,* don't you?"

"If you listen to Mel and Melda, it's a generic term for anything from a squirrel to your mother."

Jase laughed. "Did you see her face when Melda asked if she could have 'more of this ass-whompingly fine corn bread, dude?'"

Fanny's expression *had* been priceless.

Jase's gaze returned to Teo and his laughter died. "There's something about that guy I do not like."

Jase often got it into his head to dislike people. He said his Native American blood gave him a sixth sense. She thought his Native American blood gave her a pain in the ass.

But she now understood the true source of his earlier behavior. He'd taken an instant dislike to Teo. Which was too bad. She thought the two of them might have become friends. They were of an age—or close enough—and

Teo knew his way around horses. One of Jase's favorite subjects.

Laughter erupted, the sound scraping along Gina's eardrums like the cry of a dying rabbit in the depths of the night, so shrill and disturbing it caused one of the horses to skitter. Jase muttered a word he must have learned earlier that day from the Hurlaheys and aimed his seemingly eternal scowl at the final two members on their guest list.

Amberleigh, or perhaps it was Amber Lee, Gina couldn't recall, and her BFF, Ashleigh, or maybe that was Ash Lee, had asked for and been given this trip by their obviously doting parents. Or perhaps it was by their nearly deaf parents who wanted to save their last sliver of hearing by sending the girls anywhere but home. If Gina got through the next few days without a horse stampede, it would be a miracle.

"At least no wild animals are going to sneak up on you," Jase murmured.

They'd be lucky if they saw a spider with those two along. They'd never get a glimpse of a deer or a bighorn sheep or an antelope.

The girls, who attended the University of Texas in Austin, would graduate—or so they said—next spring. This was their last trip together before they got jobs or, as Gina suspected was their true mission, husbands. Why they'd picked a dude ranch for this quest was anyone's guess, although they did seem to know how to ride.

"We've been riding since we were itty-bitty," Ashleigh had told Jase that afternoon when he'd attempted, at their insistence, even though it wasn't his job, to help find them mounts. "You put a saddle on any old thang, and we'll ride it all day."

That statement had apparently caused Jase to swallow his tongue, because he'd started choking so badly he'd left the barn, abandoning the girls to Gina's ministrations until supper time. They hadn't been amused.

From what Gina could tell, the two could only relate to men and each other. Every other woman in their universe was either a nuisance or competition. Gina had learned quickly which group she belonged to when, earlier, Ashleigh flicked a dismissing hand in Gina's face, then, at Gina's blank stare, snapped, "Move!"

As soon as Gina did, the girls had begun to preen and posture like wild turkeys in mating season. When she'd glanced over her shoulder, she'd seen why.

The girls had decided what they really, really wanted to ride was Teo. He hadn't had a moment's peace since. Right now they were talking at him as if he were hanging on their every word instead of focusing all his attention on grooming an already well-groomed horse.

"They call us the As," Amberleigh said.

"Because of our *names,*" Ashleigh confided.

"Not 'cause of our grades."

"No shit," Jase muttered.

Gina cast him a quelling glance. He widened his eyes and lifted his shoulders. "What?"

"They'll hear you," she whispered.

Jase snorted. "They aren't going to hear anyone but themselves, which I think is just how they like it."

Gina didn't comment, since she had to agree.

"I'd almost feel sorry for pretty boy there, if he wasn't going to get his pole shined so sparkly he goes blind from the glare."

"You could have had *your* pole shined if you'd played your cards better," Gina said.

Jase, who'd been grinning in Teo's direction, stopped. "Why would I want to do that?"

Gina considered the As, whose artificially blond curls bobbed above equally artificial breasts. "Why wouldn't you?"

"Disease, loss of self-respect." One of the girls laughed again, and he winced. "Hearing damage. Hell, I'd probably shed IQ points just from listening to them breathe."

"That's harsh," Gina said.

"Truth hurts. Besides, what happened to the 'no bopping the customers' rule?" Jase's gaze narrowed on Teo. "Find someone you want to break it with?"

"We were talking about you."

"Were we?"

Gina sighed. Jase could be so damn . . . Jase sometimes. And while his supposed Ute sixth sense was mostly BS, he did have a sense about Gina that was often dead-on.

Gina contemplated Teo. Did she want to break the rules with him?

Oh yeah.

Was she going to?

Hell no.

Still, he *was* nice to look at.

The As couldn't keep their eyes, or their hands, off him. However, Teo kept his gaze on his horse; he didn't speak. Gina had to give the As points for being able to hold a conversation without any response, although they were probably used to it.

When confronted with hot women who were obviously interested most men would at least flirt back, even if they had no intention of following through. From what she'd observed, flirting was a game—promise but don't deliver; tease; entice; deny.

Gina wasn't any good at flirting. She'd been raised

with horses and horsemen. The latter said what they meant and meant what they said. The former had no guile whatsoever. A horse either loved you or hated you, and you knew which pretty damn fast. She liked that about horses.

Teo appeared to have the same issues she did with flirting. She liked that about him, too.

"One of us should probably rescue him," Gina said. "If he brushes Spike much longer, that horse is gonna go bald."

Spike was their most challenging mount—a roan gelding that stood sixteen hands and liked to snatch the bit in his teeth if his rider wasn't paying attention, then do whatever the hell he pleased.

Gina usually rode Spike, because no one else should. But when she'd finished finding horses for Derek and his father, she'd discovered Teo in the paddock getting acquainted with the roan as Jase watched with a smirk.

The smirk disappeared pretty fast as it became evident that Teo could handle the often-troublesome horse with ease. And, as was the way with Spike, when he had a rider who took no crap he fell forever in love.

Gina watched as the big red head bumped Teo's shoulder and Teo rubbed a palm down the horse's nose. One of the girls reached out to do the same, and Spike sneezed all over her acid-washed, skintight jeans.

"Doesn't seem like he needs our help," Jase observed.

Ashleigh—or maybe Amberleigh; it was going to be a bitch to keep them straight—stared at the mess for at least ten seconds, then started to shriek.

Jase hustled across the barn, grabbing the girl's arm and dragging her out the door. The other A followed, clucking like an irate hen and waving her arms helplessly.

Spike neighed, lifting his head, stomping his feet. Gina could have sworn the horse was laughing.

If Matt had realized all it would take to get rid of those girls was a sneeze he'd have faked a bad case of allergies an hour ago.

He rubbed his hand over Spike's nose again. "Thanks, pal," he murmured, and got bumped once more by the heavy, bony head.

"How'd you get him to do that?"

Matt glanced up so fast he nearly clocked Spike, who was hovering over him like a lovesick puppy, under the chin. The horse stamped once, narrowly missing Matt's toe, then reached out and butted Gina with similar affection.

"And here I thought I was your one and only," Matt said.

Gina scratched between Spike's eyes. "Until you showed up, *I* was his one and only. Spike's . . . difficult."

Matt was surprised. The horse seemed fine to him. He'd ridden worse.

"Jase shouldn't have given him to you."

"You can have him back," Matt said, although the thought of riding a different one bummed him out. Right now it seemed as if it were Spike and Matt against the world—or at least the As.

"No, that's fine," Gina said. "You've obviously bonded."

As if to illustrate, Spike nibbled on Matt's T-shirt, leaving a large, wet, grayish splotch at the shoulder. "Lucky me."

"So how did you get him to do it?" she repeated.

"Do what?"

"Sneeze all over Ashleigh. Or was that Amberleigh?"

"Who cares-leigh," Matt muttered. "It was his idea. I think they were hurting his ears. They were certainly hurting mine."

"You're gonna have to keep a tight rein on Spike."

The horse swung his head in Gina's direction when she said his name, and she slipped him something out of her pocket, which he began to crunch and dribble onto Matt's boots. From the shade, he guessed carrot.

"He tried to grab the bit on me earlier. But I'm wise to that."

Gina's eyebrows lifted. "You've ridden horses like Spike before?"

"One or two."

There'd been that Arabian he'd fought with across the Egyptian desert when he'd been working on his master's. He should have ridden a camel, but he really hated camels. They spit and they bit and they smelled.

The Arabian had thought it hysterical to pretend he didn't like sand. Every morning he would pick up his hooves and shake them like a cat walking through standing water. He did this for a good forty minutes, which, if done when it was time for the group to leave, meant that either everyone stared at them, sneering, or Matt got left behind with a rifle-wielding, also-sneering babysitter. Matt had learned it was best to get up early and let the horse have his fun; then he would be fine for the rest of the day.

In Belize Matt had been saddled with a donkey that liked to buck without warning, especially when traversing narrow paths along the edges of cliffs. However, when Matt refused to react—he never dismounted, he didn't cry out, except for the first time, when he'd shrieked like a little girl—the donkey stopped misbehaving. By the time the archaeologists had reached the ruins they'd hoped were Aztec but had instead been Mayan, Matt and the donkey were the best of friends. When Matt had left, the poor beast had brayed until Matt was out of hearing range.

"Teo?" Gina's voice made him realize he'd gone off in his head for longer than was normal. He did that.

Colleagues at the university were used to those little mind trips. Professors were thinkers, and thinking went on in your head. In Matt's usual circles, he wasn't the only one who became silent and still in the middle of a conversation. It was only when he ventured into the world that such behavior was considered odd.

"Yeah." He rubbed his face. "Tired, I guess."

Gina held out her hand, and Matt nearly put his into it before he realized she wanted the grooming brush. "Better get to bed. We're leaving early tomorrow."

"How early?"

"As soon as the sun's up. Breakfast at six. That a problem for you?"

Matt shook his head. Years of living in a tent had made him a perennially early riser. When the sun shone through the canvas, you got up. When the sun went down, you went to bed. In truth, he much preferred the pace of his life on a dig to the artificiality of his life everywhere else.

"If I were you," Gina led Spike toward his stall, "I'd check the bed and the closet for the As before I undressed."

Matt had been confronted with aggressive students before, but the *Dr.* in front of his name, if not his capacity to get them kicked out of school if they didn't behave, intimidated most of them. Here he had no such protection.

Matt gulped.

"Don't look so scared," Gina said, amusement lightening her voice. "You're a big boy. I think you can take them."

"Why on earth are they here?" he wondered. "There isn't going to be a mirror or a martini for miles."

Gina came out of Spike's stall, closing the door behind her. "We get all kinds at Nahua Springs."

"Yeah, but what kind are *they*?" Matt muttered.

Gina laughed, and Matt realized he was flirting with her. Usually, when girls batted their eyes or the equivalent, he tossed around big words until they went away.

He had no desire to do the same with Gina. Not only because he was supposed to be Teo Jones, schoolteacher from Arizona, but also because he didn't want her to go away. Not yet.

Talking with Gina was easy, natural, honest. Which was amazing considering everything he'd told her so far had been a lie. But as he'd lied so he could discover things, he'd best make use of this time with her to discover them.

"Nahua Springs," he murmured. "Where'd that name come from?"

The name was how he'd come across the Internet photo in the first place. He'd been plugging words that related to the Aztecs into Google Earth, working on the theory that if they'd marched into the American Southwest for any length of time there might be a place or two labeled with those words.

Bing! Nahua Springs had come up on that search and subsequent surfing had brought him to the photograph.

Spike stuck his head over the half door of his stall

and blew air between his lips. Gina set her hand on his neck and stroked absently. "There's a spring that runs through the ranch. The Ute always called it the river of the Nahua."

Matt's neck prickled, but he managed, he hoped, not to show how her words excited him. Where there was smoke, or Aztec words, there was most likely fire—or a really informative local legend.

"What's a Nahua?" he asked.

"Catchall for the ancient peoples south of the border."

"Like the Mayans and stuff?" Matt tried to sound clueless—he wanted to hear the story she knew, not influence her tale with what he did—and he must have succeeded, because her brow scrunched and she looked him up and down.

"You don't teach history, do you?"

"I . . . uh . . ." Matt didn't want to lie any more than he already had. Thankfully, Gina saved him the trouble.

"Let me guess. Phys ed?"

He shrugged, which she took as a *yes*.

"Technically, *Nahua* refers to any group that speaks Nahuatl," Gina continued, "or the language of the Aztecs."

Matt got that chill again. Sure, Gina was telling him things he already knew, but that she knew them, too, was kind of . . . hot.

"There were Aztecs here?" he asked.

"Doubtful. Like I said, *Nahua* is a catchall, and *Nahuatl* translates to *clear* or *understandable*. Isaac— Jase's granddad—says any outsider who could be understood by the Ute was called Nahua."

Matt could barely keep still at that tidbit. How would the Ute know the meaning of the word *Nahua* unless they'd encountered one? Certainly the Ute language, sometimes called Paiute, belonged to the Uto-Aztecan group of languages and was similar to Nahuatl, but—

"Isaac thinks the spring got its name because a Ute warrior came across an intruder there and they were able to communicate. Of course, considering the Ute, that intruder was probably skewered and left to bleed out in the water." Gina's lips quirked. "The Ute were never very good at sharing."

Matt stepped closer, running his hand over Spike's neck on the other side. The horse practically purred.

"Interesting," Matt said, and his fingers brushed hers. The jolt made him stare at their still-touching fingertips, expecting a spark of static electricity to flare between them and freak out the horse.

Instead, Matt and Gina's eyes met. In hers he could see the reflection of what must be in his. Surprise, nerves, wonder.

A strand of hair had sprung free of the braid and trailed down the side of her face, stirring just a bit in the breeze. He caught the scent of trees above the scent of the hay, and he couldn't determine if the aroma rose from her skin, her clothes, or actual trees.

Her lips, those eyes, that hair, and the sharp green scent of her seduced. They were alone in the barn. No one here but them and the horses, and they'd never tell.

Matt began to lean forward; so did she. Somehow their fingers had tangled together up to the joints, and he was running his thumb along the back of her hand, enticed by the smoothness of her skin against his own world-roughened flesh.

Would she taste like water in a snowstorm or perhaps fire beneath the sun? Things he didn't necessarily need but would always, always want.

Suddenly Spike threw up his head and the two of

them jerked back as his mane flapped in their faces. How could Matt have forgotten that they were separated by a great, big, snarky horse?

When Gina was around, Matt forgot a lot of things. For instance . . . what had she been saying?

Oh yes. The springs. The story. The Nahua.

He searched for a way to get back on track with his questioning yet not be obvious that he *was* questioning. "Are there . . . uh . . . any local legends? Tales of magic? Of gods? Creepy wails and howls and things that go bump in the night? Cursed land? Mysterious caverns?"

Matt thought they were harmless questions. Ones that anyone, even a phys-ed teacher, might reasonably ask in relation to legends. Every area had a few, and many of them involved the supernatural. Of course Matt was a little rusty on harmless questions, having never asked one in his life.

Something flickered in Gina's eyes, making the attraction he was certain he'd seen there die. She stepped back. Even Spike sensed something was wrong, because he snorted, kicked the side of the stall, and stretched his neck toward her, lips nibbling.

"I have to go," she said, and then she practically ran from the barn.

"Hmm," Matt murmured, watching her go. "Methinks she *has* heard a wail or a howl or a bump-in-the-night kind of legend. What think you, Spike?"

The horse licked Matt's shirt, leaving a trail of half-eaten electric-orange carrot across the front.

Matt decided to take that as a *yes*.

CHAPTER 4

Gina sat in the window seat of her room and stared at the place she could see even in the dark as though lit by a neon *X*.

There was something in that underground cavern. Something that had taken her parents away. Something that had wanted to take her.

In the depths of the night, when the wind cried her name, Gina knew with complete certainty that it still did.

She'd never told anyone what she'd felt down there, what she'd heard ever since. Sure, she'd dropped hints to Jase, felt him out. But if he'd experienced anything out of the ordinary during the hours they were buried, he'd either blocked it from his mind or decided to keep it to himself for the same reasons she had.

She wasn't keen on the idea of winding up in a mental hospital or at least in therapy. To be quite honest, she couldn't afford either one.

And that was the best-case scenario. Worst case—Isaac would believe her. He'd bring shamans from the Rez to dance and chant at the edges of the place where the Tangwaci Cin-au'-ao slept. He'd have the earth over the cavern sprinkled with salt or lye or chickens' feet or whatever happened to be the latest and greatest charm guaranteed to thwart evil. Word would get out. The curious would go there.

Then more would die as the legend of the Tangwaci Cin-au'-ao promised.

Even if Matt hadn't been in the kitchen the day before, he would easily have found it by smell alone the next morning. McCord's mother knew her way around a stove.

Matt stepped into the room, breathing in the homey scents of bacon, eggs, toast, and best of all—

"Coffee?" Fanny asked without even turning away from the griddle where she flipped pancakes with a quick, practiced flick of her capable wrist.

"Thanks." Matt crossed to the counter and served himself from the full pot.

Fanny graced him with what appeared to be a genuine smile. As opposed to her son, Fanny seemed to like Matt. "Sleep well, Mr. Teo?"

He'd tried to get her to call him Teo, but since she addressed everyone with the same combination of respect and familiarity he didn't try too hard.

"Fine," he said, which was a lie. How was he supposed to sleep with the scent of Gina in his hair? And how had her scent gotten in his hair anyway?

It was all in his head—so to speak—and he knew it.

But what had really kept him awake was the memory of Gina practically tripping over her own feet as she left both him and his obviously too close for comfort questions behind.

What had she seen? Where had she seen it? How

was he going to get her to let him—a supposed phys-ed teacher from Arizona—see it, too?

Fanny cleared her throat as she gave him a quick, suspicious glance. She reminded Matt of his mother.

Oh, not in appearance. Sure, they both had dark hair, but Fanny's was inky black like her son's and reached to the base of her spine even when gathered into a clip at her nape, while Nora's had replicated the shade of fine cherrywood, although most times she'd worn it so short the burgundy highlights had all but disappeared.

But the way they moved, quick and sure—places to go, people to feed, or in Nora's case to unearth—combined with their sharp eye for detail and a mother's loving ear for bullshit.

"I . . . uh . . ." Matt began, and Fanny waved her spatula in dismissal.

"You don't have to be polite. It's always hard to sleep in a strange place. Just because you couldn't doesn't mean there was anything wrong with the bed, or the room, or . . ." She let her words trail off, arching a brow in his direction when he remained silent.

"Oh, right!" How he could be so smart at book things and so dense at life things had always been a source of embarrassment to him and amusement to everyone he knew. "Bed was great. Room, too. Nothing wrong. Nope. Uh-uh."

"Sheesh, Jones." McCord stepped up to the coffee-maker, his massive shoulders crowding into Matt's space, making him want to move away, though he refused to. "No need to lick her shoes. She isn't going to hit you if you didn't like the bed."

"Of course not," Fanny said, then smacked her son in the forehead with the kitchen utensil.

"Hey." He picked a fleck of pancake off his face. "What'd I do?"

"Company manners," she said. "You will find them. Now."

McCord's dark eyes flashed, but he only tightened his lips, then muttered, "Yes, ma'am," before wrapping two sausages in a pancake and heading outside.

Fanny stared after him. "He isn't usually . . ." Her voice trailed off, and the crease between her brows deepened.

"Such a people person?"

Her brow smoothed as she chuckled. "There is a reason Gina deals with the customers and Jase runs the ranch."

"Because they're *partners*." Matt put an emphasis on the last word, which caused a return of Fanny's frown.

"You could say that. Technically, he works for her, but they grew up together. They both love this place as much as . . ." Her voice drifted off again as she glanced through the window over the stove.

"Each other?"

Fanny smiled sadly and didn't answer.

Any further opportunity for questions ended as the As screeched into the room, followed closely by the incredible cursing Hurlaheys and the father-and-son team known as the Gordons.

Chaos ensued as everyone attempted to speak at once while they helped themselves to coffee, juice, and plates of food. Matt's ears rang. He refilled his coffee, grabbed a pancake and sausage sandwich of his own, and slipped through the back door before the As cornered him again. If he was lucky, a day of riding in the fresh, open air would tire them out so badly they wouldn't be able to stalk him around the campfire.

But he wasn't going to hold his breath.

Excitement flowed though him. Maybe today he'd discover the place his mother had searched for and he had found immortalized on film. Then he could tell Gina the truth and find out what she needed from him so that he would be allowed to dig. There had to be some way to make this work for them both.

Although the thought of losing the camaraderie he'd found with her as Teo Jones, phys-ed teacher, and becoming again Dr. Mecate, complete with a cadre of graduate students, archaeologists, anthropologists, big lights, earthmovers, tents, and trucks, made his chest feel as if a ten-pound sack of flour had landed on his lungs.

How strange. All he'd ever cared about was proving the Mecate theory and now . . .

Matt contemplated the beautiful, peaceful landscape and winced.

Gina had worried it might take some convincing on her part to get Mel and Melda to relinquish Lily and Vi to the Gordons. However, the old couple was happy to help.

"No problem, bro." Mel lifted his hand, palm facing Gina. It took her several seconds to realize he wanted a high five. She obliged. "We don't want the youngster to fall on his—"

"Ass," Melda finished. "We can ride whatever—"

"Damn horses you want us to."

"Fantastic," Gina muttered. She was starting to wonder if the two of them had met in a Tourette's support group.

She hadn't been able to fall asleep for hours last night. Then once she had, she'd tossed and turned, her dreams full of the past. Now she was exhausted.

Gina gestured for Isaac to bring the two mid-level horses into the paddock so the couple could take a test drive. Lucy and Desi were harder to manage than Lily and Vi—pretty much any horse was—but they were a far cry from Spike.

Still, their riders needed to know the basics of horsemanship or risk a nasty fall when either Lucy or Desi decided she or he was too far from Desi or Lucy. Whenever that happened, one or the other would bolt, running full speed until he or she reached his or her true love. The best way to avoid this was to assign the horses to people who would be riding together anyway, preferably without any other guests who might get in the way and separate the love-horses.

Mel and Melda fit the profile. The cursing would probably keep the others away, but even without that quirk, the As only talked to each other or hot men and the Gordons had all they could do to manage Lily and Vi without adding conversation to the mix.

Isaac, his dark gaze on the Hurlaheys and the Arnazes, lifted a hand to let Gina know they were doing all right. The four of them—Isaac, Fanny, Jase, and Gina— worked together so well, each knowing what the others needed, often before they knew it themselves.

What would happen to them if Nahua Springs went under? Isaac and Fanny had never worked anywhere but here. Neither had Jase nor Gina. Besides, they were family. The only one she'd had since—

"You okay?"

Gina started. "I bet your students love it when you sneak up on them like that."

Teo blinked. "Why would I sneak up on them?"

"Aren't they always trying to get away with something? Smoking under the bleachers. Drinking at the dance. Making out in the parking lot."

Teo's gaze went to her mouth and stayed there. The morning sun suddenly blazed far too hot.

"You . . . um . . . ever catch them?"

"Catch?" he repeated, still staring at her lips. He licked his, and she thought she might self-combust.

"The kids. At your school?"

"No." He pulled his eyes away, but he appeared to have as much trouble doing it as she was having forgetting about it. "But I don't try."

"Why not?" She studied him. He didn't look like a bad boy, but maybe he'd reformed. "Did you get caught misbehaving when you were in school?"

"I was homeschooled."

"No way."

His lips curved, and she found herself licking her own, wondering how they'd taste after she'd pressed them to his.

"My mom had interesting ideas about education."

"Since you wound up being a teacher, did you agree with them or disagree?"

"I agree with almost all my mother's ideas. If I didn't, I wouldn't be here."

"Your mother told you to come to Nahua Springs Ranch?" She was going to have to meet his mother.

The strangeness of that thought gave Gina pause. She wasn't ever going to meet his mother. It wasn't like she and Teo were dating. They were flirting, which was bizarre enough. She never flirted with men, because men never flirted with her.

She'd been told she was pretty, and maybe she was.

But she'd come to the conclusion that there was something wrong with her, something broken deep inside that kept men from being interested for more than a minute. She couldn't remember the last time she'd had a second date.

"She did," Teo said. "She . . . uh . . . thought I should get out more."

"You a gamer?"

For an instant he stared at her blankly. Then he followed the jerk of her head toward Derek and understanding spread over his handsome face. "I've played. But I'd rather be doing."

His gaze flicked back to hers, and the unspoken word *you* hovered between them.

"Gina!" Jase's voice made them jump.

She turned her head only to discover that everyone else was mounted and ready to leave.

Everyone else was also staring at her and Teo. The Hurlaheys grinned indulgently; Melda gave her a wink and a double thumbs-up.

The As glared. If looks could kill . . . et cetera, et cetera, et cetera.

Tim Gordon appeared impatient. He probably figured that if they didn't get on the trail now, he'd lose any chance he had of getting his son on the trail at all.

That son glanced back and forth between Teo and Gina, then made a gagging motion.

Last she turned her gaze to Jase. Gina wasn't sure what she saw in his eyes before he walked away. Anger? Disgust? Disappointment? Whatever it was, it made her chest hurt when, a minute later, he thundered down the long dirt lane toward the main road, the dust from his horse's hooves nearly obscuring him.

Jase often got angry and took off. Gina had learned

long ago to let him. He'd come back; he'd be himself again. Following him only made things worse.

She glanced at the six people on horses. As if following him was even an option.

"I'll be ready in a minute," she told them, then hurried to the barn.

Lady Belle was saddled and her pack in place, as was Teo's. Weird. Nahua Springs insisted their guests saddle their own mounts and pack their own gear, not just because the ranch lacked the manpower to do it for them but also to make sure they *could* do it. Once they were on the trail, there'd be only guests, horses, and Gina. She couldn't saddle every horse; she couldn't pack every pack. Besides, why else were they here unless it was to learn how?

She checked her equipment. Even if Isaac or Jase had helped her out—and who else would have?—she still knew better than to get on a horse and ride into the wilderness without inspecting things.

Gina glanced over, thrilled to discover Teo examining his saddle and pack also. The more she knew of the man, the more impressed she became.

"You good?" she asked.

He lifted his gaze. When they'd stood in the sun his eyes had hovered between green and brown—the shade of drying moss or the new bark of a tree. Now, in the shadow of the barn, they had deepened almost to black—kind of eerie. Strange, since Teo struck her as one of the least eerie, most honest people she knew. Maybe the lenses in his glasses changed shade with the absence of or increase in light. That would explain it.

"I'm good."

He led Spike into the yard, then swung onto the horse's back with an easy, fluid movement that could

only have come with practice, making Gina wonder—
not for the first time—where he'd learned to ride.

Horses were expensive—both to rent and to own.
Lessons cost money; heck, so did a dude ranch. So how
could a schoolteacher afford enough horse time to ride
so well?

Gina followed him outside, mounted Lady Belle,
then urged her past the others to take the lead.

She'd have plenty of time to ask that question, and
quite a few others, over the next few days.

She was looking forward to it.

CHAPTER 5

Matt had figured he'd find a burr under Spike's saddle or the girth uncinched or some other cowboy trick that could have knocked Matt out of the group, if not into the hospital.

But there'd been nothing.

Of course a major injury to a guest would not only throw a wrench into the festivities but also put a crimp into their whole operation if someone was hurt badly enough.

Jase might be a lot of things—vulgar, macho, rude—but stupid wasn't one of them.

Matt on the other hand . . .

"Moron," he murmured. The man had warned him not to "eye-fuck" his girl. Yet Matt couldn't seem to stop doing it. There was just something about Gina that mesmerized him.

His gaze strayed to the front, where she rode her horse with the ease of one born to it. With each step her mount took, the curve of Gina's hip lifted and lowered, lifted and lowered as if she were riding something much different from a horse.

Matt groaned.

"What was that, Teo, honey?"

Amberleigh hadn't strayed more than three yards ahead of or behind him all day. And so he wouldn't get lonely, when she was ahead Ashleigh was behind, and vice versa. Matt was beginning to feel decidedly squished.

"Nothing," he said. "Talking to myself."

"Oh, my grandpappy did that." She turned in her saddle, pulled down her Christian Dior sunglasses, and studied him. "You aren't losin' your little ole marbles now, are you? You can't be that old."

Matt didn't bother to answer as Amberleigh—true to form—launched into a monologue on her grandpappy's senility that neither asked for nor required a response.

They'd ridden through gorgeous country—plains dotted with just-sprung flowers, woods full of new leaves—heading inexorably for the distant hills.

The San Juan Mountains were part of the Rocky Mountains and had, once upon a time, been covered in prospectors. But ore of any type had long ago run out, and now they were covered in tourists.

The mountains were steep and not exactly small— hence the moniker *mountain*—they were also the home of two national forests. Nevertheless, the place boasted ski resorts, ghost-town hotels, abandoned-mine tours, hiking, mountain climbing, and jeeping—whatever that was. Wikipedia had failed to elaborate. There was even an old narrow-gauge train that ran between Durango and Silverton and offered all sorts of touristy tours.

However, from where Matt stood, the hills were not alive but deserted. And nothing, anywhere, looked like the place he was hoping to find.

They came to an extended plain where they could all walk their horses in a line. This was unfortunate, since that gave the As an audience. Something that had been sadly lacking in Matt.

"I don't know why y'all have to ride all day like yer Billy the Boy or somethin'," Ashleigh announced.

"It hasn't been all day," Gina said. "We stopped at noon."

"For sandwiches and chips." Ashleigh's nose wrinkled. "Outside."

"It's called a picnic. Part of the ambiance."

"Part of the what?"

Lady Belle sidestepped, throwing her big ass into Ashleigh's horse. The girl fell blessedly silent while she righted her mount. Then Ashleigh opened her mouth, no doubt to complain about something else, but thankfully Derek jumped in.

"Who's Billy the Boy?"

"Oh, that outlaw." Ashleigh flipped her manicured fingers toward the just-beginning-to-darken sky. "You know. The brother of that guy on *Two and a Half Men* played him in the movie."

"Jon Cryer has a brother?" Derek appeared as confused as Matt. Who was Jon Cryer and how on earth did one come up with two and a *half* men?

"No! The *other* guy. He tried to shoot his wife. Drinks a lot, just like his character on the TV."

Derek glanced at Matt, who shrugged.

"Not shoot, dumbass." In this instance, Matt had to agree with Melda's assessment, and the expression on Ashleigh's face at her new nickname was priceless. "I think it was stab. Maybe strangle. You're talkin' about Charlie Sheen, whose bro is Emilio Estevez."

"How can they be brothers if they don't even have the same last name?" Amberleigh wondered.

"Shit happens," Mel said. "And he didn't play Billy the *Boy*. It was Billy the *Kid*."

"Oh!" Derek straightened in the saddle, wincing a little at the movement, which made Matt feel a whole helluva lot better about his own sore ass. "*Young Guns.* Got it."

"You really wanna see a great horse chase," Mel continued, "you gotta watch *Butch Cassidy and the Sundance Kid.* Now *they* rode all day, all night, all the fucking time." He glanced at his wife and together they announced: "Who *are* those guys?"

Now Matt was even more confused. "You just said they were Butch and Sundance."

Mel and Melda stared at him in shock. "You've never seen the damn movie?" Mel asked.

"I . . . uh . . ." *Hell.* Matt rarely watched movies. He was too immersed in the past.

"I've never seen the damn movie," Gina said.

"But . . . but . . ." Mel's Santa face crumpled as if the last known reindeer had just fallen off a roof and died. "It's a *western*."

"The best damn western of all time," Melda agreed.

"This . . ."—Gina spread her hand, palm extended, fingers splayed, then swooshed her arm in a half circle, indicating the panorama before them—"is the best western of all time."

For several minutes everyone observed the view. Purple mountains still capped with white, the grass gone evergreen in the dusk, the sky divided into bands of azure, gold, fuchsia, and burnt umber. The first bird they'd seen since morning—thanks to the As—even flew across the landscape just for them.

Matt glanced over to find Gina watching him instead of the horizon. When their eyes met, he experienced another moment of camaraderie that brought home to him again how much he missed his mommy. No one had understood him like Nora. He'd begun to believe that no one ever could.

"Just 'cause outlaws rode all night doesn't mean we can." Derek's voice had taken on the distinct tenor of a tired three-year-old. From the panic on his dad's face, Matt figured the kid would be pounding his head on the ground and wailing if he didn't get some food and a nap real soon.

"We aren't going to ride all night," Gina said. "Just until we reach that ridge." She pointed to a bump in the landscape that Matt knew from experience looked closer than it was. They'd be making camp at twilight. Nothing Matt hadn't done before.

Still, having something to focus on perked everyone right up. By the time they reached the ridge and stared down at the rising moon reflected in the lake below, people were singing along with Mel, who knew more funny ditties than anyone Matt had ever met. Half a dozen voices lifted in a rousing rendition of:

> *"On mules we find two legs behind*
> *And two we find before;*
> *We stand behind before we find*
> *What the two behind be for.*
>
> *"When we're behind the two behind*
> *We find what these be for;*
> *So stand before the two behind*
> *And behind the two before."*

The song seemed very apropos. Even Derek joined in. What the boy lacked in tune-carrying ability he more than made up for in volume.

"Where'd you learn all these songs?" Derek asked.

"I was a boys' school guard."

Translation: Peewee Prison.

Mel's vocabulary suddenly made a lot more sense.

As they set up camp, Mel proved adept not only at amusing everyone but also at pitching a tent and starting a campfire. Gina slipped Derek an energy bar, which caused Derek to peer after her like a devoted pet. If the kid didn't watch it Jase would want him dead, too.

Dinner consisted of premade foil-wrapped packets of beef, carrots, and potatoes stuck into the hot coals and left to bake for a half hour. Matt sighed remembering Fanny's exquisite fare.

However, when he took a bite he was pleasantly surprised. Though the meal resembled regurgitated dog food combined with something Spike had dribbled on Matt's shoes, it tasted amazing.

"Is that basil?" Melda asked around a mouthful.

"Cayenne, too," Mel said, his mouth equally stuffed.

The As were busy picking out the vegetables and leaving the meat behind.

"Dead cow?" Ashleigh tossed a piece into the fire, where it hissed and sizzled and burned. "Seriously?"

"I'm seriously gonna break your fingers if you do that again," Gina said.

Ashleigh's eyes widened. "Do what?"

Gina reached for the thick, heavy stick Mel had used to poke up the fire. Her patience had finally snapped. Matt was surprised it had taken this long.

He laid a hand over hers, and she stilled. "Why don't you give what you don't care for to Derek?" he suggested.

The boy's gaze was focused on the lumps of meat in the two girls' laps. Or maybe on the impressive lumps of meat on the two girls' chests; Matt couldn't tell.

"Thanks!" Derek leaped to his feet and collected the unwanted food.

"Aw, sweetie." Amberleigh patted Derek's arm, causing him to blush so deeply it was even noticeable in the flickering firelight. "I could have thrown it out myself."

Derek's embarrassment turned to confusion. Gina sighed and drove the big stick deep into the coals. "Here." She unearthed two more foil packets. "Take these."

Derek dumped the girls' discarded meat on top, then began to inhale the lot as if he hadn't eaten since Cleveland.

The As started to make gagging noises. Thankfully, one glare from Gina was all it took to make them stop. They weren't as dumb as they pretended.

They just couldn't be.

"How can he eat so much and still have no gut and no butt?" Amberleigh ran a palm over her own skinny butt.

"He's fourteen," Tim said. "He could eat the whole cow and beg for dessert."

Amberleigh made a face, then turned to Derek. "Do you run?"

Derek glanced up, swallowed, considered taking another bite before answering, and refrained. "Sometimes."

Amberleigh flipped her palms up. "Well, that explains it."

"V-Rex chases you," Derek shrugged, "you run."

Amberleigh froze with her hands in the air. Her gaze

went to the suddenly still night that surrounded them.
"T. rex?"

Someone smothered a laugh. Matt thought it was
Gina.

"No, V-Rex," the boy said slowly, emphasis on the
V. "Vastatorsaurus rex."

Amberleigh lowered her arms, wrapping them around
herself and hunching over as she tried to get small.

"Descendant of T. rex," Derek continued. "Just
bigger."

"B-b-bigger?" Amberleigh's gaze returned to the
tree line and when the leaves stirred she scrambled
behind Matt, talon-like fingertips pressed into his biceps and breasts pressed into his back.

This suddenly wasn't funny anymore. Should he tell
her now, or never, that a V-Rex was just make-believe?

"What's wrong with her?" Derek asked. "It's not
like the moonspiders are here."

"S-s-s-spiders!"

Her shriek scared away whatever had been rustling
in the trees. From the sound of it, a really big bird.

"That could have been a Terapusmordax," Derek
muttered. "They look like giant skinned rats with
wings and their teeth . . ." He shuddered. "Gave me
nightmares the first couple times I played."

Silence settled over the campfire. Amberleigh was
still shaking, her breasts jiggling against Matt's back
like two large, firm, warm Jell-O molds, even as her
fingernails bit into his arms like Terapusmordax teeth.

"Played?" Ashleigh repeated.

"King Kong," Tim said wearily. "You don't think
the kid was actually chased by a V-Rex do you?"

From Ashleigh's scowl, she had.

Amberleigh began to stroke Matt's arm and breathe—
make that *blow*—in his ear. Matt got up so fast she
tumbled forward without support and landed on her
face. Or she would have, if her balloon-like breasts
hadn't broken her fall.

Matt felt kind of bad, until the crescent-moon holes
in his arms began to burn.

She cast him a glare that would have blistered paint
off a Camaro, before climbing to her feet and flouncing
off.

Gina appeared at his side. "She isn't going to talk to
you for at least a whole day."

"Promise?" Matt murmured, and she laughed.

What was it about this man that made her behave so
differently from her usual self?

Gina was not a smiler or even much of a laugher.
But ever since Teo Jones had shown up—had that been
only yesterday?—she'd discovered herself doing quite
a bit of both.

Was it because of the way he looked at her, as if she
knew things he wanted to and he would be happy to
spend hours, days, a lifetime, uncovering them?

Or maybe the way he spoke to her, as if everything
she said was brilliant. He'd been to college; he was a
teacher. She'd barely gotten out of high school.

Not because she couldn't handle the classes. What
she hadn't been able to handle was the physical work of
the ranch combined with the mental work of school
and the emotional drain of dealing with customers.
Something had to give and it had been her grades. Oh,
she'd *finished*. But she'd always been a little embarrassed by how poorly she'd done.

Her parents would have been disappointed. Of course if her parents had been alive to disappoint, she wouldn't have had the issue in the first place.

Someone cleared their throat, and Gina realized she'd been staring into Teo's eyes—darkened by the night, as well as lit by the fire now reflected in his glasses, causing them to glow a lovely shade of sienna—and he'd been staring into hers while the rest of the world kept spinning on without them.

She didn't understand what was wrong with her. She never got dopey over men. Probably because men never got dopey over her.

"Everyone should get to bed." Gina turned and addressed the others. "The sun will be shining in your tent before you know it."

No one argued. They all had to be tired enough to fall asleep on their feet. The first day on the trail was always exhausting, but they needed to make it to the lake, as there was no water for the horses between the ranch and here.

The group began to drift away, but not before Mel and Melda cast Gina and Teo identical smirks. Combined with a scorching glare from Ashleigh, or maybe Amberleigh, Gina concluded everyone in the group— except maybe Derek, who was still shoveling food— thought she was sending them to bed so she could jump Teo's bones.

Right before everyone disappeared into the darkness, she caught a flash of the firelight off something sparkly tucked beneath Derek's arm.

"Whoa, kid!" Gina hurried after him. "You can't take that with you." She held out her hand for the last foil packet of food.

"But I get hungry in the night."

"So do bears." She curled her fingers inward. "Gimme."

"Bears!" shrieked one of the As. "There are bears out here?"

Gina put her finger into her ear and jiggled. "Not anymore."

Teo snorted, though bears were no laughing matter.

"Didn't everyone read the 'Safety Tips' we left on your beds last night?" Gina asked.

Usually she went over them at the campfire, because she'd learned the hard way that no one read anything you gave them, but tonight she'd been distracted by the singing, King Kong, and Teo.

She motioned for them all to come back. They stood in a semi-circle around the fading flames. "Black bears are common in the area. Most of the time they'll run off as soon as they hear us."

"And they're gonna hear us real good." Derek glowered at the As. The kid obviously had his heart set on seeing a bear. Who knows what his dad had promised just to get him out here?

"Their noses are even better than their ears," Gina continued, "and if you leave any food out for them to smell, they're gonna come searching. We like to avoid that."

"What do you do with the food?" Melda asked.

"Wrap it up, then—" Gina pointed at a nearby tree. "Hang it up."

Mel leaned back so far to see into the tree he nearly toppled over and had to be rebalanced by his wife. "Can't bears climb trees?"

"Sure. But they can't fly." Gina indicated the pulley system rigged to the end of a long branch—too flimsy to support a bear but stout enough to protect their food.

"What if we see one?" Tim asked.

"Most of the time, bears really are more scared of us than we are of them. They'll hear you and head the other way. You won't even know they were anywhere close. But if you do see one, clap, talk, sing. You don't want to startle it."

"What if we do?" Derek asked. "Accidentally."

"They might slap the ground, huff, blow, or bluff charge; then you want to—"

"What's a bluff charge?" Tim interrupted. He seemed a little tense.

"The bear runs forward, then stops. It's trying to make you move a safe distance away."

"I'll move all right," Tim muttered. "I'll run my ass off."

"No," Teo said. "You shouldn't run."

Gina glanced at him in surprise, but he *had* said he'd been camping and riding in remote areas. This was common knowledge to those who had.

"What should we do?" Derek's eyes were wide, but unlike his father, he appeared more interested than scared, which was good. That thing about animals smelling fear? Completely true.

"Maintain eye contact, talk quietly, *back* away. You don't want the bear to be any more threatened than it already is, but you can't behave like prey, either. You run, it'll chase you. Then . . ." She paused, letting her gaze meet that of every person around the fire before she continued. "It'll catch you. A bear can outrun, out-climb . . ." Gina searched for another example and came up blank. "Pretty much out-anything you."

"Maybe we should go back," Tim began.

"No." That was all she'd need. Everyone begging to return to the ranch in the middle of the night, wanting refunds she couldn't afford, from money she probably no longer had because Jase had already used it to pay off the most obnoxious of their creditors. "Bears aren't aggressive. The last person killed in the wild by a Colorado black bear was in 1993."

"What do you mean 'in the wild'?" Tim's voice was getting steadily higher and louder, encroaching into the range of the As'. "Bears have killed people in their houses? Their hotels? The candy shop on Main Street?"

"No," Gina said, keeping her own voice low, steady, and calm. " 'In the wild' means out here, like this, not a so-called *tame* bear that's a pet or a performance or a zoo animal. Those tend to flip out and attack their trainers more often than any bears in the wild jump the tourists."

She wished she hadn't had to tell them this now, before bed, which might lead to bear-induced nightmares or her needing to accompany them to the "facilities," slapping the brush with a stick to prove there was nothing hiding there in the dark. But better they knew what to do, what to expect, than that she got any sleep.

"So." Gina clapped her hands and Tim jumped, then laughed at himself for doing it. He was going to be all right. "Off to bed. I'll be right here." She pointed at her tent, which she'd pitched nearest the trees. "If you need anything don't hesitate."

"To scream," Derek said as he followed his dad toward their tent.

Tim hooked his arm around his son's neck and proceeded to give him noogies as Derek pretended to hate it but laughed nonetheless.

Gina's lips curved as they disappeared into their tent.

Let the bonding begin.

CHAPTER 6

As the others melted away, leaving only Gina and Teo behind, Teo stared after the Gordons with a bemused expression.

"What's the matter?" she asked.

His gaze flicked to hers; then he shrugged as if embarrassed. "Is that normal for a dad and a son?"

"That?"

"The shoving and the teasing, the knocking on the head."

"I wouldn't know," Gina answered. "I'm not a boy."

"Mmm," he said, the comment sounding both agreeable and slightly sexy. But then everything about him was slightly sexy.

And Gina was losing her mind.

"You didn't shove and tease your dad?"

"I didn't have a dad."

"Everyone has a dad."

"Right." He shuffled his feet, peered at the ground. "I never knew my dad. Not even his name."

"Well, that would suck." She might have lost her parents, but at least she'd known them.

"Can we get some quiet?" The shout of an A—which one Gina had no idea and didn't care—split the night. Gina opened her mouth to point out that shouting wasn't quiet, then snapped it shut again.

"The customer is always right," she muttered, and Teo laughed, then winced as the sound carried across the chill darkness.

"Sheesh!" the other A shouted.

"Sorry," Teo called, then lowered his voice. "I guess I'd better—"

"You want to come to my tent?"

Teo's eyes, nearly black in the moonlight, widened. Her question *had* sounded like an invitation for more than conversation.

"I meant walk to my tent. So a bear doesn't get me."

"Of course." He spread his hand in an "after you" gesture better suited to someone twice their age. Why she found it charming Gina couldn't say. Maybe because she found everything about him charming.

And sexy.

Hell.

No bopping the customers, she reminded herself. It didn't do much good.

They reached her tent, pitched on the outskirts of the circle, several yards from the others. Far enough away that any low-voiced conversation shouldn't carry.

Gina liked to be nearer the trees, away from the guests—especially after a day like today. Or guests like the As.

"Is this . . ." Teo indicated the two of them, "going to get you in trouble with McCord?"

Gina frowned. "I'm not following." She felt like

she'd missed an entire conversation somewhere. When Teo continued, she understood that she had.

"If I were your boyfriend I wouldn't like you spending time alone in the dark with another guy."

"Boyfriend? Jase?" Gina laughed. "He's like my brother."

"No." Teo's eyes met hers. "He's not."

"You're crazy."

"Or *he* is," Teo muttered. "He told me that he'd *end me* if I touched you."

"He what?" Gina's voice was full of laughter, but as she continued to watch Teo's face the laughter died.

He was telling the truth.

"I don't know why he'd say that," Gina murmured. "I'm embarrassed."

"You have nothing to be embarrassed about."

"That he'd assume you were interested in me." She glanced at her hands. "Guys aren't usually." Teo snorted, and she lifted her gaze. "Really. I'm not . . ."

She tried to find a word that would explain the situation without making her appear the incredible loser she must be, since few men had ever wanted to see her more than once. All she could come up with was—

"Right."

His exquisite eyes widened behind his glasses, and Gina heard what she'd said. She'd just admitted her most secret fear—that losing her parents as she had, combined with those hours she and Jase had been buried beneath the earth, had broken her in some indefinable way. Obviously men sensed this and turned away from her as quickly as they could.

So . . . what was wrong with Teo? Why did he continue to hang around? Why did he stare at her as if he thought she was fascinating? Why did he listen to her as if he thought she had something to say?

"You think there's something wrong with *you*?" he asked.

"Never mind." She'd never told anyone that, not even Jase. She'd wanted to seem like less of a loser, but instead she only looked like more of one.

"I do mind." Teo's eyes flashed. "How can you think such a thing?"

"I'm not feminine or witty. I can't carry on a conversation like the As."

"Neither one of them has ever carried on a conversation with anyone but themselves."

"I've never had a boyfriend," she blurted. "First dates, yes. Second?" She shook her head.

"Probably because McCord tells everyone he'll end them."

"He wouldn't do that."

Teo's lips tightened, as if he wanted to argue; then he sighed. "He was right to be worried."

"Worried?" she echoed.

For an instant she thought Teo might kiss her and oh, how she wanted him to. To hell with the no-bopping-the-customers rule.

Suddenly he looked down and stepped back. "I'll let you get some rest."

He headed for his tent, leaving Gina to stare after him and wonder, yet again, what she had done.

He had to tell Gina the truth. About who he was, why he was here. Before he did something stupid like kiss her, touch her, take her. If he did that, how would he ever be able to explain who he was afterward?

Matt ducked into his tent, kicked off his boots, and

crawled into his bedroll. He figured he'd lie awake, thinking of her; instead, he'd barely closed his eyes and he was dreaming.

Another tent, one of many he and his mother had shared. There Nora pored over her papers, scribbling notes, talking to herself. Matt, perhaps eight, maybe ten, lay on the cot in the corner, pretending to study math but in reality studying her as she translated Aztec to English. He did that so often that by the time she'd decided to teach him the language he already knew.

"Time for bed, *mi hijo.*"

His mother shut her books, put away her papers, and joined him on the cot. As she did every night, she told Matt the story she'd uncovered, the one that kept them searching long past the point when most others would have given up.

"One great army marched farther north than any other. And though the People of the Sun were the greatest warriors ever known, they met strong resistance, and they lost more of their own than ever before."

Matt snuggled under the covers. He might hear this tale every single night, but it was always exciting. Because it was *her* story and had, through the constant telling of it, become *theirs.* He wondered if he could even sleep if he didn't first become drowsy listening to the familiar cadence of the words.

"However," his mother continued in the slightly hoarse voice that was a mark of the Mecates, "the Aztecs, being Aztecs, weren't going to just turn around and go home."

"No," Matt said, his voice very much like hers even then. "They wouldn't run; they'd never hide."

She ran her hand over his overly long, tousled dark

hair that was but a shade lighter than hers. "That's right, Teo *de mio*. Instead, they brought forth their most powerful warrior—a sorcerer who struck fear into the hearts he would soon devour—and he mowed through the natives like a *cuetlachtli*."

"A ravenous wolf!" Matt translated.

As if in answer to Nora's tale, or perhaps Matt's words, a distant, triumphant howl pierced the night. However, neither the youthful Teo nor the yet youthful and alive Nora reacted to the call, which made the watching, dreaming Matt stir. Where was that sound coming from?

Here or there? Then or now?

"But something went wrong." Dream Teo sat up on his cot, excited over this part of the story. Because it was a mystery and he loved a good mystery as much as his mother.

"Yes, something went wrong. Because even though this . . ." She searched for the perfect word.

"Superwarrior!" Matt announced.

She smiled at him with such love the adult Matt swallowed the lump that formed in his throat, even in his sleep. No one had ever loved him like that since.

"Yes. But even though this superwarrior had powers beyond imagination, in the end he was buried there." She pushed Matt gently back onto his bed. "And where will we find him, *mi hijo*?"

" 'Where the tree of life springs from a land awash with the blood of the sun,' " he recited.

One of several phrases she had translated from the Aztec writings of the Mecates. Gibberish until you saw a photo of a place where it just might make sense.

There'd been other translations. Other places. Other pictures, legends, rumors. But none of them had ever seemed as right as that one.

They'd searched. Years upon years. Miles upon miles. Nora wasn't easily dissuaded. She read travel magazines, collected tales of the weird, haunted libraries and secondhand bookstores. She combed through everything she could find that held photos or drawings of the Southwest. She'd found two sites that way. But the true boon to her research had been the Internet.

There she'd been able to discover the next three sites that matched her translations by searching through travelogues and touristy vacation photos. Unfortunately, those pictures, some no better than fading Polaroids of trips taken by families in DeSotos, did not help to silence her naysayers when site after site produced only more dirt.

But Nora remained determined. She had believed in that superwarrior, and her son had believed, too.

Until he didn't.

Her voice whispered out of the darkness: *Find the truth. For me, Teo* de mio.

My Teo. Teo mine. The translation was actually *Teo of mine,* but his mother translated Spanish as creatively as the academic world believed she translated Aztec.

Assholes.

Matt jerked awake. Had he said that out loud? *Perhaps.* Remembering how Nora's so-called colleagues had treated her could still make him furious. Probably because they treated him the same way.

And there was the added guilt of how *he* had treated her. Refusing to go along on that final dig. Telling her she needed to grow up and face facts instead of continuing to believe in a fantasy long past the point of sanity.

Matt pushed on his forehead, wishing he could make the echo of his words go away. The only way he could atone for his lack of faith was to prove his mother's theory. He needed to remember that. But, right now, it was so difficult for him to remember anything but Gina.

Matt sat up, gathering his dream-damp hair into a tidier queue. He'd been distracted by Gina, this place, the others, but he couldn't afford to be distracted anymore. He had to find that tree that seemed to erupt from the earth. The one that turned as red as blood beneath the rays of the sun.

He dug through his pack, then pulled out the photo that had brought him to Nahua Springs Ranch. It was better than most. No Polaroid this time, not even an Instamatic. Whoever had taken it had known what they were doing, and since coming here Matt knew just who that someone was.

He'd go to her now, tell her the truth, make this journey theirs instead of his. Excitement flowed through Matt at the thought. He got dressed, shoved the copy into his pocket, then stepped into the chilly darkness that would soon give way to the dawn.

The sky had just begun to lighten. Not a hint of color yet, only that fuzzy blue-gray haze that seemed to buzz with the approach of the sun.

The fire was banked, the camp completely silent. Even the horses seemed to hold their breath. Matt knew he was.

A tent flap burst open just as the first rays of pink split the blue. A shadow trod softly in the smoky morn, moving past the horses, which now breathed and stomped and snorted again, and paused about fifty yards away, face tilted to greet the coming dawn.

Every morning on the trail, Gina rose before everyone else. It wasn't hard. In all her years of leading tours at

Nahua Springs Ranch, she'd never once gotten up later than a single guest.

Gina enjoyed watching the sun rise. It centered her for the day, made her remember why she was here, why she worked so hard.

The only thing that mattered was this place.

"Am I interrupting?"

Gina tensed, but when she recognized the voice she relaxed. Even though she'd thought she'd come out here to be alone, she realized now that she'd come to be with him.

"No." She turned, smiling at the sight of Teo, still sleepy and tousled. He'd tried to tame his hair by tying it back, but it was still kind of a mess. He'd obviously spent a very rough night. She wondered if he'd spent it thinking of her.

"Wanna watch the sun come up?" she asked.

When he didn't move she offered her hand, and as if he'd been doing it all his life he took it. He seemed to understand the need for silence. He seemed to share her awe of the almost mystical beauty in this daily birth of the sun.

People could fail you—parents, friends, lovers, employers, employees. Hell, you could fail yourself.

Banks failed. Crops failed. Marriages failed.

But the sun . . . that never failed. Even if the sky was shrouded in cobalt-colored clouds, the sun was always there, just beneath, waiting to burst free. The least Gina could do was greet it.

Together they stood—hands clasped, reverent silence shared—until the show ended. Gina drew a breath as Teo released one.

"Thank you," he said, the wonder in his voice revealing that she hadn't been mistaken. He'd understood exactly what this was.

The sharing of a part of her few others ever saw.

She nodded, acknowledging his thanks, for a moment unable to speak. They still held hands. She didn't want to let go. There was just something about him that called to her.

"The sun," she finally managed, "it's—"

"Magic," he finished. "Brilliant and beautiful, different but always the same. A mystery and an anchor."

Could he read her mind, her heart and soul? No wonder she couldn't let go of him.

Teo squeezed her hand, lips curving, eyes behind the lenses of his glasses almost catlike in the morning light. "You know the Aztecs worshiped the sun." He turned his face back to its glow. "I can see why."

Aztecs. What was it about the Aztecs that made her kind of squirrelly?

A howl split the morning stillness, pulling their attention from both the sky and each other. Any question about long-dead sun-worshiping Indians fled Gina's mind as she tilted her head and listened.

Giiiiiiii-naaaaaaa!

"I thought wolves stopped howling at dawn," Teo murmured.

She started, removing her hand from his, then shaking her head in an attempt to make her ears stop hearing what it was not possible to hear. If that howl had actually sounded like her name, Teo would have said so.

"They . . . uh . . ." She paused, took a breath, pleased when it didn't quiver, then continued. "They howl to find one another, announce a kill, freak people out. The time has little to do with it."

"What about howling at the moon?"

"Myth. Since they're nocturnal hunters, most of

their howling's done at night, under that moon, which is probably where the idea came from. Sure, you hear them less in the daylight, but you see them less, too. They gotta sleep sometime."

"You got a big wolf problem here?"

Gina glanced at him. There was no reason not to tell the truth.

"There aren't any wolves here at all," she said.

He laughed. "Sure there aren't. Wink." He winked. "Wink. Don't worry, Gina; I won't go running back to Arizona if I see a wolf, or even a bear."

"You won't see a wolf." She glanced over her shoulder at the camp. "No one ever has."

"But—" His eyes clouded with confusion, darkening them to the shade of last year's moss. "I just heard them."

"Those howls are some weird phenomenon. The wind through the rocks, the mountains, the trees. No one knows. We've looked for wolves; we've never found them."

"Maybe you just . . . haven't found them?"

He obviously knew very little about wolves. "If there were wolves, we'd see spoor. Traces of kills. We'd lose a horse once in a while. They're predators. There's a reason the ranchers hate them."

"Why haven't I heard about this?"

Gina tilted her head. "Why would you?"

"No reason," he said quickly. "It's just odd. Isn't it?"

Very. But she wasn't going to admit that, for the same reason she hadn't advertised the fact. The whole thing was a little creepy. Not the best PR. If you wanted to pay top dollar for a relaxing trip to a ranch, you didn't want to go to one with spooky un–wolf howls that couldn't be explained.

Isaac had even had some friend of his from the

war—the Big One, WW 2—who supposedly knew everything there was to know about wolves of all kinds come and study the place. And then that guy had called in his granddaughter, some hotshot "ologist." Zoologist? Biologist? Gina couldn't remember. Neither one of them had any explanation for why the wolves gave Nahua Springs such a wide berth.

"The ranchers around here are thrilled," Gina continued. "Haven't lost a foal to a wolf in forever."

Literally.

"Hmm," Teo murmured, his gaze on the trees.

"You like wolves or something?" she asked.

People did. Usually city people. Those who lived in the West and dealt with wolves loathed them. Try to discuss the success of wolf reintroduction to Yellowstone with a rancher from the area and you'd be lucky to come away with only one black eye.

"Sure," Teo said. "They're pretty."

Gina wouldn't know. She'd only seen them in movies. Where they tended to be toothy, shape-shifting, monster-type wolves and not the noble beasts of a Robert Bateman painting.

"I'll find you a bear." She patted his hand. "You'll love it."

He tangled their fingers together before she could pull away, then rubbed his thumb over the base of hers, causing a now-familiar shimmy in her stomach. "I'm sure I will."

She lifted her gaze from their joined hands to his face. His eyes, now the shade of corroded copper, captured hers. She could look into them for years and never have them appear the same shade twice. It was fascinating. *He* was fascinating.

"Love it," he said.

She blinked, trying to remember what they were discussing.

Oh yeah. Bears.

Whoopee.

No wonder no man had ever asked her on a second date if bears were the extent of her conversation. Her mind groped for something clever to say, but she came up empty. She knew horses, the ranch. That was it. She couldn't help it.

"Maybe—" Gina began, but she never finished the sentence, and later, after all that happened next, she wouldn't want to.

"You smell like . . ." He lifted his free hand to her hair, not yet braided and still trailing down her back to her waist. "Trees."

"That's probably just the trees," she murmured, captured forever by those eyes.

"Nah," he said, and kissed her.

She'd been kissed before; she was certain she had. But the instant Teo's mouth touched hers she couldn't recall a single one because she knew in that instant that this was *the* one.

The kiss. *The* moment. *The* man. How could that be?

She only knew that it was.

He tasted of mint—toothpaste no doubt, yet exotic nevertheless. He was warmth amid the chill. Solid in a world that just wasn't.

His tongue traced her lips. What should have tickled instead electrified. Her heart thundered—a rapid, steady rhythm with the cadence of hoofbeats—and her ears buzzed, almost like the ground was shaking or the air had filled with bees.

The world tilted; everything changed. She had to reach for something that might steady it, steady her.

Her fingers curled around his biceps. They flexed at the touch, bulging against her palms.

She wanted to lick his skin, see if it tasted of the oranges she smelled. Instead, she licked his teeth, his lip, his tongue, and his biceps flexed again as he grasped her hips and held on.

Her heart beat louder but slower, which made no sense; she felt it fluttering so fast and so hard it threatened to burst from her chest, yet that sound in her ears—*buzzzzzz*—had not only slowed but seemed to come closer. And how could it be any closer than this?

She became distracted by something else that pulsed. Lower, against her stomach, hard and full, with a beat that called to her own—*bump-bump*—definitely a heart and not hooves.

Gina's ears sharpened. The buzzing had stopped.

Was she dead?

She lifted her lips. His eyes behind the slightly askew glasses—had she done that? She couldn't recall—had gone the shade of those trees he insisted she smelled like. He smiled—a goofy, happy smile that made her smile, too. She was lifting her mouth for another kiss—it seemed a shame to waste one more second of her life *not* kissing him—and someone cleared his throat.

Gina closed her eyes. *Hell.* Were the others awake? Were they even now watching her and Teo, waiting to ruin magic more dazzling than the sun?

Except Gina still felt as if she were floating. Even the As weren't going to be able to bring her down. She didn't think anyone could.

She was wrong.

"Dr. Mecate." Jase's voice ruptured the once-perfect morning. "You sure do work fast."

CHAPTER 7

"Mecate?" Gina murmured, the rest of the world returning to her eyes.

Matt almost kissed her again in an attempt to drive it back out. But with McCord sitting there on a big, black dirt bike, scowling at them as if he'd caught them doing the nasty in front of the local preschool class, he doubted he'd have any luck.

Why had he kissed her?

Because, simply, he hadn't been able to stop.

"You're Teo," Gina said. "Right?"

Her voice quavered, and Matt's hands, still cupped around her hips, clenched. He wanted to put them around Jase McCord's throat and squeeze. He'd have told her the truth himself.

Eventually.

"I *am* Teo," he said; then, because he needed to tell her every truth he could to try to erase every lie, he corrected, "Or I was. Teo is what my mother called me."

"Mateo." Gina stepped away, and Matt's hands fell back to his sides. He continued to clench them; maybe then they wouldn't feel so empty. "Mateo Mecate?"

"That's him." McCord strode over, inserting his wide shoulders between Matt and Gina as if he were afraid Matt might hurt her.

Again.

"Moldy, old Dr. Mecate," Gina murmured.

"I'm sorry?" Matt asked.

"Not yet," McCord answered. "But you're gonna be."

Matt ignored him. The only thing that mattered now was her.

"Gina." Matt stepped to the side so he could see around the other man's bulk. "I can exp—"

"We called you moldy Mecate," she said. "We thought you were . . ." She looked Matt up and down, and her lip curled. "Old."

"I'm not. I'm . . ." He spread his hands. "Me."

Now those lips flattened, and suddenly he wanted the curl back. "You're *not* you. Or at least not the you you said you were. You're not Teo Jones."

Matt winced. The Jones part had been a mistake. But everything else was true.

Mostly.

"Who do you think you are, man?" McCord's grin was so wide, he appeared ready to laugh out loud or maybe break into song. He had to have been dancing since he discovered the truth. "Indiana Jones?"

"What?"

"Dr. Jones. Archaeology professor. You wanna dig deep down and discover buried treasure." McCord snorted. "Where's your whip and your hat? You got a hard-on for Harrison Ford or something?

Right now any hard-on Matt might have had was fading fast. Thank God. Because the others had begun to duck out of their tents and gather around to watch.

"You practically told me who you were," Gina murmured. "As if Teo is that far off of Mateo, and then Dr. Jones—" She rolled her eyes as if she, or maybe he, was the biggest idiot ever born.

"I don't . . ." Matt paused, because suddenly he *did* understand. He'd chosen Jones because Smith seemed too obviously a false name, but he wanted something simple, something he could remember. It had never occurred to him that the name of the Harrison Ford character all his flighty students adored was Dr. Jones.

How could he be both so smart and so dumb at the same time? It was a gift.

"I didn't—" he began.

"Oh, I'd say you did," McCord said. "Or at least you were going to."

"Will you *shut* up," Matt said between gritted teeth.

"Nope." McCord stuck his thumbs in his belt and rocked back on his boot heels, clearly enjoying this so much he could hardly stand it.

Matt wanted to punch him, something he could never before remember wanting. Violence didn't solve anything. He'd studied enough wars to understand that.

However, he thought it might make him feel better to smash his fist into that smirking face. And right now Matt felt so bad it might be worth getting his own face smashed in just for the tiny bit of joy he'd receive from popping Jase McCord in his noble Native nose.

"What happened?" Amberleigh asked, her volume causing several birds to start up from nearby trees.

"Shh, dear." Melda's bright blue gaze switched among Matt, Gina, and McCord as she chewed on her lip. "Not our business."

"Then why are we out here watchin'," Mel wondered, "when we could be in the tent f—?"

"Anyone want coffee?" Tim announced, and any

birds that had remained in the vicinity followed their friends to Canada. "I'm buying."

No one took Tim up on the offer. Because they all knew there wasn't a Starbucks for miles or because they didn't care that it wasn't their business since the scene unfolding in front of them was the most excitement they'd had in years?

You could take the kid off the playground, but you never, ever took the playground out of the kid. Even Matt, who'd never been *on* a playground, knew this as well as he knew his own name.

All of them.

If there was going to be a fight, no one wanted to miss it.

"What were you hoping to do?" Gina asked. "What possible reason could you have for not telling me the truth?"

"I . . . uh . . . well . . ." Matt took a deep breath. Why had pretending to be someone else seemed like a great idea? Now that he'd been outed, it merely seemed like the foolish stunt it was. Wasn't that always the way? Matt released his breath on a rush. "I got nothin'."

"Nothing?" Gina's voice was deceptively calm, excruciatingly soft. "You almost had me."

"No, Gina, it isn't what you think."

"You weren't trying to ingratiate yourself with the owner? Get me into bed, make me think that I was special, then beg just one little favor?"

"No." At her frown, he hurried onward, shoving that foot in his mouth so far down his throat it was a wonder he could talk at all. "I wanted to check the place out. See if it— See if you—" The expression on her face made him stop.

"You were spying on us?"

"No. Well, yes. But not you. The area."

"And this." She waved her hand to indicate what had passed between them.

"That was between you and me. It had nothing, whatsoever, to do with my work."

One of the horses snorted; then several others answered, making it seem as if none of *them* believed Matt, either.

"You wouldn't answer my calls, my e-mails, my letters," he pressed on. "When I got here you tore up the most recent message right in front of me. What was I supposed to do?"

"Find some other ranch to trash?" McCord asked amiably.

Matt ignored him, focusing on Gina. "Just listen to me, Gina. Let me explain why this is so important."

"Important enough to pretend you liked me," she murmured. "Must be life-or-death stuff."

Matt frowned, confused. "Pretend?"

"Yes," she snapped. "Lie, cheat, act like you care. Remember?"

"I told you that wasn't how it was. How it *is*."

"Right. Because a guy like you—" She waved her hand to indicate . . . His head? His face? He wasn't sure. "Is gonna be interested in a girl like me."

"Why wouldn't I be?"

She laughed, though the sound was watery. There were tears there somewhere waiting to spill out, and Matt hated himself. "Never mind," she said. "Go on. Tell me why you had to do this. What's so damn important about my land that you just can't let it go?"

There was something going on he didn't understand. But if Matt couldn't convince her now, he was not only never going to be able to vindicate both his mother's work and his own, but he'd also never find out what in hell she was talking about.

"You aren't actually thinking of listening to this guy, are you?" McCord seemed a little worried, and Matt's panic lessened.

This was the path to what he wanted. Tell Gina everything. Or almost everything. He should probably leave out the sorcerer. That usually made people stop listening, if not right away, then shortly thereafter. But he could convince her with the parts of the theory that didn't sound crazy. He had to. He just wished he didn't have to do it in front of all these people.

Once he made his case, Gina would agree to let him dig. Hell, maybe she'd even help.

Matt pulled the copy of the photograph out of his pocket, smoothed the paper, then held it up so she could see.

Gina took one look at it, paled, and said, "Get him out of here."

"Wait. What? No!" Teo, or whatever he called himself now, insisted. "Gina, you have to listen—"

She snatched the photo out of his hands and walked away.

When she reached the banked fire she crouched, poking up the flames, then feeding them twigs. As soon as they licked upward again, Gina tossed the thing on top.

She'd destroyed every hard copy she had and deleted the file. She never wanted to see that place again, not even on film. Where had he gotten it?

"Internet," she muttered. Where nothing ever died.

Gina rubbed her eyes. She felt numb, and she needed not to be. She had a tour to lead. There was no one else.

"Gina?" Melda stood on the other side of the fire. "You all right?"

"Fine." She straightened, brushing her hands on her jeans. "Everyone be ready to leave in an hour."

"What happened?" Amberleigh appeared stuck on that question.

"Why'd you send Teo away?" Ashleigh asked. "He was the only man worth talkin' to round here."

"Hey," Tim said.

Ashleigh flipped her hand dismissively. "Oh, don't get your panties in a bunch. You're okay, but I'm not stepmama material. Especially for a boy that close to my age."

"Stepmama?" Derek repeated, more intrigued than horrified.

"I thought you were graduating from college," Tim said.

"So?"

"Aren't you going to get a job before you get married?"

"Why on earth would I do somethin' like that?"

"What happened?" This time Amberleigh stomped her foot and put her hands on her hips. Maybe that worked with other people, but it just made Gina want to turn a hose on her.

"Pack up. Deal with your mount. Or so help me—" Gina took one step toward Amberleigh, and the girl ran.

She should feel bad about that, but she didn't.

Everyone got busy and left her alone. She'd done the job for so long it was second nature and she could go about preparing breakfast, packing her tent, and saddling her horse without having to think too much.

Because all she could think about was what an idiot she'd been.

She'd wondered why Teo was so interested in her so fast—or at all—but she'd been captivated by him just as quickly. She'd thought because there was something special between them, something she'd never felt before. But he'd manufactured those feelings the same way he'd manufactured his name and his background.

Her head went up as another thought crowded in. His interest in her photography had all been bullshit, too. Gina took a shaky breath, embarrassed at how much his words of praise had meant to her. He'd only wanted to find out the location of that cursed photograph.

She was tempted to remove her camera from her pack and leave it behind a rock somewhere, then never take another picture again. But photography was the one thing she had that was hers, something she did just for herself. She couldn't give it up, even though she had a feeling that every time she lifted her camera from now on she'd remember him.

While the others ate breakfast, Gina stepped into the trees and tried to get herself under control. She couldn't ride a horse, even Lady Belle, with her hands shaking this badly. And she wouldn't be able to keep an eye on her guests or give them the nature tour she'd planned for the day if she couldn't speak past the tears in her throat.

Hadn't she promised she'd show one of them a bear?

Crap. That had been Teo. Well, since she was never going to see him again as long as she lived, she wouldn't have to worry about that.

Her laughter came out sounding like a silly sob, and she drew in a breath that hitched in the middle.

"Stop it," she ordered, wringing her hands together so tightly they ached.

Teo was gone. She would forget about him. His questions. His secrets. His lies.

And that damn photograph? She'd try to forget it, but really . . .

How could she ever forget the place where her parents had died?

"I'm not getting on that," Matt protested.

"That's right you aren't." McCord lifted his chin, indicating they should head downhill. "Granddad's meeting us on the dirt road. He'll take you back in the truck."

"What if I don't want to go back?" Matt asked, even as he began to walk.

"That would just make my day." McCord moved along next to Matt, keeping pace with his hand on the clutch.

"You gonna beat me senseless?"

"Only if you ask real nice."

Matt sighed. He was screwed, and he knew it.

"Wait." Matt stopped. "My horse."

"Not *yours,*" the man sneered; however, he did contemplate Matt with a little more respect. "Gina will probably ride Spike and lead Lady Belle. Don't worry; your horse won't be left behind for the wolves to eat."

"There aren't any wolves," Matt muttered, almost as sad about never seeing Spike again as he was about never seeing Gina. He liked that horse.

Matt suddenly realized that he'd continued on but McCord hadn't, and turned. "What?"

"She *told* you?"

"About the wolves, or lack of them? Yeah. So?"

The man narrowed his eyes. "What else did she tell you?"

Matt had a sudden urge to say, *That's for me to know and you to find out.* But if he continued with the playground imagery a taunt like that would only ascertain that Jase did find out. Probably by giving Matt purple nurples until he cried uncle.

What was it he'd heard his students say?

Been there, done that. Saw the Blu-ray.

He hadn't had his ass handed to him by a bully since he'd turned twelve and grown six inches. He didn't plan to go back now. Besides, Matt couldn't think of anything else Gina might have told him that was important. He couldn't think why *that* was important.

So there weren't any wolves on the ranch. Wasn't that a good thing?

"Mecate . . ." McCord began.

"Nothing," Matt said. "She didn't tell me anything else but that."

McCord grunted. He didn't believe Matt. Luckily, they slid past a line of trees and Isaac appeared not far below, leaning against a faded red pickup. Too late for McCord to beat Matt senseless now. He doubted Isaac would approve.

"How'd you find out who I was?" Matt asked.

"I wasn't looking for you. I was looking for Old Moldy."

Matt liked that nickname less and less every time he heard it.

"Went to the Internet, plugged in your name, and up popped your pretty-boy face."

"Google sucks," Matt muttered.

"For you," McCord agreed.

"You could have waited for us to get back."

"Appears I got here in the nick of time." McCord scowled. "Or maybe a few minutes too late. You really believe sleeping with Gina would get her to agree to let you dig up her . . ." He paused, tightening his lips as if he'd almost said too much. Then he saw Matt waiting, expectant, and finished with, "Place. Guys like you think because you have a golden face, you've got a golden dick. Does every wish you make on that thing come true?"

"You really believe warning away every other man that comes near her is going to make her fall in love with you? Forever after by process of elimination?"

"I don't warn guys away," McCord said, but he suddenly became very interested in the trail ahead of them, a trail he had to have seen a thousand times before.

"I'm not as moldy as you think I am. Especially up here." Matt tapped his forehead. "How many guys have you sent packing over the years? How many times did she wait for a phone call that didn't come because you threatened to smash someone's teeth in?"

The tightness of the man's jaw told Matt the number was pretty damn high.

"Be a big boy," Matt said. "Tell her the truth before she finds out from someone else. She doesn't seem to like it when that happens."

McCord's head came up. "Don't you dare—"

"I'm not going to tell her anything," Matt said. "I'll probably never see her again thanks to you."

The sadness that flooded Matt after that statement surprised him just a little. Sure, he'd wanted her, but he hadn't realized how much he'd liked her, how much he would miss her company after only knowing her for a short while.

They continued on toward where Isaac waited, hat tilted, face in shadow. Matt might not be able to see the old man's expression but could easily tell from the way Isaac held himself that he wasn't happy.

Matt glanced at his companion. "What was it about the photo that made Gina go white as a ghost?"

McCord flinched at the word *ghost,* which only piqued Matt's interest and caused his busy brain to kick into high gear. "Is that area haunted?"

"What area?"

"The one in the picture?"

McCord smirked. "What picture?"

Matt narrowed his eyes. The man knew very well *what picture.* Of course, since Matt no longer had it and Gina had probably destroyed it . . .

Hell.

Still, McCord's reluctance to talk about the place, his refusal to even acknowledge it, combined with his response to the word *ghost . . .* There was *something* there.

A battleground? A graveyard?

A superwarrior's tomb?

People didn't behave this strangely without something to hide. Of course McCord would swallow his own tongue before he told Matt what it was.

They reached the road, and Isaac got behind the wheel without a single word of greeting. He was equally chatty all the way to the ranch.

McCord revved the dirt bike's motor, which was loud enough to be a Harley, and took off in the opposite direction. He'd travel as the crow flew and no doubt beat Isaac and Matt to their destination.

Sure enough, when the pickup pulled into the yard

the man not only was waiting for them but had also already packed Matt's things.

"Thanks for your patronage." McCord threw the suitcase at Matt so hard, Matt staggered a step when he caught it. "Never come again."

"My money?" Matt asked.

"What money?" McCord returned, already heading for the house.

That was the problem with cash. No proof of purchase.

Matt rummaged through the outside zipper pockets of his bag for the car keys. But a cry from the house had him glancing up just as Fanny banged through the screen door and handed a sheet of paper to her son. Matt was able to make out the name *Benjamin Morris* at the top.

Isaac joined his daughter and grandson on the porch, and they began to murmur among themselves. Matt caught one phrase—"sell the ranch at auction"—before McCord remembered him and snapped, "Don't you have somewhere to be?"

Matt's gaze met Fanny's, then Isaac's. No help there. While they weren't actively scowling as McCord was, they no longer looked at Matt with anything akin to welcome.

Matt nodded in lieu of "good-bye" and headed for the car, digging again for his keys. As he got in, he had an idea.

He hoped this one would turn out better than the last one had.

CHAPTER 8

Gina and the rest of the group straggled into the yard two days later. Over the past twenty-four hours, the heavens had opened and dumped every last bit of rain in the world on top of them. They were wet, hungry, tired, and just a little cranky.

But filed into the barn with their mounts. The horses were as tired and wet and dirty as they were, and it would be inhuman to leave them like that.

Gina led Spike and Lady Belle to their stalls. Jase appeared and took care of Spike with tight, annoyed movements, not speaking until he finished well ahead of her.

"Meet me in the kitchen," he said. "We've got trouble."

"What kind of trouble?"

Teo didn't seem the type to be a problem. Then again, he hadn't seemed the type to lie, and look how wrong she'd been.

Jase just shook his head and moved off to help the others.

The next few days would be spent at the ranch for

the spa portion of their getaway. The guests could order massages, travel to the nearby hot springs, schedule a yoga retreat or any number of other relaxing benefits before they left on their second, slightly more difficult than the first, trail ride.

Gina finished with Lady Belle and was able to cop a shower and a change of clothes yet still beat Jase to the kitchen. Fanny was putting the finishing touches on supper, which would consist of her famous Five-Alarm Chili and Fajita Chicken Nachos.

Despite the hot shower and warm clothes, Gina remained chilled. She poured herself a cup of coffee from the always-full pot and sat at the table.

"What happened?" she asked.

Fanny continued to stir the chili, refusing to meet Gina's eyes. "You must talk to Jase."

Gina didn't like this at all, especially since she could have sworn unshed tears thickened Fanny's voice. But no matter how many times Gina asked or how much she begged, Fanny would say nothing more. Which caused Gina to imagine all sorts of horrible things.

Teo and Jase fighting. Teo hitting his head. He was now in an irreversible coma, and the police were asking questions.

Teo dead and buried in the garden. Jase needed her to help him figure out what they were going to do with the rest of the bodies. Because they couldn't let anyone leave now, could they?

Gina shook her head. She'd watched *way* too many thriller movies on cold winter nights. Then again, so had Jase.

Taking a sip of coffee, she faced the scenario she'd been avoiding—a far more realistic but no less disturbing one. What if Teo was still here, refusing to leave until she led him to the place depicted in that photograph?

After her parents had died, it had taken Gina nearly a year to go back there. By then, the cavern had been filled with earth, packed tight, and made to appear as if nothing had ever happened there at all.

But *she* knew better.

Jase walked in, and Gina started up so fast, she nearly knocked over her chair. She did slosh coffee onto the once-pristine tabletop.

"What happened?" she repeated, a little too loud.

Jase glanced at his mom, who continued to stir the chili, staring into it as if she could find the answer to one of life's great questions at the bottom of that pot. "You didn't tell her?"

"That is for you."

"Great," he muttered.

"What did you do?" Gina demanded. "Did you hurt him?"

"I haven't even talked to him yet."

Jase crossed the room and poured his own coffee, then took the dishcloth his mother handed him, even though she hadn't turned around and could not possibly know Gina had spilled anything, and tossed it to her. "Do you want me to hurt him?"

Gina, in the middle of wiping up the mess, paused. The overhead lights caught Jase's dark eyes, making them loom black as a starless night. For an instant he looked like someone she didn't know. "Are you nuts?"

Jase shrugged. "He's gonna take the ranch. I wouldn't mind getting a few licks first."

"Take the ranch?" All of Gina's horrible scenarios

came rushing back. Teo in traction, fat lip, black eye, talking to his lawyer, instigating lawsuits. Huge earth-movers rolling up the road within the week.

"How could you?" Gina threw the sopping dishrag at Jase's head. He caught it with one hand and tossed it into the sink. She really couldn't get a good throw with something so flimsy. Next time she'd use her coffee mug. "So he lied. So he kissed me. You didn't have to break him."

Fanny stopped her stirring. "Who kissed you?"

Jase, who'd been taking an impossibly large sip of some very hot coffee, paused with the mug still to his lips. His glance flicked to his mother, then back to Gina before he lowered the mug and swallowed. "What are you talking about?"

"You hurt Teo, and now he's suing us. We're gonna lose the ranch."

Jase set the cup down so hard Gina thought it might shatter. Then he picked up an envelope from the counter and tossed it onto the table, where it skidded across the surface so fast she had to slap her palm on top of it to keep the thing from sliding off the other side.

"I'd forgotten about that asshole," Jase said. "But obviously you haven't. Maybe that'll bring your mind back to more important things than pretty boy."

He stalked out of the house, slamming the door behind him. Gina opened the envelope and discovered that Jase was right.

Any thoughts of Teo Mecate instantly disappeared as soon as she read what lay inside.

Matt made the mistake of asking his rental GPS to direct him to the nearest town, which he then drove right through without stopping, since it was composed of a few houses and several stray dogs.

After he'd driven five miles down the highway and been told by an annoyingly prim British voice that he must make a "legal U-turn," he'd done so and discovered the sign for Nomad as he'd come back in the other side.

Since Matt couldn't find a single business establishment—no gas station, no restaurant, not even a tavern—with his eyes or the damn GPS, he'd knocked on the only house with a car in the driveway (even though it was up on blocks, it was still a car) and been told by the seemingly alone ten-year-old kid that the nearest "real" town was Durango.

Matt had known this, having flown *into* it. He'd just figured there had to be another one closer to the ranch than forty miles away. Why he'd figured that he had no idea. Unless it was because the uppity British voice on the GPS had told him so.

He'd driven close to a half hour back in the direction he'd come, then another hour farther on roads that really needed some work. By the time he reached Durango, just after five, any inquiries he might have made at the courthouse or a local bank had to be postponed.

Matt had been tempted to drive directly to the airport and fly home. But the sight of the Strater Hotel convinced him to at least stay the night.

The Strater was an historic landmark in downtown Durango. Built in the late 1880s by the pharmacist Henry Strater, who didn't have the money, the experience, or enough years on the planet to enter into a contract when he started, the building had become a testament to old-time Western ingenuity. Henry built his dream with spit, grit, and imagination, and the hotel became not only prosperous but also a legend.

The place had been remodeled by the latest owners

and now boasted ninety-three Victorian rooms, each with a plumbing upgrade.

The desk clerk leaned forward, lowering his voice as if to impart a really great secret. "Louis L'Amour always stayed in room two-twenty-two."

"Okay." Matt wasn't sure why that was important.

"He said the music from the Diamond Belle Saloon right below helped him to write all those books."

"Good for him."

"Would you like to stay there? It's open."

"Why would I want to listen to music?"

The clerk glanced pointedly at the laptop case in Matt's hand.

"Oh," he said. "I'm not a writer. Just . . ."

"You don't have to explain, sir. Many of our guests are addicted to the Internet." He straightened, tapping the keys of his computer, then giving a pleased nod at what his keyboard prowess had wrought. "Would you like a room with free wireless Internet?"

Matt didn't answer at first, figuring the question had been rhetorical—who *wouldn't* want free wireless Internet?—but when the clerk continued to stare at him with his so light as to be almost invisible eyebrows raised Matt finally said, "Sure!"

A shower, some clean clothes, and a half hour with his computer and Matt was almost himself again. He found Benjamin Morris—a retired banker who'd gone into the business of buying properties in trouble, then charging the debtors a higher interest rate—through Google. However, when Matt called to set up an appointment Mr. Morris was "not available until Monday."

Though he had to wait several days to move forward, actually knowing where he was moving made him feel refreshed, renewed, and ready to prove the Mecate theory, as well as keep his job. He wasn't going to let anyone—not even the luscious Gina O'Neil—blow it for him. Besides, considering the trouble she was in, his plan would benefit them both.

He spent Friday strolling around the fascinatingly old yet intriguingly updated Strater Hotel, having a glass of wine in their Spiritorium and dinner at the Mahogany Grille next door, where he opted to ignore the elk tenderloin in favor of the Kansas City strip.

On Saturday and Sunday Matt toured the overly western but still kind of fun Durango. They'd done a nice job keeping the downtown area reminiscent of the Old West. If he didn't know better he'd think the bookstore and the candy store had actually been there since 1875.

In between his brief fits of tourism Matt did some research. Couldn't let all that free Wi-Fi go to waste.

He discovered that Nahua Springs Ranch had gone to Gina as the only child following the accidental death of her parents. What that accidental death had been was never fully explained beyond "accident," which could cover any manner of things. That it *wasn't* revealed just how high the O'Neils were in the pecking order of the area.

Nahua Springs had once been a well-respected quarter-horse ranch. Betsy O'Neil was one of the top breeders and Pete one of the best trainers. It wasn't until after they'd died that Nahua Springs had morphed from real ranch to dude.

Though it was considered one of the finest in the area, nevertheless, the place had been in trouble for a while. You had to sell a lot of "I wanna be a cowboy" packages just to make the mortgage every month, and that was before you figured in taxes that in recent years had bloomed well past excruciating.

In truth, without the intervention of Benjamin Morris, Nahua Springs would have been lost years ago.

Matt rubbed his tired eyes. Gina had been responsible for the place since she was fifteen. She could use a little help, and he was just the man to give it to her. She'd be so grateful.

He returned to the computer, figuring he should print another copy of the photograph Gina had snatched from his hand—he was certain they had an office center downstairs where he could do just that—but he Googled his brains out and couldn't find it. The picture was just . . . gone.

"Dammit," he muttered. Someone had removed it.

Gina? Or Jase? Did it matter?

He'd probably come across the image eventually—the Internet was like that—but why waste any more time? Matt didn't need the photo to remember what the area looked like.

From the expression on Gina's face when he'd shown it to her, she wasn't going to forget it anytime soon, either.

Gina would have liked to head directly into town and confront Benjamin Morris. Unfortunately, his office was closed for the weekend. Probably for the best, since she had to spend the next few days scheduling spa treatments and entertaining their guests.

SOP for the final night of the spa portion of the package was a bonfire, complete with a local crooner who sang amusing cowboy ditties with help from the guests.

Mel loved it. He and the entertainment began a dueling song contest that had begun as amusing, with Mel continuing to pull old favorites from his boys' school days like:

"A bum sat by the sewer
And by the sewer he died
And at the coroner's inquest
They called it 'sewer side'

Oh, it ain't gonna rain no more, no more
It ain't gonna rain no more
How in the heck can I wash around my neck
If it ain't gonna rain no more?"

But later the contest segued into poetry and became disturbing when a few too many Moonshine Mollys, Isaac's concoction that tasted like a weak whiskey sour but packed the punch of a double Long Island Iced Tea, led to the following:

"There once was a fellow McSweeny
Who spilled some gin on his weenie
Just to be couth
He added vermouth
Then slipped his girlfriend a martini"

"Whoa!" Gina jumped up from her perch on one of the flat stumps scattered around the bonfire for just that purpose. "And that concludes the entertainment for this evening."

"Aw, how come?" Mel muttered. "I know 'bout a hundred more."

"He does," Melda agreed, snatching the nearly empty glass that had held a third Molly from his hand. "Once he gets started, it's pretty hard to shut him the hell up."

"How do you slip someone a martini?" Derek asked. "I don't get it."

"Let's go." Tim shot both Gina and Mel a look nearly as dirty as the limerick and dragged his son into the house.

"A martini sounds good," Amberleigh announced.

The cowboy crooner smoothed back what was left of his hair, then wiped the grease he'd spread into it onto his jeans. "I could help you with that, little lady."

"Really?" Ashleigh asked. The As were sharing a sheared double log on the far side of the fire. "You have vermouth and gin?"

"No." The crooner shifted his hand from his hip to his crotch. "But I've got a—"

"Out!" Gina announced.

"But I want a martini!" Amberleigh wailed.

"Not that kind," Gina muttered. "Believe me."

She motioned for Jase to get rid of the guy, and while he hadn't spoken to her since he'd stalked out of the kitchen, he did as she asked. If it got around that they'd held a lewd-limerick contest on bonfire night they could lose what customers they had. Or maybe they'd have more customers than they could handle. Either way, the cowboy crooner needed to go now.

What *was* his real name?

"I'm gonna write a new sh-ongbook," Mel slurred. "I jush-t need music for my poems."

He was determined to create that music before morning. Gina would have gladly left him to it—she doubted he'd be able to keep from passing out within the next few minutes—except Mel wanted to compose music on a piano they didn't have, wearing underwear that existed only in his imagination.

"Isaac!" Gina shouted, and when the old man appeared she shoved a naked Mel in his direction. "Your problem."

She'd *told* him not to serve people more than one of his Moonshine Mollys.

Gina hurried to her room, retrieved a key, and unlocked the hall closet where she kept clothes she never wore.

Hanging in a plastic bag right in the center was her best dress. Sure, it had been her best dress since she'd gotten it for high school graduation. But that didn't make it any less nice. Just a little out-of-date.

Gina removed the garment from the bag, letting the full white skirt dotted with tiny purple flowers flow through her fingers.

"You aren't gonna wear that, are you?"

Both As stood silhouetted in the door of their room.

"You aren't supposed to wear white before . . ." Ashleigh frowned. "Labor Day?"

"*After* Labor Day," Amberleigh corrected. "Not *before* Memorial Day."

"Why?" Gina asked.

The girls glanced at each other, then back at Gina.

"Because you can't," Ashleigh said.

"I assure you I can." Gina leaned down and grabbed her white pumps from the bottom of the closet. Especially since she didn't have much choice.

"Ew!" Ashleigh exclaimed.

"Not those shoes," Amberleigh agreed.

Gina turned them over. They were a little scuffed on the heels, but otherwise they seemed fine to her.

"White pumps are for weddings," Ashleigh whispered as if it were a secret.

"Only?" Gina asked.

"Maybe christenings." She glanced at Amberleigh.

The other girl shrugged and murmured, "Confirmations?"

"Bar Mitzvahs!" Ashleigh announced.

"I think that's Bat Mitzvahs," Gina corrected.

"Bats don't have mitzvahs." Ashleigh laughed. "You're silly."

"That's me," Gina agreed, heading for her room with her white dress and white shoes. "Silly, silly, silly."

"Hold on." Amberleigh stepped in front of her and peered into Gina's eyes. "You really gonna wear that?"

Gina nearly walked past without answering. But there seemed to be someone home behind Amberleigh's usually vacant blue gaze for a change. "I have a business meeting tomorrow."

She didn't, not really. She hadn't bothered to call Mr. Morris and set up a meeting. That would only give him a chance to refuse.

"With a man?"

"What difference does that make?"

Amberleigh lifted a brow and waited. Gina sighed, thinking of the short, squat, strange little man who had bought her ranch from the bank. She hated the guy. But he *was* a guy. And the last time she'd visited him, asking for an extension on their loan, he'd taken one look at her dusty boots, faded jeans, and flannel shirt, lifted his lip, and said, *Next time, wear a dress.*

"Yeah," she said. "It's a man. So?"

"Important?"

"Very," Gina agreed.

"In that case, sugar." Amberleigh took the white garment from Gina's hands; Ashleigh took the white shoes, then together they tossed them into the closet and slammed the door. "You're gonna need a better dress."

CHAPTER 9

"Why are there dress*es*?" Gina asked, voice muffled as she pulled on a third, or maybe a fourth. Her head popped out the top. "For that matter why would there even be *dress*?"

"You never know when you might need a hot outfit." Amberleigh's forehead creased as she studied Gina.

"I know," Gina muttered. "Three days past never."

"This one works." Amberleigh smiled. "Don't you think so, Ash?"

Gina was shocked that she fit into Amberleigh's clothes. The blonde appeared smaller in some ways and larger in two others. But with a little tugging and pinning—why Amberleigh had pins in her suitcase was as much of a mystery as why she had dresses—Gina had to admit the dress worked.

"That's the one." Ashleigh agreed, then motioned for Gina to turn.

When she did, she found herself captured by the stranger in the mirror. The garment nipped in places and tucked in others, and the shade—a combination of red and brown that the As had insisted on calling auburn—had made Gina's plain old brown hair shine with streaks of gold.

"You wear that tomorrow," Amberleigh said, "and no man is gonna be able to take his eyes offa you."

Gina wasn't sure how that would help; then again it probably couldn't hurt.

"You can't wear a dress like that without heels like this." Ashleigh handed her a pair of ankle breakers the shade of a copper penny.

"Oh, I don't think so." Gina tried to return them, but Ashleigh put her hands behind her back and shook her head firmly.

"The whole effect's gonna be ruined if you don't wear the shoes."

"The whole effect's gonna be ruined when I fall on my face and break my nose," Gina muttered.

"Even itty-bitty girls wear heels," Ashleigh said.

"*Especially* itty-bitty girls," Amberleigh agreed. "Makes their legs look *lo-o-ong*. Makes men wonder how those legs would feel naked and wrapped around—"

"I'll wear the heels!" Gina interrupted, not only because if she heard the rest of that sentence her eardrums might go pop but also because she'd needed to put a stop to the image that had leaped into her own head.

Of her long legs, naked and wrapped around Teo Mecate's—

"Thanks," she told the As, feeling kind of fond of them for a minute.

Gina had never done anything like this before. No sharing of clothes and shoes, no discussions of men, no slumber parties. The few friends she'd had in school had never really felt like friends because they were always talking about all the fun things they did while Gina worked at the ranch.

Sure, she'd had Jase. She'd always have Jase. But there was something to be said for a girlfriend.

"Why are you helping me?" she asked.

Had she expected apologies for rudeness, perhaps an explanation of girl power, or a sudden profession of friendship, which in her current state she might have accepted, Gina would have been disappointed.

Because what she got was a yawn from Ashleigh. "We were bored."

And a shrug from Amberleigh. "It's not like you're gonna come out ahead in any competition for a man. Not even in that dress."

"Like there are any men left to compete for," Ashleigh muttered, disgusted. "Two old guys, a dad, and a little kid."

"What about Jase?" Gina asked, then bit her lip. Why on earth was she trying to sic these two on her best friend?

"He'd never leave here, and I'm certainly not stayin'," Ashleigh answered as Amberleigh nodded in agreement.

Every once in a while the As said something that made Gina think they were smarter than they pretended. Because they were right. Jase would never leave Nahua Springs, and neither would she.

Gina was a bit disgusted with herself. For an instant after the As had declared she couldn't beat them in a competition, she'd actually experienced a burst of competitiveness accompanied by the thought: *I'll show you!*

Gina rubbed her forehead. The dress and the shoes

and the brainless twits were getting to her. She wasn't *in* a competition, for men or anything else. The outfit was supposed to make her feel good about herself, give her the confidence to slay the dragon ex-banker in his den.

And if Mr. Morris got distracted by her cleavage or her legs and gave her another sixty days before he sold the ranch . . . Gina gave a mental shrug. It was no more than he deserved for looking in the first place.

There was a wrench in her logic somewhere, but Gina decided not to look for it.

The As kept her up long past midnight—she'd had to wait for her nail polish to dry—and Gina overslept the next morning. Then the unfamiliar clothes, the needle-heeled shoes, which fit fine with the addition of some newspaper in the toes—Ashleigh had freakishly big feet—the styling of Gina's hair, and the application of makeup so old she had to add water in order to smooth some of the dry cracked stuff onto her face meant she was parking the truck in front of Benjamin Morris's office at 9:30 instead of the 8:45 she'd planned.

"Tough." Gina slammed the door of the truck. It wasn't as if Mr. Morris wasn't going to be in his office on this fine May morning. He always had been in the past.

As before, Mr. Morris sat behind a desk that was much too large for him. Gina had to wonder if he'd in-herited the furniture from an extremely tall previous owner of the building or the desk itself was the usual male compensation mechanism. She'd been around enough men to know what big cars, big hats, big boots, and big horses meant.

She also knew better than to say so.

As her mother would have told her, now was the

time for honey, not vinegar. Since Gina was more of a vinegar type she had her work cut out for her.

Maybe the dress *would* help.

"Gina," Morris murmured, his voice so low it still startled her to hear it coming from a man so small in stature his feet couldn't possibly be touching the floor from the height of his gigantic office chair. "What can I do for you?"

"I . . . well . . ."

Get it together, Gina. Smile. Dance. Show him what you've got!

Gina smiled, straightened her back, and walked to the guest chair, swishing the skirt for all she was worth. And Mr. Morris *did* notice. His gaze went from her face to her breasts, then did a quick leap to her feet and stayed there.

"Nice shoes." He licked his lips.

"Thanks. I've come about this." Leaning over, she set the letter in front of him. Instead of peering down her dress, as any red-blooded American male should, or so she'd heard, he leaned to the side so he could keep his gaze on her feet.

Gina tapped the paper, then snapped her fingers beneath his nose. She was starting to think that the dress had been a mistake. The shoes certainly were.

She snapped again when Mr. Morris continued to salivate over parts of her much lower than he should be and was at last rewarded with his attention.

His tiny dark eyes flickered over the letter before he pushed it back toward her. "There's nothing I can do."

"I'll have the money next month."

She wouldn't, but she had to say something.

He stared down his also-short nose at her. "It wouldn't matter if you did."

"Because you don't like money?"

"I adore money. Which is why I accepted the offer of the gentleman who was in my office this morning a single moment after I arrived."

"I don't understand."

He leaned back and spoke to the ceiling: "They never understand."

"Who's they?"

He lowered his head. "People who can't pay their bills. I warn them and I warn them; then when I sell off the merchandise they're so confused."

"Sell?" Gina stood, towering over the man. He didn't appear intimidated. He was no doubt used to it. "You sold my ranch?"

"Not yours. Not mine, either, anymore." He wagged a finger at her. "I *did* warn you."

Gina sat again. Her legs weren't going to hold her much longer. "What happens now?"

"That's up to the new owner." Morris's attention had returned to Gina's shoes. "A doctor . . ."

"Crap!" Gina sprang to her feet just as Mr. Morris murmured, "Mecate."

Matt returned to the Strater and began to make phone calls. He put a decent-sized crew on alert. They'd come just as soon as he found the area of the ranch that matched the photograph. A few more calls and he'd rented all the equipment he'd need for the dig.

He'd thought the meeting with Benjamin Morris would take longer, that the man would require convincing, that Matt might even have to bid against other interested parties or wait for a public auction. Instead, he'd walked out of the office a half hour later with the paperwork.

Cash worked wonders. Or at least the ability to complete a wire transfer.

Matt tossed the few things he'd removed from his suitcase back in. He couldn't wait to tell Gina.

He'd just set his glasses on the bedside table, then yanked off the tie and scratchy dress shirt he'd bought the day before when someone tapped on the door. Figuring it was a bellman—even though he hadn't requested one, he had called to inform the desk he was checking out—Matt glanced up, saw he'd left the door ajar in his hurry to return to the ranch, and called, "Come in."

It wasn't the bellman.

At first he wasn't sure who the woman was. She flew across the room so fast Matt, without his glasses, only got the impression of tall, curvy, lots of legs, and miles of flowing hair. Then he caught the scent of the forest an instant before he caught her.

His mind, full of those legs and that hair and the smell of her, stuttered once before it came to the conclusion that she'd found out about him saving her ranch and come to thank him. Personally, so to speak. So he wrapped his arms more tightly around her.

Their chests bumped, their hips, too. She murmured his name as they both lost their balance; then one of her obscenely high heels came down on his foot. Next thing Matt knew they fell onto the bed.

He landed on top. They bounced once. All the air in her lungs flew out, blowing back his hair. Her dress had bunched up; his palm now cupped her thigh. Her skin was so damn soft he couldn't help but stroke.

Her lips parted; her eyes darkened to smoke, and then he was kissing her, tasting her, wanting her as he had kissed and tasted and wanted her not so long before. But this time no one would interrupt and tell her his secrets. She knew his secrets—all of them—and still she had come to him here.

His hair made a curtain, shrouding them from the world. She reached up, her fingers tangling in the strands, hard; it kind of hurt.

He tugged on her lip with his teeth, and her grip relaxed, turning from torture to temptation. She pulled him closer, opened her mouth wider on a sigh, and he caught the flavor of . . . lipstick?

How strange. He wasn't a fan. Then again, he'd eat a tube if it meant he could kiss her some more.

Her tongue met his, sliding along the underside, then tickling the edge. Her hands had moved from his hair to his neck, her fingers cupping the back of his head, urging him on.

He discovered his fingers were cupping her ass, shifting her so that they fit together just . . .

There, that felt better. Except they were wearing far too many clothes, or at least she was. He spared a moment to be glad his shirt had scratched and he'd yanked it off, because now her palms were on his chest, stroking him as he'd just stroked her.

It had been so long since anyone had touched him. Or at least anyone he'd wanted as badly as he wanted Gina.

His hand had just lifted to the tricky fastening at the front of her dress when someone cleared their throat. Matt ignored the sound. It couldn't be real. He and Gina were in his room. On his bed.

Alone.

Someone coughed—loudly—and they didn't stop. Whoever was out in the hall sounded like they'd just swallowed a whale down the wrong pipe and they were going to die if the Heimlich wasn't performed immediately.

Matt's concentration was shot. He lifted his head, then blinked at the slightly fuzzy assortment of hotel personnel and guests assembled just outside his open doorway. How could he have forgotten that he'd told Gina to *come in*? Neither one of them had shut the door. They'd been a little preoccupied.

With the fingertips of one hand brushing the swell of a breast and the palm of the other cupped around a butt cheek, not to mention his erection cradled between her legs, her thumbs poised over his almost painfully perky nipples, and his lips no doubt as swollen and wet as hers, Matt understood why none of the passersby had been able to pass by.

Who'd want to miss this show?

"Get off me." Gina's voice sounded as if it were coming from between a set of tightly clenched teeth.

He glanced down. *Huh.* It was.

No doubt she was embarrassed. She was the one with her dress rucked up to her hips and her breasts almost bursting from what he could see now was a very un-Gina-like bodice. What was going on?

Matt needed to be a gentleman. If he could only remember how.

With all the dignity he could muster Matt got up, crossed the floor, and slammed the door. Then he leaned his forehead against it while he tried to tame an erection the size of Tokyo—one that continued to thunder with a pulse that reminded him uncomfortably of Godzilla's footsteps.

The bed creaked. Clothes rustled as Gina put herself

back together. Matt waited for her to cross the room, maybe put her hand on his shoulder, even give him another kiss, and murmur, *Thanks.*

Perhaps he didn't need to tame that erection after all.

He turned, and his shirt hit him in the face.

"Put that on." She waved at his chest, her gaze landing everywhere but on him.

Matt shrugged into the shirt, but he left the buttons alone. He was too busy staring.

The dress was all wrong; the shoes were ridiculous. Her hair was nice; he liked it down, and the way the light played across the strands made him think of the sun slanting through autumn leaves. But whatever she'd put on her lips, which he'd done his best to lick off, had stuck there, along with the brown gunk on her eyelids and some orangey stuff on her cheeks.

She didn't look like Gina at all. However, when she spoke she sounded exactly like the Gina who'd kicked him off her ranch.

"What the hell was that?" she demanded.

"You forgot to close the door."

She waved her hand again, and he was distracted by the copper sparkle on each and every nail. He hated it.

"I meant, why did you kiss me?"

"I thought . . ." He had to pause and force himself to stop staring at her nails, her lips, those stupid, stupid shoes. "You wanted me to."

She snorted, sounding more like Spike than Spike. "Why would I want that?"

"You ran into the room, threw yourself into my arms, said, 'Matt,' and—" He frowned. Then things kind of blended together.

"I did run into the room—the faster to kill you, my

dear." Matt's frown deepened. "Then I tripped, said, *'Ass!'* and grabbed onto you to keep from falling." Her gaze went to the bed, stuck on the tangled bedclothes, then jerked back to his. "It didn't work."

"You're sure you said 'ass,' not 'Matt'?"

"Since you introduced yourself as *Teo,*" she practically spit the name across the room like a rotten watermelon seed, "I'd hardly call you Matt."

He went back over what had happened, which did not help the erection from Tokyo. Even though she didn't look anything like Gina, she smelled like her and she talked like her and when he'd touched her and kissed her she'd *been* her—the woman he'd probably never stop wanting to touch.

And why was that? He'd had his hands on plenty of women. They'd been nice, but he'd never been desperate for one brief brush of their lips the way he was desperate, even now, for one more brief brush of Gina's.

"Wait a second," he said. "You stroked my hair."

"Yanked on it. I was trying to get you off me."

Now that Matt thought about it, she had pulled kind of hard. At first. Then she'd shoved her fingers in, right before she'd wrapped them around his neck and given him the tongue.

Matt shook his head.

Gina's gaze narrowed. "Why are you shaking your head?"

"You kissed me back."

"In your dreams, Mecate."

She *had* been in his dreams, and from the sudden blush across her cheeks, the color so much more appealing than the false one she'd brushed there, he'd been in hers.

"I know a tongue when I feel one," he said. And her

hands had been all over his chest, not pushing him away, either, but stroking his ribs, his collarbone, his shoulders, and more.

He shifted those shoulders, feeling again those hands. Her gaze lowered to his stomach and stuck there. Then her blush deepened, and he couldn't help but smile.

Bad idea. Because her gaze jerked back to his and she flipped.

"I know someone's hand on my rear when I feel one, too. You play a lot of grab ass with your students?"

"No!" His smile folded into a grimace. "That's disgusting."

"I bet three-quarters of the coeds are far from disgusting. More like the As than like me."

"There's no comparison."

"I know."

"You're so much more beautiful than they could ever be." Her quick glance, the expression on her face, made him realize she didn't believe him. *Damn Jase McCord and his manipulative bullshit. How many men had told her she was beautiful, then never talked to her again?*

"Is that what this is about?" Matt waved his hand at the dress, the shoes, the makeup. "A competition with the As?"

She made a sound of derision, but she wouldn't meet his eyes. "I had to talk to a man about some business. The As thought I needed help."

"The As are the ones who need help. They should leave you alone."

"I wish they would. Unfortunately, they've still got several more days on their ranch package. Unless . . ." Gina lifted her gaze to his, and her lip trembled.

Matt took a step forward, hand outstretched: What

was there on this earth that could cause Gina O'Neil's lip to tremble? Whatever it was, he would make it go away.

"Unless you're going to close the place down right away."

"I'm going to . . ." Matt let his hand fall back to his side. "What?"

"You bought the ranch." She glanced out the window, and her shoulders slumped, making the dress pooch across the bodice. He could see the smooth, supple curve of one breast, and right now he didn't even care.

"I did," he agreed. "But—"

"Must be nice to be rich. To be able to buy anything you see that you might want."

He knew there was a trap in there somewhere, but he couldn't quite figure out what it was. "It is."

Her gaze flicked back to his. "You spoiled, elitist, rich-boy snob." She lifted her chin. "You can't buy me."

CHAPTER 10

What had happened to her honey-versus-vinegar plan?
It had lasted about as long as her patience.

Gina didn't have the money to buy back the ranch.
Hell, she didn't have the money to buy lunch. So she
might as well scream, throw things, maybe even pop
Teo in the nose. It might make her feel better as she
packed up and left the only home she'd ever known.

"What I don't understand is why?" Gina took a step
closer. Smart man that he was, Teo kept his gaze on her
face, even as he took a step in reverse. "Did getting
thrown off infuriate you so much you just had to throw
us off back?"

Confusion flickered in his still-gorgeous eyes, more
green than brown now that they were free of the lenses.
"Throw you off?"

She took several more steps, quick like a bunny
despite the obnoxiously high heels, and poked him in
the chest, concentrating on shirt and not actual chest.
She was having a hard-enough time forgetting what it
felt like, smooth and firm and hot— Gina swallowed.
She didn't need to feel it again.

"What the hell are you going to do with a ranch anyway?" she asked. "I mean after you dig it up and make it crap? Do you have so much money that you can just shrug and walk away?"

"Yes," he answered. Then, when she narrowed her eyes, he hurriedly said, "No!"

"Which is it? 'Yes'?" She purposely took another step forward, grinding the spike of her heel onto his toe. "Or 'no'?"

He hissed in pain, but he didn't push her away, and a trickle of admiration pierced her fury. "I . . . uh . . ." He winced, and she removed her foot. No need to make him bleed. Yet.

"I *am* that rich." He lifted his hands. "I can't help it! My family. I was the last one. I got it all."

"How much is all?"

"Millions."

"Three? Four?"

"Hundred."

"Three or four *hundred* million?"

He shrugged. "Don't hate me because I'm rich."

"No problem," Gina muttered. She had plenty of other things to hate him for.

Like the way his unbuttoned shirt kept fluttering every time he moved, giving her tantalizing glimpses of pecs and abs. What kind of professor had a body like that?

"I'm not going to dig up your ranch."

"I know," she said, and he let out a relieved sigh. "You're going to dig up *your* ranch."

"No. I mean yes. But—"

"Sheesh, for a teacher, you sure have a hard time expressing yourself."

He tilted his head, and his hair slid across his cheek,

making her remember how she'd threaded her fingers through it and held on. *Damn!* What was wrong with her? Nothing a good dose of bitchy couldn't cure.

"I suppose you're better in print. Your letters were certainly . . ." She let her lips curve. "Amusing."

His eyes went blank as he thought back on what he'd written. "They weren't meant to be amusing."

"Which is what made them so damn funny."

She was being mean, but she couldn't help herself. He'd *bought* her ranch!

" 'It would *behoove* you to allow me to dig on your property,' " she quoted. "Who talks like that?"

"I try *not* to talk like that." He glanced at the floor. "When I was a kid, it used to get me beat up. Until I hit my growth spurt anyway."

Gina stilled. The idea of him as a kid—skinny, bespectacled, picked on—caused a sudden rush of protectiveness. If she'd been there, no one would have dared.

Then she heard her thoughts. *She* wanted to beat him up *now*. Why on earth did she care if he'd been beat up then?

"But it comes out in my writing," he continued. "And when I'm nervous."

Gina searched for something to bring back her anger. She didn't have to search very far.

"You said you were homeschooled. Or was that as much of a lie as your name?"

"I was. My mom took me on digs with her, and they weren't very often near a school." He shrugged, making his shirt shift again. Was he doing that on purpose? "They weren't very often near a road."

"How'd you get beat up if you didn't go to school?"

His gaze met hers again. "There are more places than a playground to find a bully."

True enough.

"Don't look so mad," he said, and Gina realized she was scowling, clenching her fists, thinking about retro-active violence again. "Getting picked on got me off the couch. Or the cot in my case. I started working out. I learned how to defend myself. Without that experi-ence I might have turned into a perennially hassled, geeky, four-eyed, overweight professor."

As if.

"You said your mother took you on digs. She is . . . like you?"

"Yes and no."

Gina would hate to be a student in his class. You'd never know the correct answer on a test, the way he waffled around. Of course, the view might make up for it.

Her gaze strayed to his stomach again, and her palms burned. She had never been this attracted to a man in her life. Why in hell did it have to be him?

"My mother was brilliant," he continued.

"Like you."

He actually blushed. It should have made him ap-pear feminine; instead it only made her chest ache. He was such an appealing combination of confidence and self-doubt.

"She was eons more brilliant than me," he said. "And she was beautiful."

Like you, her mind whispered, but thankfully her mouth did not.

"She was funny and articulate and brave."

Hmm, Gina thought. One word just kept coming up over and over in this recitation of Mama Mecate's at-tributes.

"Was," Gina murmured, and he glanced up, eyes suddenly wary. "What happened?"

He remained silent for so long, she didn't think he was going to answer, and that was probably for the best. Hearing about his mother, that he *had* a mother, made him too human, too real, too easy to like. Seeing the shadows in his eyes that reminded her far too much of her own was going to make it really hard to keep hating him.

And she needed to hate him. Hating Teo Mecate was the only way she was going to be able to survive Teo Mecate.

"My mother had some odd beliefs about the Aztecs."

"What kind of beliefs?"

He hesitated, making her think that he was hiding something. But why would he hide anything about his mother's academic theories? Maybe he just didn't want to talk about her. Gina, of all people, could understand that.

"She believed the Aztecs marched into the Southwest and attempted to conquer one of the tribes there."

"From what I remember of the Aztecs," Gina said, "they tried to conquer tribes everywhere."

"True. Their main occupation was war. Everything in their lives supported that. Food was raised to feed the soldiers. Priests prayed to the gods to smile favorably on the soldiers. Boys were raised to be soldiers. Girls were raised to give birth to soldiers."

"Why?" At his confused expression she elaborated: "Because they were easily bored? Or because they were a society of psychopaths who really liked killing?"

"Ah." He nodded. "The Aztecs believed that the only way to make the sun rise was to appease it with a sacrifice."

"A soldier's death appeased the sun?"

"No. Dying in war assured them of Tonatiuichan.
The sun heaven reserved for those who died in battle.
A true sacrifice had to be done by the priests in a certain way. They usually cut open the chest and tore out
the heart with their bare hands."

"Not a common priestly activity."

"It was for them."

"Let me guess," Gina said. "Instead of sacrificing
Aztecs, which would have eventually made them damn
short on Aztecs, they went out and nabbed some captives."

"Hence their constant state of war."

"Which led them to venture farther and farther
afield to round up more captives."

Teo cast her a quick glance. "Correct."

Gina's chest got a little tight and warm, like someone she admired had just patted her on the head. Because *that* happened a lot.

Maybe she would have done all right in college. Not
that she cared. Not that she needed college. She was
doing fine without it.

Then she remembered that she'd just lost her ranch.
To *him*. And all her warm-and-fuzzy feelings fled.

"Who cares if the Aztecs invaded the Southwest or
not?" Gina asked. "They're all dead and buried."

"Not all. There are nearly a million descendants.
I'm one of them."

"Is that why your mom was so interested? Why you
are?"

"Maybe." He lifted a shoulder, and his shirt slid off.
She got a tantalizing glimpse of bare honey skin before
he yanked the garment up again. This time he absently

buttoned the top few buttons to hold it in place. Gina tried to contain her disappointment.

"My mom spent her life studying the Aztecs." He turned to the window. "She gave her life trying to prove her theories."

Ah, at last they'd reached the root of that word *was*.

"It was my fault," he said.

Gina remained silent. Either Teo would continue or he wouldn't. Urging him to share his pain would only make him clam up about it. On this she was an expert.

"I should have been there. But I . . ." He lifted his gaze. She'd seen enough sadness and guilt in the mirror to recognize them instantly. "According to one of her assistants, someone thought they saw Aztec glyphs and called for her. The area was farther into the cavern, not well lighted yet. But she was excited—probably thinking that she could show me—" He broke off with a long, pained sigh. "She ran, her gaze on where she was going, not *how* she was going there, and—"

He slapped his hands together, the sound so sharp, so startling, Gina jumped.

"Low-hanging rock connected with her head." He tapped his temple. "Out went the lights." He swallowed. "And they never came on again."

Silence settled between them, broken only by muted voices in the hall. Gina knew she should say she was sorry. She was. She also knew how worthless saying it would be.

"What about the glyphs?" she asked instead.

"Scratches from falling rocks. Water stains. Not really drawings at all."

"How old were you?"

"Eighteen. It would have been my last dig before I

left for college. We planned to keep searching every summer, working our way through a list of places she'd translated from ancient writings she found in the family library."

"Aztec writings?" Gina couldn't begin to imagine what those would be worth. Probably ten times more than whatever they'd find digging around in the earth.

Of course the Mecates didn't need the money. Gina wondered what that might be like.

"Yes," he said, then: "Well, not exactly. There are only two known codices—" He paused at her curious expression and translated, "Painted hieroglyphic books. Just two predate the Spanish Conquest: the *Tonalamatl Aubin,* or Book of Days, and the *Codex Borbonicus.* Some scholars aren't even sure those are original."

"What happened to the rest?"

"Spaniards burned them."

Gina clucked her tongue, although she wasn't surprised. From what she could remember of her history, the Spanish had burned a lot of things—including people.

"The conquistadors considered the codices idolatry. You know the Aztec language was Nahuatl, but their written language was direct representation." He spread his hands. "If you were writing about a cat, you drew a cat. A drum, a deer, the water. Running." He used his fingers to show the movement. "Flowing." His hand made waves. "Up. Down. Big. Little." He continued to act the words out with finger and hand and arm movements. "Nouns easy, verbs kind of hard. But you get the drift."

"Then the Spanish showed up," Gina continued. "Someone opened a book, which was to them just pictures—"

"Very beautiful pictures—artwork in many cases. They handed it to an Aztec priest, who probably still had the blood of his last sacrifice under his fingernails, and he started reading those pictures."

"How very witchy of him."

"Now you're catching on." Teo made a tossing motion. " 'Burn them all.' "

"Including the priests."

"I'm sure they did. What my mother found in the family library was most likely a codex produced after the conquest, when the Spanish realized the Aztecs were on to something by using those freaky little pictures for words."

"Had a bit of a language barrier?"

"Deep and wide." He used his hands to illustrate again, and Gina was momentarily distracted by the contrast of his white nails against smooth dusky skin beneath a dusting of curly black hair. Those hands might look like the hands of a scholar, clean and slim, but they'd felt like the hands of a laborer—strong and capable, the palms calloused just enough to entice.

"They bridged the gap with hieroglyphics," he continued, and she yanked her gaze, and her thoughts, from his hands. "Pacifying the masses by allowing them to re-create the codices. Under strict supervision of course."

"Of course," Gina murmured. "But re-creations aren't originals."

"So every codex has to be taken for what it is— someone's retelling of what they, or maybe someone they knew, heard, or saw, or read. Not to mention that many of the priests decided to Christianize the Aztec tales, either by forcing the scribes to do so or by writing their own versions in Spanish."

"All in all, not the best source of info."

"But the only ones we've got left."

"And the writings your mom found?"

"Tell the tale of a superwarrior, birthed by the moon, to protect the People of the Sun."

"Pretty."

He smiled. "That's what you get when you turn pictures into words. As the story begins, the Aztecs marched north and engaged the enemy."

"What enemy?"

"To the Aztecs, anyone not them was just asking for it. According to the codex, these natives fought back hard and they began to win. But the Aztecs never lost, and now we know why."

"Why?"

"This superwarrior was also a sorcerer."

Gina started to get uneasy. Teo wanted to dig where her parents had died. In a place the Ute believed was cursed. Where she had heard strange whispers and felt . . . something.

An Aztec sorcerer perhaps?

But that was crazy. Wasn't it? There was no such thing as a sorcerer. Not then and definitely not now.

"Are you kidding me?" she asked.

"Yes." He smiled at her confusion. "I don't believe the warrior was a sorcerer, but the Aztecs did." He spread his hands. "Hey, back then the sun was a god. Sorcerers and magic would have fit right in."

"Maybe some guy figured out how to throw his voice, use herbs to make people froth at the mouth, then he 'cured' them." She made quotes around *cured* with her fingers.

"I'm inclined to agree. But as my mother always insisted, the legend came from somewhere. Something out of the ordinary had to have happened for the story to be repeated and passed down and eventually *written* down. Take out the sorcerer and you've still got super-warrior."

"A soldier who was bigger, stronger, or *super* in some other way," Gina reasoned. "He went north, kicked some native ass; then the rest of them snatched a few hundred captives and everyone hightailed it south of the Rio Grande."

"Except that's not what happened. According to my mother's translations the Indians had a sorcerer of their own and he confined the superwarrior to a cavern beneath the earth."

Gina's neck prickled as the bad feeling she already had deepened. "One sorcerer is far-fetched enough," she managed, "but two? Really?"

"Hieroglyphics are hard to interpret. For instance, are the colors used just for decoration or do they add meaning to what they symbolize? Does a different color indicate a different direction? Day? Night? Male? Female? A certain connection to the glyph on the right or the left?"

Gina shrugged.

"Exactly," Teo agreed. "Maybe yes, maybe no. Maybe yes on this page but no on that one. It can be maddening. In the end, my mother interpreted the location of the superwarrior's tomb in six different ways. We dug at five of the sites. We didn't find anything." He glanced at her. "The sixth translation is: 'Where the tree of life springs from a land awash with the blood of the sun.'"

Gina closed her eyes.

"I don't know if I would ever have found it if it weren't for—"

"That damn photograph." She opened them again.

His gaze held hers. "I can't give up until I've checked every site on that list."

Gina needed to convince him otherwise. That area was bad luck. Cursed. Haunted. Dangerous. Unfortunately, he seemed as obsessed with it as she'd once been. Still, she had to try.

"That isn't the place," Gina said, though her lips felt stiff and the words were very hard to get out.

"How do you know?"

"If the Aztecs had come to Colorado and the Ute had beaten them, or close enough, old men would be telling that story around the campfire until the end of time. I've never heard it. Not once."

And she hadn't. Then again, telling such a story would make people want to go there more, not less. The Ute weren't stupid.

"I can't just quit," Teo insisted. "My mother gave her life trying to find that tomb. She became . . ." He took a breath, let it out on a rush. "Kind of a joke in scholarly circles."

"Why?"

His eyes met Gina's. "She believed that sorcerer was real. And she wouldn't let it go."

"And now *you* won't let it go."

"I can't." His shoulders drooped along with his head. "I told her to grow up. That she was embarrassing me. She was living in a fantasy world."

"You were a kid."

"We'd looked for that tomb my whole life. The search was exciting, fascinating." He took another breath. "But I was going off to college. I knew people would laugh at me the instant they heard my name. I wanted her to stop looking. Or at least stop talking about magic."

"She wouldn't?"

"Of course not. She knew what she believed, and once I'd believed it, too. I refused to go with her on that last dig. And then she died."

"You think she wouldn't have hit her head if you'd been there?"

"Maybe she wouldn't have been so distracted by my *not* being there or so anxious to prove to me that I was wrong that she would have looked where she was going instead of charging into the gloom."

"You don't know that."

"In here?" He tapped his head. "Maybe. But here?" He tapped his heart. "It hurts."

For an instant she felt sorry for him, until she remembered that to assuage his guilt he planned to dig up a place that needed to be left the hell alone.

"I've become kind of a joke, too," he continued, his scratchy voice even scratchier after having spoken for so long.

"I thought you didn't believe in magic or the sorcerer."

"I don't. But I believe there's a tomb and it's located north of the border. That would be a find in and of itself and would go a long way to vindicating my mother's research. She deserves to have her name spoken with respect. Because the Aztecs *were* here. As soon as I saw that photograph, I knew."

Damn her infatuation with cameras. Gina had no one but herself to blame for this fiasco.

"Proving this theory was her dream." Teo's earnest gaze captured Gina's. "You understand why I can't give up?"

"For the same reason I ignored your letters. I couldn't

let you run around putting holes in my parents' dream. But I guess I have nothing to say about it now." Which made her feel kind of sick.

"I don't want the ranch," Teo said.

Gina's head jerked up. "What?"

"I'm a professor. What am I going to do with a dude ranch?"

"Dig it up, then sell it?"

"Don't you get it?"

"Spell it out for me."

"You show me the area in the picture . . ."

Gina wrapped her arms around herself, trying to stave off the sudden chill his words invoked. She began to shake her head, and he held up one hand, palm facing outward to stop her.

"Then, once I find what she gave her life looking for, I'll sign the place over to you, and you'll never have to see me again."

CHAPTER 11

"Are you fricking nuts?"

Gina winced at the volume of Jase's voice and the horrified expression on his face.

"You can't let Old Moldy back on the property. You can't let him dig around. Especially there."

"I'm not going to be 'letting' him do anything. It's his place now. And he isn't old or even very moldy."

Jase's eyes narrowed at her final comment. "You on his side now?"

"I'm on the same side I've always been on. The side of Nahua Springs Ranch," Gina clarified. "Which will be gone unless I find a way to get it back. I don't know about your checking account, but mine is tapped. So the only way I'm gonna be able to save our *home* is by doing this."

Jase let his gaze wander from the top of her now-tangled hair, over the low-cut neckline and high-cut hem of Amberleigh's dress, to Ashleigh's spiky copper heels. "Looks to me like you've been workin' on that already."

Gina started for the door. She really needed to change

out of this getup and back into her own clothes. "I don't know what that means."

"Did you sleep with him?"

Gina froze with her hand on the door. "Do not screw with me, Jase; I've had a very bad day."

"You think mine's been any better?"

She turned. "What happened?"

"What didn't?" He threw up his arms. "I wake up and you've taken off. I'm stuck with the guests." Jase yanked the ends of his short hair. "Those blondes are enough to drive any man mad."

"With desire?"

He grimaced. "I'm rather stick my dick in a knot-hole."

"Thanks for that image."

"At least a knothole's quiet."

He had a point.

"Then the old folks keep singing campfire songs, when the old guy isn't reciting dirty limericks. Which the kid likes but his dad does not."

"I already caught the matinee of this show. You aren't going to get any sympathy from me."

"I don't deal with the guests."

"At least not very well," Gina agreed. "Unfortunately, you're going to have to deal with them from now on."

"Oh no." Jase backed away, shaking his head, waving his hands. "Not me."

"You don't have any choice. I have to show Mecate the place he bought the ranch to find, which means you have to leave with the As, and all their little friends, on the second leg of the program this afternoon. You should have gone this morning."

Jase stopped backing away and dropped his hands.

"You can't take Mecate there. Granddad says that place has bad juju."

"I have never in all my life heard Isaac utter the word *juju*."

"You know what I mean."

She did. The Ute had believed the place cursed even before her parents had died there.

"It doesn't matter," Gina said. "I still have to take him."

Quickly she gave Jase the CliffsNotes version of Teo Mecate's life story, watching Jase closely when she mentioned the sorcerer, the magic, but his only reaction was an eye roll and a sneer. He obviously hadn't heard a similar tale from any of the Ute elders. Nor had he suddenly remembered hearing insidious whispers during the time he and Gina were buried down there.

Only she had.

Should she feel better knowing that or worse? On the one hand, if she was imagining things, then the place they were headed to was just a place. Full of bad memories, sure, but nothing more than dirt and rocks and trees.

On the other hand, she was *imagining* things. And had been for nearly ten years.

"He isn't going to give me what I want unless I give him what he wants," Gina finished.

Jase shot her an evil glare, but thankfully he kept his no-doubt obnoxious comment to himself.

She'd considered leading Teo on a wild-goose chase until he gave up and went away, but considering what he'd told her about his mother—her life and her death—she'd be wasting her time. Since he owned the ranch now, he didn't have to leave. Ever. If she wanted it back, she had one choice.

Take him where he wanted to go.

Maybe if she faced the place again, saw that it *was* just a place . . . watched him dig and find nothing . . . maybe then she'd start to believe it herself. She'd stop hearing her name on the wind. Avoiding the area certainly hadn't helped.

"I'll do it," Jase said.

Oh, that would be grand. One of them would wind up buried in the forest. And she had a pretty good idea which one.

"You ended any chance of him putting up with you for more than a minute when you blabbed his true identity before God and everyone else."

"I shouldn't have?"

"There are better ways to handle something like that than an ambush."

"You're just mad because I interrupted him before he could get in your pants." Jase's mouth tightened as his gaze scanned her face. "Or did I?"

"Kiss my ass," Gina said sweetly. She'd never discussed her sex life, or lack of it, with Jase and she certainly wasn't going to start now. He might be her best friend, but he was really more like a brother, no matter what Teo said, and that was just icky.

"Fine," Jase growled. "Just show him the tree, let him do whatever the hell it is he has to do there, then get rid of him as fast as you can."

That was the plan. The longer Teo stayed, the harder it would be for everyone.

"I'll distract Granddad," Jase said.

"What? Why?"

"You think he's gonna let you go anywhere near the end of Lonely Deer Trail again no matter what reason you have for it? I wouldn't be surprised if he locked you in the barn and used his shotgun to get rid of the professor." Jase's lips twitched. "Permanently."

"Hell," Gina muttered. She hadn't thought of that.

"Don't worry about it. Just get Moldy out of here as quick as you can."

"No problem," Gina said.

Unfortunately, from that moment on problems were all that she had.

For the second time in a week, Matt drove his rental car toward Nahua Springs Ranch.

Gina had agreed to his terms. She hadn't really had any choice. Matt should have felt bad about that, but he didn't. Sure, he'd bought her ranch, but he'd give it back. All she had to do was show him that place.

The one that made her turn white and swallow back puke.

The ranch appeared on the horizon, and Matt pressed the accelerator. He wanted to get there. He wanted to see—

"The tree."

Not Gina. Any chance he might have had for a relationship with her was as dead as he was gonna be if Jase McCord got him cornered in the equivalent of a Colorado dark alley.

As Matt drove into the yard, Gina led Spike and Lady Belle from the barn. The horses were saddled and packed. Where was she going?

He got out of the car. "I thought you were taking me—"

"I am," she interrupted. "Let's go."

Gina tossed him Spike's reins. Matt was so surprised they hit him in the face and slithered to the ground. Spike tossed his head, stomped, and gave Matt a look that plainly said, *Nice one.*

"Sorry," Matt muttered, picking them up. "Where's the fire?"

Gina had already mounted Lady Belle. "Under your ass if the As see you."

"They're here?"

"Where else would they be?"

"The French Riviera if we had any sort of luck at all," he muttered.

"We don't. So let's make some time."

She urged Lady Belle down the road, and after a quick glance toward the house, where he could see several people milling beyond the sun-sparkled windows, Matt mounted Spike and followed.

Two hours later, Gina and Lady Belle stood on the bank of a raging creek.

"Huh," Gina murmured.

She wasn't sure how, but she'd spaced off the day in the deluge with the As, the Gordons, and the Hurla-heys. In her defense, she'd had a lot on her mind during the hours in between. And at the time she'd been intent on urging everyone back to the house, not concerned about what the downpour would mean to the creek on the opposite end of the ranch.

She hadn't considered it today, either. Because if she'd been paying attention and not doing her best to avoid a conversation with Teo, while at the same time playing the truly obnoxious game of *what if* in her mind—What if she and Teo had met somewhere else?

What if she'd gone to college and he'd been her professor? What if he hadn't been obsessed with his mother's work to the exclusion of all else? What if he hadn't lied? What if he hadn't bought her ranch?—she might have considered that the creek would be flooded and taken a different route.

Gina dismounted and kicked a large rock into the water. "What if you'd been watching where you were going, and then you wouldn't have wasted hours riding to an area you can't get across?"

The thud of hooves and the snort of Spike announced Teo's arrival. To his credit, when he'd discovered that she wasn't in the mood to be sociable he'd stopped trying to keep up and let Gina ride ahead.

He stopped next to her. "Huh." He peered right, then left. "Anywhere not so frothy?"

"Frothy?"

He made a motion with his hands to indicate the swirling, grinding, *frothy* water.

"No."

"There has to be."

"Really, there doesn't. The rain makes this thing impassable. Until it runs off, there's no getting across."

"Can we go around?"

"We're gonna have to."

The sun had begun to fall by the time they reached a locale where the creek narrowed and died. The horses picked their way across the rocks that had tumbled downstream, driven by the force of the water.

"How far?" Teo asked. He was like a little kid on a road trip: *Are we there yet?*

Gina hoped they *never* got there. Although . . .

She lifted her gaze to the sky. She'd prefer not to get there in the middle of the night.

"We need to make camp."

"But you said tonight."

She indicated the still-raging water to their right.

"Oh." Disappointment washed over his face. "Yeah."

They were going to have to travel farther still to reach a decent place to camp. Here was too rocky, too damp.

Gina let her gaze trail over the horizon. She pointed to a grove of trees that populated a hill. "We'll head for that."

Teo looked at the sun. "It'll be dark before we reach it."

Gina urged Lady Belle forward. "I know."

Night fell. Clouds shrouded the moon and the stars. Gina hoped the horses could see, because she couldn't.

This had been *such* a bad idea. And she had no one to blame but herself. She'd never let her mind wander to the extent she'd let it wander today. Had her subconscious highjacked her brain, assuring that they wouldn't reach the grave site as planned, gifting her with one more day of peace?

Giiiii-naaaa!

She started, her hands jerking the reins, causing Lady Belle to throw up her head and nicker.

"Something wrong?" Teo asked.

"You hear anything?"

Giiii-naaaa!

"The wind?"

Wasn't it always the wind that called her name? Whenever it wasn't the wolves that weren't there.

The night had gone cool, brushing her face, stirring her hair, making her remember—

God, she *so* didn't want to be here.

As if in answer to that thought, Lady Belle stopped

dead, the movement so sudden Gina slid sideways and grabbed at the pommel to right herself.

Spike, who'd been a few steps ahead, stopped, too. Then he snorted, pawed . . . and reared.

She gave Teo credit; he held his seat. At least until the horse's hooves returned to the ground and Spike began to buck. Teo flew sideways. Gina had an instant to register that he hadn't caught a foot in the stirrup—if he had, he'd have been dragged across the plain, head bouncing against the rock-strewn ground as Spike bolted—before Lady Belle began to buck, too.

Gina held on longer than Teo, but in the end she landed on the ground a few feet away. If a horse wanted you off, off you would eventually be.

Gina lay there, listening to the thunder of Spike's and Lady Belle's hooves as they raced back in the direction they'd come. She took stock of her body. Everything moved. Nothing was broken.

"You alive?" she asked.

"No," Teo groaned. But he sat up. "What the hell was that?"

Gina didn't want to move. Because once she did, she knew what she'd see. In her experience, horses at Nahua Springs Ranch reacted in that way to just one thing.

She turned her head as the clouds parted and the moon shone down. "Remember when I said we wouldn't get where we were going until tomorrow?"

"Yeah?" Teo rubbed the back of his head, then squinted at his hand, letting out a sigh of relief to find no blood.

Gina rose, then lifted her chin, indicating the horizon behind him, out of which an old, craggy, half-dead tree appeared to grow.

"I was wrong."

CHAPTER 12

Matt glanced over his shoulder. He could just make out the spiky branches of a tree reaching for the ebony night. Beneath the moon they shone silver instead of red, but—

"That's it," he said.

Gina got to her feet, emitting a surprised grunt, even as she tightened her lips against sudden pain.

"You okay?" Matt stood as well, reaching for her.

She pulled back. "Fine."

Matt let his hand drop to his side. Would she ever let him touch her again?

Doubtful.

"I think they stopped."

Matt followed her gaze, catching just a hint of equine shadows several hundred yards in the opposite direction. "I'll get them."

"They aren't going to come," she said. "Horses have never liked it here."

Matt, who'd already started toward them, turned back. "Why?"

She shrugged. "Any horse that's ever come within a hundred yards of this place bolts."

Though he felt like a two-year-old who'd just discovered his favorite question, nevertheless, Matt was forced to ask again: "Why?"

"None of them have ever said."

"Har-har." Matt considered the distant silhouettes of Spike and Lady Belle. "What are we going to do?"

"Sleep over there." Gina brushed her palms against her pants and began to walk.

Gina couldn't believe they'd been this close to the site and she hadn't been aware. Sure, it was dark, but shouldn't she have been able to feel a change? The horses had.

Yes, she'd heard the wind calling her name, but she heard that all over the damn place.

Gina increased her pace. She didn't like the horses being so far away. Not that a wolf was going to get them. But there *was* the odd bear or pack of raging coyotes. Not to mention that Spike might just take it into his head to run home.

Teo's scurrying footsteps scattered rocks and dirt every which way as he hurried to catch up. "Animals sense what we don't," he said. "If there's a tomb below, that's gotta feel . . . I don't know . . . hollow to them."

Gina didn't bother to point out that when the horses had actually lost it the area had still been a good hundred yards away.

Because they *had* sensed something. She just didn't think it was that hole beneath the earth.

Gina approached Spike and Lady Belle, murmuring reassurances. The mare lifted her head and nickered a welcome, as if nothing had happened at all.

Spike snorted and stomped and shook his mane, but he didn't bolt, and if he was still bothered by . . . whatever, he would have. Unfortunately, the bolting he'd done thus far had been enough.

"My tent's missing," Gina said, then cursed. "My camera bag, too."

Why she'd brought the thing along she wasn't sure. She certainly didn't want to take any more pictures of this place. The first one had caused trouble enough.

Teo stared back the way they'd come. The moon had disappeared behind the clouds again. They could barely see three feet in any direction; they certainly weren't going to be able to find anything now.

"You can have mine." Gina felt rather than saw him glance at her. "I'll sleep outside."

"I promise I won't jump you if you don't jump me." Gina'd meant the words to be flippant; instead they came out kind of bitchy. And really, she was okay with that.

"I . . . uh . . . well, certainly," Teo managed. "I would never force my attentions on a lady."

Gina's lips curved as she turned away. Since he'd started to talk like an eighty-year-old man with a stick up his butt, she'd made him uncomfortable.

Join the club.

The idea of sharing a small, enclosed space with Teo made her as twitchy as a horse in a barn full of flies.

"It's going to rain." She heaved the tent in his direction. He caught it with a muffled *oof.* "You can't sleep outside."

An hour later the horses were taken care of. Gina had made a fire; Teo had pitched the tent. They'd eaten, and now they lay inside the shelter, staring at the canvas ceiling as distant thunder loomed.

Or at least Gina stared; she wasn't sure what Teo was doing except tossing and turning, every shift of his body reminding her of that body shifting against hers on his bed in the hotel. The constant movement also squirted the maddening scent of oranges and sunshine across the far too short distance that separated them.

He was driving her batty!

"Okay." She sat up. "Let's play cards."

"I'm sorry?"

"You aren't, but you should be."

"What?"

"You should be sorry for coming here, for lying, for trying to seduce me, for stealing my ranch. But you aren't. Because you got what you wanted. Or you soon will."

He moved again, making more noise than Spike on a rampage. An instant later, the portable tent light—a combination of lantern and flashlight—flared to life, illuminating Teo sitting cross-legged on his bedroll, hair mussed as if she'd just run her fingers through it over and over and over.

Gina clenched her hands until the knuckles crackled in the sudden stillness. She could still feel that hair against her palms and that mouth against hers.

Hell.

"I am sorry." He lifted his gaze, which, unfettered by his glasses, had softened to the shade of the sage in Fanny's spice garden. "But not for everything."

Gina wasn't sorry about everything, either. She might be mad about some of it, but she wasn't sorry.

"Cards," she blurted. "What can you play?"

"Nothing."

"You don't know how to play cards?"

"Oh, I know how. What do you think we did on digs when the torrential rains came?"

As if in answer to his question, raindrops began to patter against the canvas and the wind shook the tent just a little. But worse was coming. Gina could smell it.

"I don't know," she answered. "Read a book?"

"That was my mother. I played cards with the workers." He cracked his knuckles. "I'm really good at poker."

Gina's lips curved. "Not as good as me."

"I'd love to prove you wrong, but I don't have any cards."

Crap. Neither did she. And she had no one to blame but herself, since she'd done the packing. Which just proved how out of it she'd been. Cards were usually one of the first things she tucked into the pack.

"Great." Gina fell back onto her bedroll. Another sleepless night with nothing to do but think. Just what she needed.

A rustle drew her attention to Teo. He'd put on his glasses and now peered at a notebook he held in his hands.

"What's that?"

"My mother's translations." He shrugged, appearing sheepish and very young. "Do you want to see?"

At her nod, Teo scooted over on the bedroll, making room for Gina to sit at his side. Which was probably a really bad idea.

"I promised not to jump you," he said, surprising a laugh from her.

What was it about this man that made her want to like him, to trust him even though he'd proved he was both unlikable and untrustworthy?

Though it was probably a bad idea, nevertheless, Gina leaned forward, placing her palms on the ground; then she crossed, on her hands and knees, the few feet that separated them.

She hadn't realized how suggestive the pose was until his breath caught, then his eyes flared, gaze lowering and fixing on something just below her neck. She glanced down and discovered that her shirt gaped, revealing the easy sway of her breasts beneath.

When she lifted her head, the expression on his face, the stark wanting, made her chest ache. No man had ever looked at her like that before.

Gina sat back on her heels and considered returning to her side of the tent.

"Sorry," Teo murmured. "You're just so lovely I can't help myself."

Her cheeks heated. *Lovely.* Such an old-man word, though the look in Teo's eyes had been anything but old. Or maybe it had been ancient—the same look men had been giving women since the beginning of time. And since she now knew exactly what it felt like when he touched her, all he had to do was glance at her and she remembered his hands, his mouth, that taste.

She remembered, and she yearned.

"Stare all you want, but keep your hands off," Gina muttered, even though that wasn't what she wanted. Not really.

How pathetic. Lie, cheat, steal, attempt seduction under both a false name and false pretenses, yet still she wanted him.

"No touching," Teo agreed. "Swear to God."

"Which god?" Gina asked.

"Any god. All the gods. Whatever you want."

She lifted a brow, but she scooted the few feet left to

his bedroll in an odd, crab-like movement that kept her from flashing him again.

Gina crossed her legs, stilling when her knee brushed his. Teo shifted, as if he just needed to change positions, but she knew better. The electricity that had jumped between them at that simple touch was disturbing. Would her body ever stop calling out for his?

He pointed to the notebook. "These are the glyphs that led me here."

Gina leaned closer, careful to avoid brushing any more body parts. "Reminds me of kindergarten stick figures."

"Not everyone was van Gogh."

"More like Picasso."

"Yes!" he agreed, both surprised and pleased. "The colors, the glyphs that appear to be half person, half something else. Excellent comparison."

Gina felt again the warm rush in her chest and stomach that his praise brought to her. Why she craved it, craved him, she had no idea. But she couldn't seem to stop.

"This is the section about the superwarrior." Teo pointed to another picture. "The Aztecs marched to—" He slid his index finger, dark against the creamy sheet, to another glyph. "A land north," he tapped what appeared to be a yellow and black knife, "of the big river."

Gina leaned closer, barely registering the graze of her shoulder against his in her eagerness to see what he meant. The drawing of the river next to his nail was definitely bigger than the other drawings of rivers elsewhere on the page.

"There isn't another big river in Mexico?" she asked.

"Not like the Rio Grande. Hence the moniker Grande."

"Good point," Gina said, and he turned his head to

smile. Because she was leaning against his shoulder their faces were far too close. His nose nearly brushed hers as his breath breezed across her cheek.

She straightened, cleared her throat, and made herself glance away. "How do you get *north* out of this?" She indicated the bumblebee-shaded knife.

"The Aztecs believed each direction was the realm of a particular god. Tezcatlipoca governed the north; he was the god of night and destiny, of war. His glyph was a *tecpatl*—the weapon used for sacrificing victims."

"Weren't all Aztecs—from the farmer in the fields to the warrior on parade—ruled by sacrifice?"

"Yes."

"So why did this guy have the sacrificial knife as his symbol? Was he more vicious and violent than the rest?"

Teo's eyes seemed to lose focus. He'd gone away for a minute in his mind. Gina was starting to understand that sometimes he had to.

"No," he said at last. "North was also associated with the xerophyte tree, which grew at the northern reaches of the empire in a place called the land of death."

"Cheery group of people, those Aztecs."

His lips quirked. "It would make sense to them to use the weapon of death to symbolize the god of the land of death."

"I suppose so," Gina agreed. "What else?"

"Uh . . ." He stared at the pages for several seconds as if he'd forgotten what the pictures meant or perhaps just didn't know where to begin.

Gina slid her finger beneath a string of colorful drawings all in a row. "What about these?"

Teo pushed his glasses up his nose, even though,

from what she could tell, they hadn't moved at all. "Those describe the superwarrior. A glyph can have several levels of meaning—the actual thing it represents, as well as a trait, and sometimes even a letter of the alphabet."

"I don't get it."

"You've seen those games where you have to figure out a sentence from a string of pictures?" Gina shook her head. "Like this."

Frowning, he patted the pocket of his shirt, then his pants, then, muttering, patted the bedroll surrounding them, triumphantly pulling a pencil from beneath his ass, before flipping to the back of the journal and scribbling.

He offered the page so she could see what he'd drawn. An eye. A heart. An alligator. "What does that say?"

"Your heart sees alligators?"

He laughed. She really enjoyed his easy laughter, both the sound of it and how it made her feel. As if she was funny, witty, and smart.

"Or . . ." He rapped the pencil's eraser against the eye. "I." Then the heart. "Love." Then the alligator. "Alligators." He lifted his shoulder, rubbing against her again despite their continued efforts to remain apart. "I don't, but I'm really good at drawing alligators."

"You are," she said, hearing the laughter in her own voice.

He turned the page in his direction again, scratched a few lines, and turned it back. "This is the symbol for teeth, called *tiantli* in the Aztec language. But it was also used to represent the letter *t*. And this," he tapped what also looked like teeth, except these had a roof on top, "is the symbol for *la,* which is used to indicate an 'l' sound at the end of a word."

"What is that thing?"

"I don't know. Something that sounded to the Aztecs like 'la.'"

"How could anyone know *what* was being written with all those possible meanings?"

"The Aztecs knew, or at least those who could read and write did. And while the Aztec may have been the only civilization at that time with universal schooling for both sexes, the majority of the population was still illiterate. They didn't need to read or write unless they worked for the government or the church."

"So how do we know *now* what they were saying *then*?"

"Some of the codices reconstructed after the conquest have Spanish translations below them." He frowned. "Of course many of those translations were merely what the Spanish *wanted* the texts to say."

"Let me guess: Any bearded guy was labeled Jesus, even in a story about an ancient god of the sea."

"Stop me if you've heard this before," Teo murmured.

"I did a report on the Crusades," Gina said. "Imposing their own interpretations on every ancient legend appeared to be SOP for all Christian conquerors. So my question remains—how do we know what the Aztecs were really saying?"

"We don't. To make it even harder, Aztecs didn't write in a linear fashion like we do." He used his finger to draw a line across the page, left to right. "They drew a picture. Things that were farther away at the top, things that were closer at the bottom. All of them interacting in strange and mysterious ways. To translate, one has to pick through and interpret."

"Kind of a 'Where's Waldo?' for the sacrificial crowd?"

"Yes. Although I've never found Waldo in any of them."

"Thank God," Gina muttered. The idea of that be-spectacled candy-cane shirt–wearing doofus peeking out from behind an Aztec pyramid was both amusing and a little creepy. "I don't understand how, with all those options, you manage to figure out anything at all."

"That's why my mom had six possible places where the superwarrior could have been buried."

"Did she also have six possible translations for what else a superwarrior might be?"

His eyes, darker in the dim light and shaded behind the lenses of his glasses, narrowed. "I don't follow."

"If the place of his burial could be one of many, maybe he could be one of many, too?"

"One of many what?"

"How should I know?"

"Here." Teo scooted closer again, flipping pages until he found what he wanted. "These are the glyphs my mom interpreted for the superwarrior legend." He pointed to an obvious soldier. "You see how this draw-ing is much bigger than the others?"

"Yeah." It was, in fact, twice as big as the others. "Like I said, maybe they labeled him as super just be-cause he was taller than everyone else. I read some-where that the reason David was able to fell Goliath was because the giant wasn't exactly gigantic, just larger than the average Philistine."

"David was still a pretty good shot. The smaller the head of the giant, the better that shot becomes."

"Good point," Gina agreed. She studied him a moment. "You believe the stories in the Bible?"

"Yes," he said, shocking her. As he was a scholar, some might even say a scientist, she'd expected him to say no. He was just one surprise after another.

"If I don't believe those stories, how could I ever believe these?" Again he tapped the notebook.

"You said you didn't believe the superwarrior was a sorcerer."

"That doesn't mean I don't believe he existed at all."

Gina's gaze returned to the extremely large stick soldier. "So you think the super part of the superwarrior was his size?"

"Maybe. Or it could just relate to his personality, his essence, his spirit. In many of the codices, glyphs relating to royalty were also drawn larger than everything else. The Aztecs used size not only to mean *size* but also to indicate a largeness of intangible things. A largesse of being."

Gina wasn't exactly sure what largesse was, but she got the concept from the drawing.

"What about these?" She indicated a string of symbols beneath the great big warrior.

"We think it describes his attributes." Teo moved his finger from icon to icon as he explained. "The wind, which also means strength. A lizard, which indicates endurance, the rabbit for speed, a dog for loyalty; the monkey symbolizes agility. No other warrior in any codex was ever described with this many superior traits."

Gina studied the glyphs. In her opinion that dog looked far too vicious to symbolize loyalty. Perhaps he'd been viciously loyal.

"Maybe the super part of his warriorhood," she pointed to the final image: a skull, which loomed larger than all the others, "was not just that he was a very big boy, but also that he was fabulous at killing people."

"The skull does mean death," Teo agreed. "But it can also indicate life force and vitality."

"So he was either king of the killing," Gina said, "or just larger than life."

"Or both."

"You said the pictures could actually mean what they represent." He nodded. "What if the army just ran into a dog, then a rabbit, a lizard, and a lot of skulls on their trip?"

"How do you explain a monkey this far north of the border?"

"Maybe it was a pet. Were there monkeys somewhere in the Aztec empire?"

Teo nodded as he considered the row of glyphs. "If that's the case, this could be nothing more than a travelogue."

His eyes had lost some of their light.

"Would that be bad?" Gina murmured.

He didn't answer for a long time, just continued to stare at the page until Gina touched his elbow. "Teo?

He came back to the here and now with a start. "Uh . . . well . . ." He pushed his glasses up again. "It's an interesting concept. Perhaps the large soldier merely represented a large army. Nothing earthshaking there."

"But you said this," she pointed to the bumblebee knife, "indicates north. And this." She tapped the big water. "The Rio Grande."

He sighed, and his chin lowered toward his chest. "It could mean anything." He slapped the book shut. "It could mean nothing."

Gina felt like she'd kicked a kitten.

"Even if the so-called superwarrior didn't exist," she

argued, "the translation still points to the Aztecs traveling north of the Rio Grande. Isn't that important?"

"Not if there's no way to prove it. Without that tomb, I'll never be able to vindicate any part of my mother's work or my own."

"Well, what do I know?" Gina asked. "You and your mother have been translating this stuff for decades. I never saw it before today."

Although, strangely, she felt like she understood it. That with a little practice she could read those writings and, even more strangely, that she wanted to. Perhaps Teo's enthusiasm was catching.

"My mother *did* spend her life on those translations," he agreed.

Gina suddenly saw what she'd done. He'd been doubting himself, doubting his mission, and she *wanted* him to doubt. She wanted him to give up and go away. Instead, she'd managed to turn him back to the idea that what he believed about this place was true.

What was *wrong* with her?

Teo's head lifted. "There *is* the part about the tree of life springing from a land awash with the blood of the sun. And we both know that's here."

"There's nothing underneath that tree," she lied.

"Gina," he murmured, voice both soft and rough. "If there was nothing there, you wouldn't be trying so hard to keep me from it. Why don't you just tell me what happened?"

Her eyes, though she tried to make them stop, flicked to his. He was closer than he should be, or maybe she was. Their knees knocked. Their faces hovered a foot apart. She didn't want to tell him. She didn't want to tell anyone, ever. Instead, she touched her lips to his.

He stilled, and for an instant she thought he might

pull back, might stick to his promise of not touching. So she flicked out her tongue. Just a quick swipe along his slightly parted lips and he was as lost as she was.

He came to his knees; she came to hers, and they were touching thigh to thigh, hip to hip, chest to breast, mouth to seeking mouth.

His palms rested at the curve of her waist; his thumbs stroked the fluttering muscles of her stomach, chasing them across the taut skin, first above her shirt and then blessedly, thrillingly, below. His calluses scraped, and she caught her breath.

"Sorry," he murmured, but as he began to withdraw, both hands and mouth, she nipped his lip, snatched his wrist, and he swept his hands upward, cupping her breasts along with her bra. Despite the chill of the night, they both wore far too many clothes.

Gina's fingers went to his shirt even as his went to hers. But there were too many buttons, too many fingers, too many arms criscrossed every which way.

They broke apart, breathing heavily, mouths damp, eyes dark. Then, as one, they unbuttoned their own shirts.

"You first," he said, his hanging open, revealing a far too small slice of chest and torso.

Gina shrugged free of the flannel. His gaze hung on her every move. Slowly, she undid her bra, letting the straps slide down her arms the same way the shirt had.

Though the tent was cool, his eyes had gone hot, seeming to warm her flesh wherever they touched.

"I can't breathe," he murmured. "You're so beautiful."

Right now she *felt* beautiful.

"Your turn." She indicated his shirt with a lift of her chin.

The flannel fell away with one quick shrug, revealing gorgeous, gleaming skin. She wanted to touch him so badly; she licked her lips and reached out.

He grabbed her wrist, pulled her close, but being on her knees, she wasn't very graceful, and she fell forward, crashing into him. They both tumbled to the bedroll, then lay there all tangled together, breathing hard. Gina began to giggle.

"Why is it every time I see your bare chest I fall?"

"I don't know." He touched her cheek. "But don't ever stop."

The light shone off his glasses like a beacon; she couldn't see his eyes. Lifting her hands, she touched the frames. "Can you take these off?"

"Sure." He set them atop his mother's notebook. "You mind if I turn off the light? Everything's fuzzy now."

Gina reached over herself, the movement rubbing her breasts against his chest in new and enticing ways, then flicked the switch. Navy-blue night settled over them with an audible hush.

His hair brushed her cheek; she buried her face in his neck and took a taste. Something that had been slightly hard against her hip became definitely hard and she smiled into the velvet darkness. Reaching down, she slid her thumbnail up his length, and he choked.

"Sorry." She pulled her hand away, but he caught her wrist and tugged it back.

"Don't be."

He let go of her wrist and slid his palm up her body, cupping first one breast, then the other, rolling each nipple until they hardened like him. When his mouth closed over one and his teeth worried it, she muttered a word she'd learned from the Hurlaheys and slid her hand inside his jeans.

He rose, palms at her back, lifting and holding her to his lips as he teased and taunted and took. Her jeans fell away, as did his. Though the tent surrounding them was dark, the night beyond it ever darker despite the distant rumble of thunder, nevertheless, Gina saw in her mind's eye the contortions of their bodies, the slide of legs, of hands and fingers, of lips, and it excited her.

He urged her onto her stomach so he could run his mouth from her ankles to the soft curves at the backs of her knees, then up her thighs, across the swell of her buttocks, where she felt again his teeth, then to her spine. His fingernail ran gently upward, over each ridge, before his hands spread across her shoulders, down her ribs to her hips. Her skin on fire, she began to turn, but his voice stayed her.

"Ever since you crawled across this tent, I've had this image I can't get out of my head."

"Me, too."

"I wonder if they match," he said, and lifted her onto her hands and knees again.

Then he waited, touching her nowhere but his palms at her hips. She felt his heat, the pulsing weight of his erection so close but still so far. She wanted him inside of her.

"Yes," she said, then, as he pushed fully within, "yes."

Though this had begun as just sex, rooted in a need to forget, to avoid, perhaps even to break free, it changed. One instant she reveled in the sharp slap of flesh, the pulse and the push that ground so deep. The next he had curved himself over her, chest to back, fingers to breast, lips to neck, and her chest, her belly, her very being, stilled.

"Gina," he whispered in a voice full of wonder, as if he'd seen a shooting star, a meteor, or maybe just her.

His other hand settled atop hers where it rested on the ground, and without thought she linked their fingers together.

The catch in his breath rushed along her skin, giving her goose bumps despite the seeming heat, then he throbbed, once, twice, again, and she was falling, rising, coming as she reached for a place where she no longer remembered anything but him.

He shouldn't have touched her with so much strife between them. But one look into her endless eyes and Matt had been lost.

Or maybe he'd merely been found. Because making love to Gina had felt like coming home.

Ridiculous. He'd never had a home. How could he possibly know what coming back to it would feel like?

Gina stirred at his side, and he tightened his arms around her. He didn't want her to move. Not now. Not ever.

He kissed her and again experienced that tug in his chest that made him want to hold on, to never let go. She'd told him that she'd rarely had a second date with a man; he'd rarely had a second date with a woman.

Because no first date had ever felt like this.

She licked the seam of his lips as she lifted her mouth. He could see nothing beyond the slightly darker outline of her head, but her breath brushed his cheek, her hair stroked his chest, and his body yearned all over again.

"I need to check the horses," she said.

"I'll do it."

Her laughter flowed across his skin, and his penis

leaped. He reached for her, but she was already rolling away, grabbing her jeans, her shirt. "I won't be long."

Matt lay back, hands beneath his head, and listened to her move about the tent. His mind wandered, as it often did, and he remembered what he'd asked right before she'd suddenly kissed him.

"What happened?" he repeated. "Beneath that tree. You can tell me."

The rustling stopped. The tent flap opened. She stepped out; the scent of rain rushed in.

It took Matt several minutes to realize she wasn't coming back.

CHAPTER 13

A loud crack sounded directly above; then rain fell in a deluge and the heavens erupted with lightning. Gina caught a glimpse of the horses, standing with their butts to the wind, heads down but calm enough, right before the world went dark again and she ran.

You can tell me. In other words . . . *you can trust me.*

But she couldn't. Mateo Mecate was after one thing, and it wasn't her. It had never *been* her.

Sure, she'd been the one to kiss him. She'd wanted to forget. And she had.

Until he'd made her remember. Now all she could think about was the time she'd spent underground.

The wind battered her face, whipped her hair, sang to her a name.

"Giiii-naaaa!"

"Hell," she muttered. One of these days she was going to have to either figure out why she kept hearing that or check herself into a place where she couldn't.

The sky lit up like a carnival midway, and she stopped so fast she slid several inches in the mud, arms pinwheeling as she tried to avoid falling on her ass. She managed, just barely.

She might not want to *talk* about what lay at the end of Lonely Deer Trail, but it appeared she was pretty intent on *standing* at the end of Lonely Deer Trail. She was nearly there.

And the wind kept calling her name.

"Giiii-naaa!"

"Fuck you," she muttered, but she kept moving.

She didn't feel any change beneath her feet as she approached. But then she wasn't a horse.

The night was so dark. Just as it had been back then. No rain that time, but the clouds had covered the moon.

The complete darkness all around made her feel as if she were in space, where gravity was skewed and up could be down or the other way around. The startling flashes of light caused the barren, glistening landscape to resemble the surface of the moon.

The sky flared again, and she started as Teo's damn tree of life—her harbinger of death—sprang up in front of her. If she'd kept going—half-walking, half-jogging, was that wogging?—she'd have run smack into it.

She slipped, and this time no amount of pinwheeling could prevent her from falling. The movement did, however, keep her from landing on her ass. Instead, she landed on her face. Or near enough.

Despite her disorientation, she brought her arms up and broke her fall. She still smacked her head into the ground. But she turned her neck sharply, so instead of crunching her nose, she felt her temple connect with a dull, squishy thud.

Then she lay there, letting her pulse return to normal. It didn't matter that she wallowed in the mud or that water sluiced across the ground as if running desperately downhill, despite the flat nature of the plain, skirting her body like a dam in a creek. She was already soaked.

But her pulse *didn't* slow, even though her breathing did. She felt fine. She wasn't hurt. Her heart shouldn't be beating so fast and so loudly the very earth seemed to shake with its force.

Gina rolled sideways, placing her palm against her chest.

Bu-bump. Bu-bump. Normal rhythm.

She laid her hand on the ground.

Ba-bump-ba-bump-ba-bump.

She snatched her hand away. The earth seemed to be shaking because it *was* shaking. Or at least beating to the tune of a very fast heart.

No wonder the horses flipped whenever they walked here. The vibration made her teeth itch, and horses had a *lot* more teeth.

Gina sat up, curling her legs into her chest and wrapping her arms around her knees; then she again touched the ground.

With the exact same results. The heart of the earth beat against her palm with such force her skin crawled.

She wiped her hand against her jeans, but the thud continued beneath, vibrating through her butt and up her spine. She felt as if her hair, despite being plastered to her scalp by the needle-like rain, was actually standing on end.

"Giii-naaa," whispered the wind, and she shivered, causing the hairs on her arms to dance.

"Hey!"

Her head lifted; her eyes scanned the darkness. Had

she heard someone shout? Perhaps the whispers of *Gina* had actually *been* the word *Gina* coming from a human mouth instead of a—

Well, who knew?

"Teo?" She stood. The beat of the earth rumbled against her feet. She swayed, but she stayed upright, gaze straining, breath shallow, as she waited for the flash. She'd run away from him, but now all she wanted was to see him again.

The world went bright white, and there he was, still a good hundred yards away. The air rushed from her lungs as relief swamped her, right before the whole world settled back to black.

Teo had been calling her name. It hadn't been the wind at all.

Of course that didn't explain the *ba-bump* beneath her heels. She wasn't sure anything could.

Unless there *was* a sorcerer down there.

Gina began to walk in Teo's direction, but as she did the *ba-bump* smoothed into one long, rolling rumble. She threw her arms out for balance; the sky lit up, and everything that had once been solid disappeared.

Every time the lightning flared, Matt lifted his head. The tree was always there—where was it going to go?—but Gina . . . Gina was another story.

The first flash, he'd seen her, running hell-bent for that spooky old tree.

During the second, she no longer ran but stood still as a photograph, the sky gone white, both the massive tree and the tiny human etched in black.

The third time the sky erupted in silver shards, what he saw made him stumble, nearly fall.

She was gone.

Which was impossible. This was a plain. The only thing sticking out of it were that tree and her. There was nowhere to go except—

His breath caught and he shouted, Hey!" And: "Gina!" Then he listened. But between the wind and the rain and the thunder, all he could hear was the ever-increasing rhythm of his heart, the thud so loud it echoed in his feet. He feared an imminent heart attack. Nevertheless, he began to run.

The next flash revealed Gina again. He didn't realize he'd been holding his breath—no wonder his heart was pounding in his brain—until it exploded from his mouth at the sight of her.

But his relief was short-lived, because suddenly the thunder of his heart was the thunder of the earth as it opened and swallowed Gina alive.

The ground gave way—first solid and then simply gone. Gina hit bottom, but instead of the dry dirt all around caving in, spilling onto her, some mud oozed down the walls, a bit plopping on her skin.

"Gina!"

Her gaze swiveled around the dark interior, trying to pinpoint the source of her name. Then another big clunk of mud fell from above, this time right on her head. She glanced up just in time for lightning to reveal Teo's anxious face peering over the edge of the hole in the ground. "You okay?"

Gina took stock. Odd, but she felt better physically than she had when she'd been tossed from the horse. Mentally was another thing entirely.

Mentally, she was screaming. Her parents were down here.

Her attention returned to the eternal blackness that surrounded her.

Somewhere.

And . . . What if her parents were the least of her worries?

"Can you stand?" Teo's voice drew her gaze upward. She needed to focus on him, not—

"Yeah." She stood. "I'm okay."

"Why did you run?" he asked, then lowered his voice. "Why did you run *here*?"

She wasn't going to admit to the wind calling her name. Teo would haul her out and deposit her in the nearest nuthouse. Not that she didn't belong there, but if she was going, she was going on her own.

"Gina?" he murmured again.

"You asked about my parents."

"I did?"

The surprise in his voice was comical. She could just make out his face against the suddenly lighter blue of the sky. The rain had slowed considerably; a few stars had begun to peek out.

"You asked what happened here."

Understanding blossomed, quickly followed by regret. "The accident . . . ," he began, then paused. "If you don't want to tell me, that's all right."

Gina rubbed her wet hands against her wet jeans, sucking in a breath when her palms burned like fire. She'd scraped them—either when she'd fallen out there or when she'd fallen in here.

"What's wrong?" Teo's voice, which had been so lovely and calm, took on an edge of panic.

"Nothing," she said quickly, then peered into the gaping teeth of darkness that lay behind her.

Everything.

"Maybe I should get a rope," he said.

"No!" The thought of being left alone down here made her swear she could hear those teeth snap at the air far too close to her heels.

Teo would have to get a rope eventually, but if he did so now, she just might cry. And if she started to cry, when would she stop?

So, while she'd just run *from* him rather than share the past of this place, Gina took a deep breath and set that past free.

"Isaac told us not to go here. He said at the end of Lonely Deer Trail was death. Everyone who'd ever come here had died."

"Everyone?" Teo sounded as skeptical as she'd once felt.

"According to Isaac. Of course the warnings only made me want to see the place even more."

"Of course," Teo echoed, in a voice that said, *Who wouldn't?*

She smiled against the darkness. "I bullied Jase into coming along."

"McCord doesn't seem like the kind of guy who'd be bullied by anyone."

"Call him a wuss and a girl sometime and see what happens."

"A broken nose most likely," Teo muttered.

"For you, probably. For me . . ." Gina shrugged. "It took months, really almost a year, of constant badgering. The only reason Jase came at all was because I threatened to go alone."

"Why so obsessed?"

"Good question." One Gina didn't have an answer

to. All she knew was that this place had been the only one forbidden her and she'd been unable to keep herself from seeing it.

"What happened?" Teo repeated.

"We came over the ridge and . . ." She paused as her breath caught in her throat now as it had then. The vista that had spread out before them had been so irresistible she'd scrambled like a kid with a broken piñata for her camera. "I took that damn picture as the sun set."

And even though Jase had wanted to turn back then—they'd found the end of the trail; now they could go—she'd been captivated by a tree that had appeared to be on fire.

"By the time we got close, the sun was gone; the moon was coming up." She'd planned to return to the exact same place where she'd taken the sunset photo and take another of the moonscape, but by then her camera had been crap.

She lifted her face and received a few final plops of rain on her cheeks. "The horses threw us at about the same place ours did today. But those didn't stop where Spike and Lady Belle did. They kept going. Jase and I walked around, trying to figure out what was so bad about the area. How could people die? It was flat. Nothing dangerous that we could see. Unless someone climbed the tree and fell on his or her head."

Gina remained silent for a few seconds, bracing herself to share the recurring nightmare that had begun right here. "The ground gave way, and the dirt just kept pouring in, the walls collapsing." She swallowed, remembering how the dust had filled her throat, forced her to close her eyes.

"How did you survive?"

"Must have been an air pocket."

"Unusual."

"I don't have any other explanation." She didn't have an explanation for a lot of things.

"The air wouldn't last forever."

"No." Gina remembered the panic, the darkness, that sense that something "other" was there and that it was so very, very glad they'd come. "But every time one of us moved, the dirt would shift, and we were afraid we were only making it worse. We tried to talk, but that uses oxygen." And caused dirt to cascade into their mouths.

"What did you do?"

Held hands and waited to die.

"The horses ran home," she blurted.

"Awful long way."

"We'd already been missed. My parents were almost here when they blew past."

Teo sucked in a loud, sharp breath. He knew what she was going to say. She said it anyway.

"They tried to come in from the side so they wouldn't dislodge more earth. Instead—" The words stuck in her throat just like all that dirt had.

"The earth dislodged on them," Teo finished.

"It was like . . ." She paused, uncertain how to say it and not sound crazy. So she said the first part and kept the second to herself: "In pouring onto them, it poured off of us."

As if the earth, or something else, had chosen who would live and who would die.

Duck. Duck.

Goose.

"I guess that could happen." Teo sounded skeptical.

"It did," Gina said flatly. "We dug, but couldn't find them. By the time Isaac arrived, it was too late."

"What do you mean, you couldn't find them?"

"Dug here, dug there, no bodies."

"That's . . ." His voice faded. Obviously it *wasn't* impossible or there'd be bodies. "Weird," he continued. "Didn't you bring in earthmoving equipment? Professionals?"

"Things just kept collapsing. Some geologist figured there were underground catacombs. Every shift of the soil only caused the bodies to break through another layer, falling deeper and deeper. Therefore, the more we dug, the farther away they fell."

She'd had nightmares for years about reaching for her mother, only to have the earth give way beneath Betsy's feet an instant before Gina touched her, the echo of her scream fading as she fell and fell and fell.

"Not long after they got us out Isaac had the hole filled in."

"But if there are catacombs," Teo said, "it would eventually cave in again."

"Really?" Gina muttered. "Ya think?"

Silence descended. The sky had cleared, the moon just visible over the lip of the hole.

"I understand now why you didn't want me here," he murmured. "But I still have to look."

She almost told him everything—what she'd heard, what she'd felt—except she was trying to convince him *not* to dig farther. If she told him that, she'd only intrigue him more.

"It's dangerous," she said instead.

"I've done this before; the people I'll have helping me have done this before. The machinery and tools we'll be using are made for this situation. It'll all work out. You'll see. We might even find—" He broke off, but Gina knew what he'd been about to say.

He thought they might find her parents. Was that what she wanted?

Gina glanced around the hollow where she'd fallen, no longer pitch-black but beginning to gray with the glint of a rising moon.

She'd never understood the need to bury a body. Her parents' funeral hadn't been any less final without twin coffins at the front of the church. The headstones Isaac had insisted they place in the cemetery weren't any more upsetting because they marked empty plots.

So, no, Gina didn't care if they found her parents. In fact, she'd much prefer they did not.

But what she wanted didn't matter. Teo would dig, and there wasn't a damn thing she could do about it beyond watch.

"I'll get a rope, some light, the hors . . ." He paused. "Well, at least the rope and a light."

"Crap," Gina muttered. It wasn't as easy as it appeared on TV to haul a person out of a hole. If there was a horse available to help, you used the damn horse.

Unless the creature planned to behave like the wildest bronc at the rodeo as soon as it came anywhere near.

"I'll be right back," Teo said, and then he was gone.

Gina wrapped her arms around herself and kept her gaze on the sky so she wouldn't be tempted to let it wander around the cavern.

However, creaks and crinkles, whistles, and was that a whimper? tempted her. She cast quick glances—first forward, then up, then to the left, the right, back up, and finally to the rear, where she could have sworn she saw something move.

She began to hum, uncertain at first of the song, until another loud *reech* forced the words right out.

> *"In a castle, on a mountain,*
> *Near the dark and murky Rhine,*
> *Dwelt a doctor, the concocter*
> *Of the monster Frankenstein."*

Gina laughed, though the sound gurgled weak and watery. Of all of Mel's songs to remember right now, it had to be that one.

She hoped singing would make the swirling shadows back off. Instead, the sound of her own voice echoing out of one helluva big empty hole only made them seem to swirl closer, brushing against her skin, cool as fog. So she sang louder.

> *"In a graveyard, near the castle,*
> *Where the sun refused to shine,*
> *He found noses and some toeses,*
> *For his monster Frankenstein."*

Gina's gaze flickered downward again. If there were any spare noses or toeses, she figured she'd find them right over . . .

There.

She yanked her gaze back to the shimmering, silent moon.

Really, really, *bad song choice, Gina.*

However, now that she'd started, she couldn't make herself stop. Probably because when she stopped, she kept hearing the damn song anyway. The words were set to the tune of "Darling Clementine" and *that* was a rhythm that just wouldn't go away.

> *"So he took them and he built him,*
> *From the pieces he did find.*

And with lightning he animated
The scary monster Frankenstein."

Bizarrely, lightning blazed in the distance, thunder rumbling in from the east.

Once the flash of silver cleared, a ray of gold appeared against the sky, bobbing closer and closer, as if the biggest firefly in the world flitted near.

"Scared the townsfolk, scared the po-lice,
Scared the kids, did Frankenstein,"

she sang softly, gaze on that flickering light that spread and spread like the sun across a field at dawn.

"Till with torches they did chase him,
To the castle by the Rhine."

"Did someone ask for a torch?" Teo's head appeared haloed in the golden glow of the tent light in his hand.

She was so glad to see both him and the lamp, she laughed. Why did he have to be who he was? Why did she? Whenever they forgot themselves, they almost had fun. She had so little fun in her life; she cherished it. Even if it was with Dr. Moldy.

Who wasn't very moldy at all.

"Aren't you going to finish?" he asked.

"You weren't supposed to hear that."

"Gina," he said. "Everyone within thirty miles heard that."

She winced. "Oops."

"You have a nice voice. I, on the other hand—" He straightened and began to sing the chorus at the top of his lungs.

"Oh, my monster, oh, my monster,
Oh, my monster, Frankenstein.
You were built to last forever,
Dreadful sca-a-a-a-ry-y-y-y-y . . ."

He drew out the last word, voice warbling—that just *had* to be on purpose; could he really be that awful?—then moving on to the big finish with:

"Fran-ken-stein!"

"Wow," she said when the off-key echo had faded. "That was truly . . ." She shook her head. "Horrendous."

Teo bowed. "Now you know why I dig in the dirt." He set the lantern at the edge of the hole. "I'm gonna tie this . . ." He held up the rope. "Around the tree."

Gina nodded, but he was already gone. She was getting a crick in her neck from staring up, so she lowered her head and rubbed at the ache.

The golden light chased the shadows back far enough that Gina could see—

Frowning, she dropped her hand and stepped forward.

Was that a wall?

CHAPTER 14

Matt secured the rope, then returned to the gaping maw in the earth. When he glanced into the hole, she was gone.

"Gina!" he shouted, alarm causing his voice to come out louder than he'd expected. He jumped as the sound echoed back from below.

"I'm not deaf," she said. "Or at least I wasn't."

"Where are you?"

"Right here." She leaned into the light. "I saw a wall." She disappeared again.

"There's gonna be walls or you'd be—" He broke off. *Buried* was not a good word to use right now. Actually, it probably wasn't a good word to use with Gina, ever.

"Not dirt walls." Her voice came from a little farther away. "Stone." Matt got a chill. "And there are some marks."

Oh shit, oh shit, oh shit, his mind jabbered.

Matt very calmly asked, "What kind of marks?"

"The kind you just showed me."

"I'm coming down."

He nearly grabbed the rope and rappelled over the edge before he remembered more light would probably be a good idea and if he was *down* there there'd be no one *up* here to help him with that.

Matt took several deep breaths, slowing his heart, centering his mind. When he did things too fast, he only wound up wasting time.

First, send the lantern down to Gina. Second, send him.

"Gina," he said, thrilled when his voice came out calm, as if he were speaking to a student in class. "Can you grab this?"

He leaned down for the light, but when she didn't return he straightened again, leaving it at the edge of the cavity.

"There's what looks like a man," she called. "He seems to be fighting the vicious dog-being you showed me before. You said that meant loyalty. So . . . he's fighting his loyalty?"

Matt stood, rope in one hand, the other empty, fingers curling inward, making a fist as he tried to keep himself from jumping in. He wanted to see that wall, read those icons, but he could tell from Gina's voice she was as fascinated by them as he'd always been. She wasn't going to come back until she read them all—or at least tried. After what she'd gone through, she deserved that.

"Maybe he was fighting an enemy that fought like a vicious dog," Teo suggested.

"Hmm." She didn't sound convinced. "The guy himself seems a little doglike."

"Not everyone was van Gogh," Teo repeated, and she laughed.

"Right. I suppose all your people have alligator teeth."

Come to think of it, they did.

"Is one of the men bigger than the other?" Matt continued.

"Yes," she said.

Matt got a tingle again. This *had* to be the tomb of the superwarrior. Then again—

"That could mean a big man or an army of men."

"The Nahua," she said.

"Yes." Except the Aztecs hadn't called themselves that. They'd called themselves Tenochca; however, the icon to indicate either one would probably have been the same.

"Wait." Matt heard Gina move; he could almost see her hair swaying, her hand reaching for another drawing, her finger resting just below whatever she'd found. "You told me this one. The teeth, which is the letter *T.*"

Matt got excited again. *T* could indicate *Tenochca,* which meant whoever had written that on the wall had been Aztec.

"Not *T,*" she murmured as if to herself. "But the roof on the teeth, which is the 'l' sound. And it's right next to the dog-faced man icon, which would make it—"

Matt glanced at the sky. *That* put an entirely different twist on things.

"Nahual," Gina concluded.

From the depths of the cavern, something howled.

Gina could have sworn she heard a *click.* Then a howling, swirling black cloud whooshed past, its force blowing back her hair, blowing back *her* a few steps. Her ears rang, and the inside of her nose stung, as if she'd just taken a large sniff of below-zero air.

The smoke spun around her, twirling up her body

from her feet to her head, and as it curled around her face it whispered, *Giii-naaa*.

Then it was gone—*phht!*—and she was left shivering. It took her several seconds to realize she could still hear her name.

Because Teo was shouting, his panic so audible, she stumbled away from the wall and into the circle of light. When she glanced up, she could have sworn she saw the outline of a black wolf against the backdrop of the silvery moon.

"What the hell was that?" she asked.

"I'm coming down. Grab the light."

Before she could protest—right now she'd prefer to be up—he swung the lantern over the edge. Either his hands on the rope were shaking or he was hurrying too fast to keep the contraption steady, because it pitched wildly back and forth, sending blares of light into her eyes, making it hard for her to see or catch the thing.

"Watch it." She grabbed the lantern right before it clocked her in the head.

"Sorry," Teo said, but he didn't sound sorry; he sounded as shaky as she felt. What had the strange black smoke looked like from his end?

He yanked the rope so hard and so fast the tip nearly flicked her in the nose. She didn't bother to complain. He was *excited*. She got that.

Instead, she lifted the lantern and moved closer to the wall. Dog-faced man, teeth with a roof. There were other glyphs, too, tiny, colorful sketches of animals and people, moons, or maybe suns, and stars, with a thin brown line encircling the entire panorama.

Teo landed with a thud and a grunt, crossing the distance between them with long, choppy strides, then crowding in to see the etchings with a muttered, "Excuse me."

Gina let him peer at the pictures, holding the lantern so the wall was better illuminated, until she just had to ask, "What was that black smoke?"

"Hmm?" Teo leaned closer, nearly putting his nose to the rock. Only then did she realize he didn't have his glasses.

"The black smoke that shot out of here so fast it blew back my hair. The black smoke that was so cold my nose hairs froze."

He turned his head, expression blank. "What black smoke?"

In the circle of golden light, Gina paled. "You didn't see it?"

"I . . . uh . . ." Matt reached up to push his glasses into place, but his finger encountered only nose. He'd left them in the tent. No wonder he was starting to get a headache from squinting. "No."

She switched her gaze to the long hallway, which disappeared into the dark. "What about the howl?"

"That I heard."

She glanced back, her eyes both startled and relieved. "Well, at least I'm only half-crazy today. Seeing things, yes, but for a change I'm not the only one hearing them."

"For a change?" he repeated.

She waved him off. "What do you think howled?"

She peered at the corridor again; Matt followed her gaze. He was going to have to go down there.

"Might just have been the usual unwolves," she murmured, still staring into the dark.

"But you don't think so."

Her eyes cut to him, then quickly away. "The howl came equipped with icy black smoke that swirled past and went—" She pointed at the opening. "The unhowls have never had visuals."

"I didn't see any smoke, but I was—" Matt tried to remember what he'd been doing after he'd heard that howl and couldn't. He'd been so excited about what they'd found he'd been kind of out of it. Still, there was really no logical explanation for a swirl of icy black smoke. Not that there was a logical explanation for the unwolves, either.

His gaze returned to the long, dark stone hallway. "A gun would be nice."

"I've got one." Matt glanced at her, and she shrugged. "In the tent."

"Oh, that's helpful."

"This place has been buried for nearly ten years. There shouldn't be anything left to shoot." Gina wrapped her arms around herself, peering into the darkness as if she could make it disappear just by wishing it to. "Right?"

"Right," he repeated. It was probably nothing.

So why, then, did he distinctly feel something?

"I'm gonna look." He stepped forward.

"I'm gonna come with you."

"No." He extended his hand for the light.

She held it out of his reach. "Yes."

"It's better if you stay here."

"In the dark? Not happening."

Matt wouldn't want to stay here alone, either. And he hadn't even seen the weird black smoke.

"All right." He curled his fingers toward his palm in a beckoning gesture, and she gave him the lantern. "Stay behind me."

As they moved past the wall, Matt couldn't keep his gaze from the drawings. They depicted a battle, many dead. Then there was a big Aztec warrior and—

Matt stopped, and Gina crashed into his back. "Hey!"

"Sorry." He lifted the lamp. "There were *two* big guys. See?"

She followed his gaze to where another, only slightly smaller man with an avalanche of stars pouring from his fingertips confronted the man-dog figure. "What does that mean?"

"No idea."

"This?" She pointed at another tableau of the man-dog beneath two suns, or two moons, maybe one of each, since the left circle was yellow and the right pure white.

"Got me," Matt said. He could probably study this wall for a year—he planned to—and not decipher all of the glyphs.

"This is interesting." Matt indicated a herd of what appeared to be dog-horses with stars around their hooves.

For an instant he thought Gina recognized it; she blinked, leaned in closer, frowned. Then she shook her head a little and lifted her chin to indicate the dark path in front of them. "It'll still be here when we get back."

They needed to move forward. Except when Matt faced the glistening blackness he didn't want to. And that wasn't like him. Usually he couldn't wait to explore every shadowed nook and cranny.

"Want me to go first?" Gina asked.

"No." The only thing he wanted less than to move forward himself was to have Gina do it.

Matt put one foot in front of the other, wondering as

he did so just what was the matter with him. He should be charging down the corridor, searching for the tomb of a superwarrior that would vindicate both him and his mother. Instead, he really wanted out.

It was as if a foul stench emanated from that darkness, even though every breath Matt took smelled fine. A little musty, a little dusty, a little cold, but not bad.

Luckily, he and Gina didn't have far to go; he wasn't sure if he would have been able to continue if they had. Matt covered maybe ten yards, the lantern illuminating their path, Gina determined to step on his heels at every opportunity, and then—

Her arm shot past his cheek, and he inhaled the scent of trees. He wanted to turn his head and rub his face on her skin and smell only that forever.

"What's there?"

The urgency of her voice brought his attention back where it belonged, and he followed the line of her finger to an opening in the wall. Matt forgot all about the scent of evergreens on smooth, supple skin.

"Burial chamber," he said.

Gina bent to examine the floor. "This swung inward."

She pointed at the marks in the dirt, and Matt joined her, insinuating himself between Gina and the uncharted darkness beyond.

He lifted the lantern so he could examine the back of the door. "There's no handle."

Gina followed, frowning at the sheer panel on the other side, before her face smoothed and she lifted one shoulder. "Why would there be? If it's a burial chamber, what's in there isn't coming back out."

"We should probably see what that is." And Matt should probably be more excited about it.

"Ready when you are."

Matt shifted the lantern so the golden glow illuminated the small room.

"That can't be good," Gina said.

Right now, staring at the empty room, Matt had to agree. Although . . .

"The Aztecs often burned their warriors, then stashed them in burial pots."

Gina took a pointed look around the room. Nothing there but dirt and stones and walls.

"According to the codex my mom translated, the superwarrior was buried in the land to the north. Which means he could have been interred by whomever he defeated, according to their practices. I need to research the Ute—"

"The Ute wrapped their dead," Gina interrupted, "then buried them in rock-covered graves beneath the earth."

"Which might explain this."

"The rock-covered grave, yes. But lack of a body?"

Matt contemplated the tomb. "The wrappings, being natural, not synthetic, *would* have disintegrated by now. But in dry, cool conditions, like these, bones can last for centuries." Which made it odd that there was nothing left at all.

Odd, but not impossible.

"If there was no way to open the door from the inside," Gina said, "then someone had to have pushed it from the outside."

"Theoretically."

"Maybe whoever pushed it took the body. Or the burial pots."

"Probably," Matt agreed, but then his gaze caught on something interesting. "Except . . ." He pointed at the ground. "The only footsteps here are ours."

CHAPTER 15

"What does that mean?" Gina asked.

"I haven't a clue."

"But you've got that Ph.D. thingy after your name."

Teo smiled. "Sometimes that Ph.D. thingy isn't worth the paper it's printed on."

Interesting. Gina had always thought it must be worth a helluva lot.

"Why the glyphs?" she continued. "Why the door, if there was never anything in there at all?"

"Never's a long time."

"Now you're just talking gibberish."

He glanced at her, and his eyes had gone dark in the lamplight. They almost didn't look like Teo's eyes at all. "Maybe someone took whatever was in here, then covered their tracks."

"If someone found a mummy, don't you think we'd have heard about it?"

"Not necessarily. Tomb raiders have been around as long as the tombs. And when one of them snatches something to sell to private collectors, or even witch doctors, they usually do so without letting anyone know about it."

"Witch—" Gina stuck her finger in her ear and wiggled it. "What?"

"Certain spells require all sorts of weird things for ingredients."

"You said you didn't believe in magic," Gina pointed out.

"Just because I don't doesn't mean there aren't others who do. Others who'd be willing to do anything, or pay anything, to get what they think they need."

Gina opened her mouth, then shut it again. He should know. She certainly didn't.

"This place was cursed. No one ever came here."

"Grave robbers love curses," Teo said. " A curse pretty much puts an *X* right on the spot."

She hadn't thought of that.

"What happened to the footsteps of the grave robbers?"

"They brushed them out, or maybe they were here so long ago . . . Other things that happened afterward . . ." He paused, casting her a concerned glance. "They could have changed everything."

If grave robbers had come before she and Jase had been buried, before her parents had died and the cavern had been searched and then filled in again, the idea that footsteps would still be visible was ludicrous.

Gina had another thought. She'd been avoiding shadowy corners, afraid of what she might see, but now her gaze flicked around the room, back through the door, and down the shadowy hall. She hadn't seen any bodies out there, either. Maybe, just as the "experts" had said, they'd only fallen in deeper, being pulled lower in a maze of catacombs as every granule of earth was dislodged. Then again, maybe they hadn't.

The idea of strangers snatching up what was left of her parents and—

"If grave robbers were looking for bones," Teo said softly, "they'd take any bones they found."

Therefore, what remained of her family might very well be resting in a jar on some shelf in a voodoo shop in Louisiana. That really pissed her off.

However, if the remains were gone—removed by thieves or sifted through to a lower level—she could stop worrying that she might stumble over them at any moment.

Hey, there was a silver lining to every cloud just as Fanny had always told her.

"If the crypt was already open," Gina murmured, "then why did I hear a click?" *Or a howl, for that matter?*

"Click?" he repeated.

"There was a click, the howl, a whoosh." And the smoke.

Teo stared at the door. "Whoever took the body could have shut the door."

"Then how did it open again?"

Teo went silent, and Gina did, too. But not for long.

"What if it was like *The Mummy*?" she blurted.

"It *was* a mummy," he said slowly. "But it's gone."

"No. The movie."

"I don't see many movies," he admitted. "*Raiders of the Lost Ark* once." He shrugged. "I liked it."

Gina stared at him. *No movies? What kind of life was that?*

One in which more exciting things happened to him every day than he could ever see on the screen.

"There was a movie about a mummy," she said.

"Brendan Fraser." Teo opened his mouth, and she shook her head. "Never mind. Anyway, this guy boinked the Pharaoh's honey, and they—the Egyptians, I think—buried him alive."

"*Never* boink the Pharaoh's honey," Teo murmured.

"I think that was the lesson they were going for. Anyway, they buried him and his minions with all these booby traps so that anyone who came across the crypt had bad things happen and then the tomb raiders would run away before they got to the big prize."

"What kind of things?"

"Acid flew out of some of the graves when they opened them. And there were these creepy-monkey priests."

"Creepy-monkey?" he repeated.

"You had to see them. They could run sideways on walls. Very scary. Then there were these nasty beetles that crept under your skin. They'd crash through your toe and scuttle all the way up to your—" Gina shuddered. She'd always hated that part of the movie. "Believe me, you wanted to leave soon after you came."

"Explain to me why you think this movie connects to . . ." Teo waved his hand at the empty room.

"What if the howl was a booby trap, or at least a sound effect to frighten away the amateurs? Open the door, a howl erupts."

"That might explain the smoke, too."

"Okay," Gina agreed. She was willing to agree to anything if it would explain that smoke.

Who knew? If they could logically explain howling, freezing black smoke, maybe they could also logically explain the unwolves and the singsongy Gina voice.

However, Gina doubted she'd be that lucky.

"Show me where you were when you heard the

click and the howl." Teo moved into the hall, crowding Gina forward, sweeping her along with both his body and his enthusiasm. "What did you do? What did you say?"

She tried to remember exactly what had happened and in what order and in doing so fell behind. Teo simply reached back, snatching her hand in his as if he'd done the same a thousand times before and therefore knew where both she and her hand would be.

Gina's throat went thick with need, not for sex but for this. A connection to someone that went beyond sight, beyond mind, beyond body—the kind of connection her parents had had.

Before she'd killed them.

Teo squeezed her fingers, rubbing his thumb along the base of hers, a comforting gesture that aroused feelings that went beyond comfort.

Had she made an involuntary movement? Had she gasped or whimpered? She didn't think so. Nevertheless, he had sensed her distress and answered it. Her longing intensified.

What was wrong with her? She should hate him. He was a liar, an imposter, a thief. Her mind knew these things, but her body didn't seem to care.

Teo arrived at the wall of glyphs. Lifting the lantern, he squinted, then he dropped her hand, and Gina had to clench hers until her nails bit into the palm to keep from reaching out and taking his back.

"The dog-headed man and the *la* symbol." Teo tapped his fingernail, usually so clean and white but now slightly tarnished with dirt beneath the glyphs. "You stood here?"

He turned, his eyes more spring leaves than winter moss, and tilted his head. His hair slid over his shoulder.

She clenched her other hand to stop herself from touching it.

"Um." Gina took a breath, striving for calm. Instead her heartbeat increased in tempo as her nose filled with the scent of dust and oranges. She glanced at the floor, where his boots stood right next to the imprint of hers. "Yeah."

"Show me." Gina blinked, and he made a "be my guest" gesture with one long-fingered, dirty hand. "Where you were, what you did."

Gina stepped forward, positioning her feet directly atop the prints she'd made earlier. "I was looking at the pictures, thinking about what you'd told me. You said this . . ." She put her finger beneath the man-dog figure. "Might be an indication of an army and not a single man. Which made me think Nahua."

"Except the Aztecs called themselves Tenochca."

He leaned over her shoulder to see better, and his hair brushed past her cheek, causing a shiver. His hands landed on her shoulders and he rubbed her arms, quick and fast, as if to warm her. Gina couldn't help it; she leaned into him, pressing her back against his front. They'd both been drenched; they should be equally cold, except he gave off heat like a bonfire.

"Wh-what does *Tenochca-la* mean?" she whispered, afraid if she spoke too loudly he might move away.

"Diddly."

Teo leaned closer. Gina had to bite her lip to keep from arching into him. He was just too hot, and she was oh, so cold.

"I don't get it," she said. But boy, did she want it.

"Me, either," he muttered, and now his breath brushed her cheek, the heat of it warming Gina all the way to her icy, stiff toes. "These are Aztec figures. But I don't know why any Aztec would draw this."

He reached past her and tapped the man-dog head, then the *la* symbol. His arm rested on her shoulder; she wanted to turn her head and rub her cheek against it.

"Is there any such thing as a Nahual?"

"There is. I don't know that much about it, since my specialty is the history and writings of the Aztecs. The Nahual is more a mystical thing."

"A god?"

"No. A Nahual was a spirit that took the form of an animal. A guardian. Everyone received a different Nahual, which was tied to the day of his or her birth in the ancient calendar. If you were born on the dog day, for example, your Nahual would take the form of a dog."

Gina frowned at the figure. "You think this guy was born on the dog day?"

"Could be."

"So that would mean this glyph refers to a single person, rather than an army of them."

"Maybe. A Nahual was considered extremely personal. Not something to be advertised, or drawn on walls. An Aztec would only speak of his Nahual to a very close friend or relative."

Gina shrugged, the movement rubbing the back of her all over the front of him, creating a friction she wanted to continue so badly she immediately stopped. "That just means whoever drew this was his pal."

"Hmm," Teo murmured, the reverberation in his chest trailing up her spine and settling at her neck, causing goose bumps to erupt everywhere.

He rubbed her shoulders and arms, again almost absently. Had she shuddered? She didn't think so.

"I'm gonna need to talk to an expert on this."

His right hand left her arm. She wanted to reach for him and bring it back. He cursed, and she turned her head to find him staring at his cell phone.

"No bars," he muttered.

She let her gaze wander over the ceiling of the *cave* they were in. Why on earth would he think there would be bars? The man was so smart yet sometimes, also, so dumb. Why did that make her want to hug him?

Gina sighed. She was in so much trouble.

Teo put away his phone. "We need to go back."

She started to move away, and the hand still on her arm tightened.

"First," he said in that ruined voice that made her yearn, "finish telling me exactly what you said, what you did."

Gina contemplated the glyphs in front of her for several seconds, remembering. "I combined what I thought was *Nahua* and that symbol, which you said was an 'l' sound at the end of a word into *Nahual*. Then I heard a click—" She jerked her chin in the direction of the tomb. "Down there. Something howled; then this dark smoke barreled past and disappeared out the hole I put in the ceiling."

"Hmm," he repeated. "Words wouldn't open a tomb."

"They did in the movie," she muttered.

"I don't think the Aztecs saw it." Gina glanced over her shoulder to see if he was kidding, but Teo continued to stare at the glyphs. She doubted he even knew what he'd said. All he cared about was the wall. "Did you touch something?"

"Yeah." Gina pointed to the area below the man-dog figure, and Teo reached out to touch it, too.

Their fingers met, hers leaving, his going. Teo's breath caught; Gina's did, too. Then several soft thuds from above were followed by a louder, lower thump to the right.

"What was that?" Gina asked, just as Teo muttered, "Shit," and Jase called out, "Gina?"

Matt stepped away from Gina, stifling a groan. When their hands had touched, he'd felt it all the way down to his toes. For just an instant, he'd entertained the notion of spinning her around and taking her against the glyph-strewn wall.

Thankfully, he'd refrained. What if he'd been buried deep inside of her when McCord showed up?

Matt winced and rubbed a hand over his face. How in hell had the guy found them and why?

McCord's boots begin to stomp down the corridor in their direction. Light bobbed to the right, and Jase Mc-Cord appeared an instant later. His frantic gaze went directly to Gina; then so did he. He wrapped his huge hands around her arms, his wide shoulders blocking Matt's view. "You okay?"

"I'm fine."

"What the hell, Gina?" He scraped his fingers through his short, glistening hair. "I found your camp, the horses, then the hole. I thought I'd have a heart attack. When you didn't answer—" His hands fell back to his sides, and he turned, his cool, dark eyes narrowing when they encountered Matt. "Why didn't you answer?"

Matt couldn't help it; he smiled.

McCord took one step toward him, and Gina grabbed his arm. She would never have been able to hold him back; he was built like a bull, and he wanted Matt to be his own personal china closet. But the instant she touched him, murmuring, "Hey," the man stilled. Talk about taming the savage beast.

"I'm sorry you were scared." She rubbed McCord's arm, and all the tension flowed out of him. His broad shoulders slumped; his thick neck seemed to lose strength so that his head fell forward. "But why are you here?"

McCord's head came up, his nostrils flaring like that bull. "I didn't mean to *interrupt*."

"I fell in a hole, Jase. There isn't much to interrupt except an extreme need for TYLENOL."

The fight went out of him. The guy changed directions so fast Matt was starting to get whiplash. "You said you were okay."

"I am."

"Why are you . . ." He peered around the cavern, seeming to see it for the first time, and his perpetual scowl deepened. "Where did this come from?"

"Must have been here all along."

He stared at the wall and the icons. "I never saw it."

"We never saw anything but dirt."

He turned in a circle. "And where is that dirt? It was supposed to be filling this in forever."

"A cavern's a cavern," Matt said. "Filling it in won't change that."

McCord cast a withering glare in Matt's direction. "We did change it. This place has been buried for ten years."

"*After* it caved in."

McCord glanced quickly at Gina, and she shrugged, which only made the man's face darken. McCord wasn't happy she'd told Matt about their experience here. Matt had to wonder if she'd ever told anyone, and the thought that she might not have, that he was the first, made him bold.

"You can fill this place with dirt over and over again," he said in his Dr. Mecate voice, "but what the earth wants to be it will be. There's some underground stream or drain or soft spot that makes the ground above collapse. You should just leave it alone."

"Fat chance," McCord muttered. "Granddad's gonna fill this back in the instant your ass is out."

"Jase, you're supposed to be leading the second half of the tour, and that isn't on this side of the ranch."

McCord glanced down. "Well, we— I mean, they—"

"He changed the itinerary," Matt murmured.

Gina's brow creased. "Why?"

"So he could keep an eye on us."

"Eye?" Gina repeated, then glanced from Matt to her childhood friend and back again. "Huh?"

"He's jealous."

"I've told you before, Teo—"

"His name's not Teo!" McCord erupted. "It's Dr. Mecate. Matt. Moldy to you."

Gina's lips tightened. "I met him as Teo, and Teo he is to me. You call him whatever you like. Now, explain why you brought paying customers to the shitty side of the ranch."

McCord's own lips went tight. His face turned dark red. In an instant, steam might come out of his ears.

Matt should have known better, but sometimes he just didn't. "Tell her what you did," he said. "How you've warned every man away from her. How you warned me."

McCord might be big and bulky, but he moved faster than a thin, lithe snake. He stepped forward, popping Matt in the chin before anyone could stop him.

As if anyone *could* have stopped him.

Matt's head snapped back and Gina cried out, but he

didn't go down. He was quite proud of that. Because his face hurt like a bitch.

He was able to stare calmly at the man, whom Gina held by the arm. "Hitting me doesn't make what I said any less true." Matt transferred his gaze to Gina. "Doesn't it seem a little too weird that no one's ever come back after a first date? You aren't *that* bad."

She laughed. Just once, a sparkling, happy sound, and Matt realized *he'd* done that. He'd made her doubt there was something wrong with *her,* made her consider there was something wrong, instead, with all of *them.* What man would let another warn him away from Gina? She was worth fighting for. Hell, she was worth dying for.

Gina's laughter faded, and her forehead creased as she added two plus two and got, of all things, four. "Jase." She let go of his arm. "Why *are* you here?"

The man's gaze met Matt's, and in it Matt saw coming retribution. Maybe not today, maybe not tomorrow, but someday, and someday soon, McCord was going to get him.

"We've got trouble," McCord said. "Someone's dead."

CHAPTER 16

"Dead?" Gina repeated. "Who?"

For an instant she thought of Isaac, of Fanny, and she couldn't breathe. Then she realized that if Jase's granddad or his mother were dead, he certainly wouldn't be questioning her and punching Teo.

Would he?

The Jase she'd thought she knew wouldn't. However, the Jase who'd emerged lately, the one Teo insisted had been there all along . . . him she didn't know at all.

A shadow passed over Jase's face. There and then gone, disturbing because she'd never seen that expression before. It made him appear young and uncertain— a boy's expression, not a man's.

She couldn't help it; she reached out and took his hand. "What happened?"

His fingers tightened around hers, clinging, also something he'd never done. "We were camped by the stream. We had to go around and then it was late, getting dark."

"We were there," Gina said, hoping to speed things up. *Who* was dead?

"Everyone was headed to their tents. Mel had taught us a new song."

"Uh-oh," Gina murmured, and Jase's lips tilted just a bit before they stopped, straightening again into that tight, stressed line.

"Yeah. The first one was about a guy named Frick who tried to balance on his—"

"Got it!" Gina interrupted.

"I made him teach another. 'Ghost Chickens in the Sky.' It was catchy. People liked it. They were still singing, which made it easy to hear when—" He broke off, gulped. "They stopped."

"What do you mean they stopped?" Teo asked.

Jase's hand in hers jerked. He'd forgotten Teo was there.

"They stopped," Jase snapped. "First singing, then not."

"Okay," Gina soothed. Had Jase's hand begun to shake? "What's so bad about that?"

"That wasn't the bad part. The bad part was the screaming."

"The bad part is always the screaming," Teo muttered. "You probably should have started with that."

Jase shot him a glare. Gina squeezed Jase's fingers until he returned his attention to her. "Go on."

"The screams were coming from all directions. I—I didn't know which way to run first. I went to the As because, well—"

"They were the loudest?" Gina guessed.

"No."

"They weren't?" Gina asked. "No way."

"Not *they*. When I got there, only one of them was left."

"Which one?"

"Who knows?" Jase put the heel of his free hand between his eyes and pressed. "Who cares?"

Gina let that go for the moment. "Where was she?"

"Gone."

"She couldn't just be gone," Gina insisted. "What did the other one say?"

Jase lowered his arm. "After she stopped shrieking like someone was sticking an ice pick in her eye?"

Gina could imagine. She was surprised she and Teo hadn't heard the girl down here.

"Yeah, then," Gina agreed.

"It didn't make much sense."

"Which would make it equal to a lot of what the As have said so far."

Jase's lips curved again. Making jokes seemed to help him focus or at least calm down enough to continue. "She said they were singing, then there was a *whoosh,* a swirl of black, and—" He paused, then snapped his fingers. "*Ashleigh* was gone."

Gina and Teo exchanged a glance. He opened his mouth, but she shook her head. Better that she asked the questions of Jase.

"A swirl of black?" she asked. "What's that mean?"

"How the hell should I know? Amberleigh said the darkness took her. She's still gibbering about it."

Gina couldn't blame her. She was starting to feel a little like gibbering herself.

"Anyone else see 'the darkness'?"

"No," Jase said. "But they all heard the howl."

Matt had been studying the glyphs again, listening with one ear as McCord and Gina talked. Certainly Matt was concerned about who was dead, but there was something about that wall and the pictures on it that was off.

Before he could really begin to ponder things, Matt heard McCord's last sentence, and his gaze flicked to Gina's. Hers was already waiting for him.

"What kind of howl?" Matt asked.

"The same kind we always have around here."

"The one that isn't made by actual wolves."

"Do you know how ridiculous that sounds?" Mc-Cord asked.

Matt shrugged. Just because it sounded ridiculous didn't mean it wasn't true.

Too bad he hadn't figured that out before he broke his mother's heart.

"Any tracks?" Matt asked.

"No."

"How can that be?" People didn't just disappear into thin air.

"You figure it out, pal, you let me know."

Matt's mind began to flirt with images of pterodactyls swooping out of the night and King Kong–like beasts reaching down from nearby trees to snatch up an unsuspecting A as she sang about *ghost chickens in the sky*.

Maybe *they'd* taken her.

Any and all of those ideas were, sadly, no more strange than whooshing darkness and unwolves. However—

"You said someone was dead."

Gina glanced at Matt, then back at McCord expectantly.

"And here I thought you weren't listening," McCord murmured.

Now that the man had told his tale, his nerves appeared to have settled and he was back to his annoying, sarcastic self. How had Gina put up with him all her life? Matt had known the guy less than a week, and he could no longer count on two hands the number of times he'd wanted to kill McCord.

"If Ashleigh's 'gone,'" Matt made quotation marks in the air with his fingers, "then how do you know she's dead?"

McCord's dark eyes met his. "I never said we didn't find her."

Gina, who'd still been hoping Ashleigh was just fucking with them, released a sigh that sounded more like a whimper. Jase, whose hand she still held, didn't seem to notice. He was too busy having a testosterone staredown with Teo.

"Where?" Teo asked.

"Couple hundred yards away."

"How?"

Gina wasn't sure if Teo were asking how Ashleigh had died or how they'd found her. Didn't matter. Either one was on Gina's list of questions as well.

"She—" Jase began, and then a scream, followed by several shouts, erupted from above.

The other guests! Gina had forgotten all about them.

Jase, Gina, and Teo ran for the opening. Jase reached the rope first, grabbed it in his huge, hard hands, then paused, glancing at Gina before handing it to Teo. "You go first."

"Kiss my ass," Teo murmured conversationally.

"Jesus." Gina snatched at the rope. "I'll go first."

Jase held the rope out of reach. "You aren't going up there alone. Who knows what's going on."

The screams and the shouts continued, accompanied by a lot of scuffling.

"*Someone* better get up there," she snapped.

Jase gave Teo an evil glare, as if *he'd* done this,

whatever *this* was. "Fine." Jase started to climb. "It's not as if *he'd* be any good at handling a catastrophe."

Gina's gaze met Teo's as the end of the rope danced like a cobra between them. She thought he'd be very good at handling just about anything.

"Hurry up!" Jase shouted, disappearing over the lip of the cavern.

"Go," Teo said.

Gina bit her lip and contemplated the distance from floor to opening. She'd climbed ropes in gym class, but she'd never gotten more than ten feet off the ground.

"You first." She held out the rope in his direction, and when he began to argue she interrupted. "I might need help."

Teo glanced around the cavern. "You'll be okay down here?"

"I'll be better up there," she said; then when another shriek sounded, she muttered, "Maybe. But we gotta go, so—" Gina jerked her thumb toward the sky.

Teo leaned over and brushed her lips with his. The action was both surprising and somehow just right.

She almost told him again what she'd heard when she'd been buried here, admitted that she'd heard it ever since, along with the uneasy feeling that the sorcerer Teo didn't believe in was not only real but also still very much alive.

Then he grasped the rope and scooted upward with easy, coordinated movements of hands and legs and feet. She watched him all the way, ignoring the sudden increase in the chill of the air now that she was alone.

"Okay." Teo stared at her from above, hair hanging around his face, the moon bright at his back. He wiggled the rope. "Tie the end around your waist. Walk up the wall. I'll pull from here. Piece of cake."

It wasn't, but she made it, Teo hauling her in as soon as she crept close enough to haul. As his arms came around her she realized that though she'd been scared of what was down there, what she might see, what she might find, she hadn't worried once about being trapped. Because from the instant she'd fallen in she'd known that he would get her out.

Teo released her, frowning into the cavern.

"What?" She spun, afraid she'd see more black smoke shooting out.

Teo snatched her elbow, drawing her back from the edge. "We left the lantern."

The hole in the earth seemed to glow, golden flickers dancing around the opening like a flame.

"Probably better we did," Teo continued. "Don't want anyone to fall in accidentally as they run around like chickens with their heads chopped off."

"What is it with the chickens?" Gina murmured.

The moon shone brightly, the storm that had caused this mess no longer rumbling even in the distance. The scene that spread out before them was illuminated in shades of silver—the sky gray, the mountains charcoal, the swaying grasses white. Everything that moved across the moonscape appeared etched in black.

"What happened?" she shouted.

No one bothered to answer. No one even bothered to glance her way.

The screams had stopped. Gina wasn't sure if that was good or bad. Did it mean the horror was over? Or that it was just over for whoever had been screaming.

She cast Teo a worried glance, then hurried toward the nearest outline that resembled a person.

"Hey," Gina murmured as she approached.

The outline threw up its arms and shouted, "Fuck!"

Melda. Gina should have been able to tell by the short, squat, Mrs. Claus–shaped shadow even before the woman turned, revealing the shimmering tracks of her tears.

"Where's Mel?" Gina asked.

"Gone," Melda whispered. *"Whoosh."*

Gina wanted to shout, *Fuck!* herself, but she figured that would be redundant.

Teo appeared at her side. "You heard?" she asked, and he nodded.

His gaze, gray-green in the moonlight, scanned the area. "Did you see anything, Melda?"

"The darkness took him," she said; then she sat, right down in the dirt as if her legs could no longer hold her.

"The darkness is really starting to piss me off," Gina muttered, and moved to the next outline.

"Derek," she said as soon as she recognized the kid, hoping that if she used his name, she wouldn't scare the shit out of him as she had Melda.

No such luck. He wheeled toward her, fists raised. Gina started to bring her own fists up, but before she even got them waist high Teo had inserted himself between them. "Whoa, buddy," he murmured, his scratchy voice strangely soothing, perhaps because it was so recognizable.

The boy's hunched shoulders relaxed, though he didn't lower his fists until Teo set a hand on them and pushed them down.

"Where's your dad?" Teo asked.

Gina's own shoulders hunched as she waited for the inevitable *gone*. Instead, Derek pointed to two figures standing far enough out on the plain that they appeared small.

Considering whom Gina and Teo had accounted for

so far and the distinctly male-shaped silhouettes, Gina checked off Jase and Tim on her mental list as present and accounted for.

"Where's Amberleigh?"

"Probably still chattering in a corner," Derek answered, gaze fixed on his father.

"There is no corner, Derek."

The kid threw Teo an "are you for real?" glance, then jerked his head in the direction of the tree.

Amberleigh sat at the base, sucking her thumb.

"Peachy," Gina muttered, and started for the girl.

As Gina walked away she heard Teo ask, "What did you see?" and Derek answer, "Not one damn thing."

Amberleigh wasn't any more help than anyone else had been. Of course the incessant sucking of the thumb didn't allow her to say much, but considering all she seemed *able* to say was: "*Whoosh!*" Gina let Amberleigh have at it.

The crunch of footsteps had Gina glancing up. Jase and Tim had returned. She patted Amberleigh on the shoulder. "You okay?"

"*Whoosh!*" Amberleigh said around the thumb.

Gina stalked toward Jase. "What were you thinking to bring her out here?" She threw out an arm to indicate Amberleigh. "She's slipped a cog. She needs a doctor."

"She didn't have that many cogs to slip."

"Jase, so help me—"

"Gordon's a doctor."

Gina cut her gaze to Tim, who shrugged. "Don't tell me you agreed that dragging her on horseback farther *away* from medical care was a good idea?"

"Uh—no," Tim said. "But then, no one asked me."

Gina narrowed her eyes on Jase, and he held up his

hands—one now held a rifle—in surrender. "Okay. Bad idea. I figured she'd snap out of it."

"Does that . . . ," Gina stabbed her finger at the tree, "look like she's gonna snap out of it anytime soon?"

Jase contemplated Amberleigh, then sighed. "No. That just looks like she snapped."

Behind him, Melda still sat in the dirt. She was rocking and humming, but at least she wasn't, yet, sucking her thumb.

Teo and Derek joined them. Tim put his arm around his son's shoulders. It was a testament to what had happened in the past twenty-four hours that the boy let him.

"What did you find?" Gina asked.

Jase and Tim exchanged a glance. Tim's eyes shifted toward Derek, and Gina tried to think of something she could send the boy away to do.

"I'm not leaving," Derek said. "Whatever's out there could get me, too. I need to know what's going on."

"He's right," Teo murmured. "Tim?"

The man pulled his son closer, as if he could keep him safe by proximity alone, then nodded.

"Mel's out there," Jase said.

"Shit," Gina murmured. "Dead?"

"Throat torn out."

Gina's eyes widened. She didn't know what she'd expected but not that.

"Same as the girl's," Jase continued.

Gina frowned. "We're talking animal then?"

"God, I hope so," Jase muttered.

"Why would you hope so?"

"Because if a human did that, we've got bigger troubles than we can handle."

CHAPTER 17

Gina soon discovered that the troubles they couldn't handle were only just beginning.

The men, minus Derek, who'd been deemed old enough to hear about death but not old enough to see it, were headed for the horses, planning to use one to bring back Mel's body. Gina and Derek were headed for Melda to break the news when Tim's voice drifted across the cool, silent night: "Where's Ashleigh?"

"It's *Amber*-leigh, Dad. And she's by the tree."

"Shit," Jase said, and Gina got a chill. "The body's gone."

"That's imposs—," Teo began, and then: "Shit."

Gina pointed to the ground next to Melda, who was still humming what sounded like "Row, Row, Row Your Boat" over and over and over. "Stay here." Derek opened his mouth, and Gina snapped, "I mean it."

The kid emitted a long, grievous, put-upon sigh, but he sat and he stayed.

The men stared at the ground, where an empty sleeping bag and several pieces of rope lay scattered about. The horses seemed unperturbed, though they could have been stomping and neighing earlier and, in the mayhem, no one would have noticed. The dirt around them *did* appear overly churned up.

Jase walked a few yards to the east, bent, and peered more closely at the ground. Gina joined him. She saw immediately what he was staring at.

Tracks. Going thataway.

Gina lifted her head, squinted into the gloom, but she saw nothing, no one.

"Boots," Jase muttered. "Of a small man."

"Or a woman with freakishly large feet." Gina remembered the unpleasant scrunch of newspaper against her toes as she attempted to walk in borrowed copper high heels. "Like Ashleigh."

Jase glanced up, eyes widening. "She's dead, Gina."

"You're sure?"

He looked away. "No one could survive that."

"Instead, someone snuck in here, unwrapped the body, tossed it over his or her shoulder, and left without anyone seeing a thing."

"There's a lot of that going around."

"Jase—" Gina began.

"You got a better explanation?"

Not one that she wanted to go into right now, so she shook her head.

"Ready?" he asked, assuming—rightly—that they would now be the ones to go.

Gina turned, and her gaze met Teo's. She didn't even have to tell him to stay here, to take care of things. He nodded as soon as their eyes met, then put a hand on Tim's shoulder and led him toward the others.

"Should we take a horse, bring back Mel?"

Jase shook his head. "Let's see what's going on first."

Probably a good idea. Kind of hard to handle a horse and a—

What? An invisible Aztec sorcerer who had somehow survived thousands of years and was now on a rampage?

She kept that thought to herself, but she left the horses behind.

Gina and Jase followed the boot tracks for maybe a hundred yards before Jase stopped and said, "Shit." There also seemed to be a lot of *that* going around. Then he glanced to the left, the right, behind them, head swiveling faster and more frantically with every turn.

"Lose something?"

"The other body."

Gina blinked, opened her mouth, shut it, tilted her head, and— "You sure?"

"Would you quit asking me that?"

"If you'd quit saying things that make me."

Jase turned in a slow circle, gaze scanning the ground. "It was right there." He pointed to a spot directly in front of them. A spot the tracks seemed to be headed right for.

Neither one of them spoke; they followed the trail, which ended at a big circle of dark in the dirt. Even in the waning moonlight, Gina knew blood when she saw it.

"And you're certain Mel was dead?"

Jase didn't even bother to answer. Really, from the amount of blood, he just had to be.

"Whoever snatched Ashleigh must have come over here and snatched Mel, too," Jase said.

"I'd agree with you, except for one thing."

"What?"

Gina pointed to the other side of the big, dark splotch. "There are two sets of tracks."

A sudden howl, followed quickly by another, brought their heads up. What they saw brought Jase's gun up, too.

The horizon had just begun to lighten with the first hint of dawn, illuminating the silhouettes of two wolves, snouts lifted to serenade the dying moon.

"You see that?" Jase murmured.

"Uh-huh." Gina even blinked a few times, but they didn't go away.

"Explains a few things."

"It does?" In her opinion, the wolves only brought up more questions.

"*They* tore out Ashleigh's and Mel's throats."

"Wolves don't do that," Gina said.

"I bet these do."

Gina didn't answer, because she bet they did, too.

They had two dead people with their throats torn out by an animal—something that had never happened here before. Then they saw two animals of a type that had never been seen here before.

One plus one equaled two. Always. And it was a much saner explanation than an escaped sorcerer. However—

"The wolves don't explain the *whoosh,* or the darkness, or the disappearing bodies surrounded by human tracks."

Jase nodded, still staring at the horizon. "We need to get back to the ranch."

Returning to Nahua Springs proved both easier and harder than Gina had anticipated.

Easier because while Melda and Amberleigh were

not themselves, they weren't lobotomized or deaf. The instant the two heard the party was headed home, they hopped on their horses and took off. The only hard part was keeping up with them.

On the other hand, Teo refused to leave.

"You can't stay here," Gina insisted.

"I can't leave the cavern open and unguarded for just anyone to crawl around in."

"We've had this talk. No one *comes* here."

"Someone came here and took the damn mummy," he muttered.

Gina bit her lip. She wasn't so sure.

She glanced at the wolves, which continued to sit on the horizon and watch them, still as statues guarding an Egyptian tomb.

She and Teo needed to figure out what in hell was going on. *How* they'd do that she wasn't sure. But it wasn't going to be out here where God only knew what was hovering.

"I can start translating the glyphs," Teo began. "If you'd just call my assistant and—"

"No."

He blinked, the eyes behind the glasses he'd retrieved along with their tent, bedding, and horses confused. "No?"

"It's the opposite of *yes*." She threw the saddle on Lady Belle.

"But . . . why?"

"That's more your department than mine."

His confused expression intensified.

"I have no idea why *yes* is the opposite of *no*. Isn't that the kind of crap you study in college?"

"Gina," he said, exasperated. "Tempting me with linguistic puzzles will not make me stray from my goal."

When he talked all stick-up-the-butt like that she wanted to—

Kiss him. Which was a big change from how she used to feel whenever she read one of his letters.

When had the change happened? She wasn't quite sure.

What she was sure of was that she couldn't leave him here. Who knew what would happen by the time she got back? What if he was *gone* like the others? The thought of losing Teo Mecate was not a thought Gina could live with.

"I need better lights," he muttered. "Certain equipment, people trained in uncovering the truth."

Oh yeah, more people wandering around out here would be a fantastic idea, Gina thought.

"I'm not gonna call anyone," she said.

"My phone doesn't work."

"Aw." She pouted like an A. "If you want to call someone I guess you'll just have to come back to the ranch and do it yourself."

The confused expression returned. "Why are you being difficult?"

Gina turned away, messing with Lady Belle's saddle even though she'd already tightened everything that needed tightening and checked everything that needed checking. "I don't want you to be gone, too," she whispered.

He didn't respond; she wasn't sure he'd heard her. The activity all around them—the saddling of horses, chewing on granola bars, slugging water, talking—was loud and distracting. Even though Gina was totally focused on Teo, she didn't hear him approach, only knew that he was near when the scent of oranges arrived an instant before he did.

He slid his hands over hers where they rested on the saddle, set his lips to her hair, and murmured, "I won't be."

She couldn't help it; she turned her hands in his, tangling their fingers together and holding on tight. "No one saw what took them. A *whoosh,* a howl, the darkness. What *is* that?"

"Mass hysteria," he said. "You don't really think they were taken by the night."

"I don't?"

He chuckled, his breath puffing against her cheek. "That's impossible."

She knew that in her head, in the light of day, but in her gut, in the middle of the night . . .

"What *did* take them?"

"The wolves." Teo shrugged, sliding his front all over her back. She leaned into him, enjoying the flex of his muscles against her skin, despite the layers of clothing in between.

"Wolves are fast, but I doubt they're faster than the speed of sight."

He squeezed her fingers, like a hug with hands, the movement making his biceps bulge against hers. "People see things when they're frightened, Gina. Or, in this case, they don't see things."

He sounded so sure, so rational; her crazy suspicions wavered.

Gina turned, and Teo stepped back but not too far. "You need to spell it out for me."

"A wolf snatched Ashleigh and dragged her off. Amberleigh's mind was so horrified by what she saw, it shut down and refused to remember anything but darkness."

"And Melda?"

"Power of suggestion. Once she'd heard Amberleigh's tale, when the same situation occurred she saw what Amberleigh saw—or rather she didn't see it."

·Strangely, that made sense.

Of course, when compared to a whooshing darkness stealing, then killing people, pretty much anything would.

Perhaps Teo's explanations could be applied to what she'd heard and felt as well. Tricks of the mind. Posttraumatic stress. Anything was preferable to what she had imagined.

"I'll be fine, Gina." Teo brushed his knuckles against her cheek. "You don't have to worry about me."

"I know." She stepped out of his reach. When he touched her she couldn't breathe, let alone think. "Because you're coming back to the ranch with us if I have to hog-tie you and have Jase toss you over Spike's back."

"But—"

"You think we have superfast, supersmart, superhungry, vicious wolves on the prowl. I'm not leaving you anywhere near them."

Teo's expression of surprise morphed into one of annoyance as he realized his own explanation had doomed him. "I'm an idiot," he muttered.

Gina shrugged. "Saddle your horse."

She let out a long, silent sigh of relief when he did.

Matt didn't waste time thinking about how he could have avoided returning to the ranch. Looking back on what had happened thus far, returning had been inevitable. Gina wasn't going to let him, or anyone else, stay behind when they might wind up dead.

Although going back to Nahua Springs after Mc-

Cord had seen him and Gina murmuring and snuggling next to Lady Belle . . . probably not the best idea. Matt had intercepted no fewer than half a dozen "I'm gonna kill you" glares from the man already.

And if Matt was going to wind up dead or missing, he'd rather do it while he was hard at work in the place he'd spent a lifetime searching for. However, that was the problem with dead or missing—one rarely got to choose when and how it happened.

They arrived at the ranch as the sun fell from the sky. The place appeared deserted, and Matt experienced a tingle of unease, although considering Isaac and Fanny were the only ones here, he doubted it could appear anything but.

Then Matt glanced at Gina and caught her worried glance at McCord. The creepy, not-right feeling Teo had had . . . she was having it, too.

"Mom?" McCord yelled at the same time Gina sprinted for the house shouting, "Fanny?"

The front door opened, and Fanny stepped out. A collective sigh of relief swirled around the yard. The others dismounted and led their horses away, Tim and Derek quietly coaxing Melda and Amberleigh along.

Fanny's dark gaze stayed on the guests until they'd disappeared into the barn; then she motioned for Jase and Gina to come inside. Matt decided to go inside, too.

He left Spike ground-tied with Jase's and Gina's horses. "Be right back," he murmured.

Spike snorted his opinion of that, but right now Matt didn't have the time. Something was up; he had to know what it was.

He slipped into the hall just as Fanny announced: "He was there, and then he was gone."

"Whoosh?" Gina asked.

"Yes."

"Who?" Matt hoped it wasn't Isaac.

McCord whirled, a scowl already crinkling his face. "Get lost."

"No." Matt joined them. "Who's gone?"

"Part-time worker." Gina turned to Fanny. "Tell us exactly what happened."

"They had just put away the horses. It was late, dark. Juan was headed to his car. Then there was a howl, the sound like a big wind, and the darkness took him away."

"You saw this?" Matt asked.

Fanny shook her head. "This is what my father saw."

Gina flicked Matt a glance. "Isaac is the least likely person to see something that isn't on this earth. And since he didn't know about what happened out there," she jerked a thumb over her shoulder, "he certainly couldn't repeat the exact same occurrence back here."

She was right, of course, but what did that *mean*?

"Did Granddad find Juan?" McCord asked.

Fanny's lips tightened as she gave a sharp nod. "Dead. Throat torn out."

Gina placed her hand on the older woman's arm. "And then?"

Fanny removed her arm from Gina's touch, hugging her elbows, swaying back and forth, as if she was cold or scared, maybe both. "Dead is dead. What *else* could happen?"

They all waited, because from Fanny's behavior, her expression, the shadows in her eyes, something else *had* happened.

"Father came to get a horse to carry the body. But when he returned it was no longer there."

"Tracks?" McCord asked. His mother nodded. "What kind?"

Her wide brow creased. "What kind?"

"Boots? Shoes? Man? Woman? One set? Or two?"

"I do not know."

"Where's Granddad?"

"He took his rifle. He has been gone all day."

"Have you seen any wolves?" Gina asked.

"Not before Juan died. Since then, there is one that watches the house. That's why Father left with his gun. He said it is the creature that killed Juan and that creature must die."

The others began to file inside, and Fanny rubbed her hands on her apron, face clearing. "I must return to the kitchen. Everyone will be hungry." She peered at the group crowding into the hall. "Where are the other two?"

Amberleigh gasped. Melda choked. Then they were both crying.

Ah, hell.

Gina glanced at Matt, and he moved forward, putting his arm around Melda, even as Gina cast him a dirty look for choosing the easy one and headed for Amberleigh. Gina jerked her head at Fanny, and McCord drew his mother aside to explain that what had happened at the ranch had been repeated away from it times two.

Fanny began muttering in Ute, and Jase herded her and the others down the hall toward the kitchen.

"We need to take," Gina indicated Amberleigh, who'd folded herself into Gina's embrace like a baby, with a downward tilt of her chin, "into town."

Matt nodded. *The sooner the better.*

"Let's get everyone cleaned up and settled first."

Matt tilted his head, patting Melda as she continued to cry on his shoulder. "You think that's a good idea?"

"It's a better idea than dragging a traumatized woman into town covered in mud and just—" She mouthed the words *leaving her there.* "Besides, we need to talk to the police. I'd prefer not to do it dropping dried mud all over the station."

Matt wasn't so sure. He figured their appearance would lend weight to their story. But . . . What *was* their story?

"What are you gonna say?"

Gina climbed the stairs, Amberleigh moving along compliantly at her side. "Give me an hour," she said. "I'll come up with something."

A half hour later Gina stood beneath the heated stream of the shower, letting all the mud and grit slide down the drain. Too bad all the confusion didn't wash off the same way.

She'd been afraid she might have to climb into the shower with Amberleigh, but cleanliness appeared to trump craziness, because as soon as the girl saw indoor plumbing she stopped whimpering and tore off her clothes.

Gina sat on the bed until Amberleigh came out of the shower wrapped in a robe—pale, with purple circles under her eyes, at least she'd stopped sucking her thumb—and kicked her out.

"I just wanna sleep," Amberleigh said. "Go away."

Before Gina was out the door, Amberleigh was snoring. Maybe sleep was the best thing. Maybe they'd take her to the doctor tomorrow. That might give Gina a chance to figure this out.

She pulled back the shower curtain with a half laugh. There *was* no figuring this out.

Although she would like to have a long talk with Isaac.

The sun had set while Gina dealt with Amberleigh. She heard the others going into their rooms, turning on their showers. She threw on sweatpants, fuzzy socks, and a T-shirt, then went to find food, coffee, and her family. All three were in the kitchen.

Fanny and Jase sat at the table, steaming bowls of soup and cups of coffee in front of them. Fanny made a move to get up, but Gina shook her head. "I'll get it."

Before she'd finished, Teo entered, wearing nearly the same outfit as she—minus the fuzzy socks. His were just socks, white, athletic; he had a tiny hole in one heel. His wet hair was tied back; the ponytail had left a damp patch between his shoulder blades.

"Private conversation," Jase muttered.

Teo opened his mouth, no doubt to tell Jase to perform an anatomically impossible act; then his gaze went to Jase's mother and, instead, he smiled and crossed the room to help Gina—who'd filled a second bowl and cup upon his arrival—carry everything to the table.

"Did Isaac get back yet?" Gina asked.

"No." Fanny glanced at the windows, her eyes as dark as the night beyond the panes. "Where could he be?"

No one answered, no doubt thinking of what had happened to the others whose location was now a mystery. Everyone hoped Isaac hadn't met the same fate.

"The guests will be leaving tomorrow," Gina said. "Then we can deal with this."

"With what?" Fanny asked.

Gina took a deep breath, prepared to lay everything out—from the first time she'd fallen through the earth to what had, she hoped, been the last, but a movement in the doorway had them all lifting their heads. Derek hovered between hall and kitchen.

"Growing boy," Fanny cooed. "You would like more soup?"

"Uh . . . no." Derek stepped into the room. "Thanks," he said as an afterthought, then turned to Gina. "That one blond chick who's left?"

Gina nodded, tensing. From the instant the blond chicks had come, any mention of them had been followed by something unpleasant.

"She's standing at the window in the upstairs hall, sucking her thumb and muttering, 'No, no, no.'" Derek shrugged. "I figured that wasn't good." He left as quickly as he'd come, his footsteps thundering up the stairs.

"Damn," Gina muttered. "I thought she'd sleep the night and we could take her in the morning, but—"

"Let's take her now." Jase shoved his chair away from the table and stood. "I'll get the car; you get the blond chick."

"How come I always have to get the blond chick?" Gina muttered, but she headed for the front hall. Teo fell into step behind her. Explanations would have to wait.

As they reached the stairs, Jase opened the door. Instead of walking through, he cursed, then slammed it shut again.

Gina, who'd just planted her foot on the first stair, spun. Jase stared at the closed door as if he wasn't quite sure what to do with it.

"What's the matter?" Gina asked.

He glanced over his shoulder, then, without a word, stalked into the living room and opened the curtains. Gina followed.

What she saw through the window made her blink, rub at her eyes, glance out, then rub at them again. No matter what she did, the scene remained the same.

A semi-circle of wolves stood in the front yard, barring their exit from the house.

CHAPTER 18

"Everyone's seeing what I'm seeing, right?"

"Dammit," Jase muttered.

"I'll take that as a *yes*."

Gina glanced at Teo. He stared at the wolves with a thoughtful expression. At least he wasn't staring at her with the same look, one that brought to mind a mechanic who just loved to take apart every motor he saw and lay the pieces on a tarp until he figured out what was wrong with it.

"I told you never to go there."

Gina spun. Isaac stood in the archway between the living and dining rooms. He still held his rifle, which was strange. What possible good could come from a firearm in the house? Although—

She peered at the wolves again. What possible good could come of not having one?

"Now you've let it out," Isaac continued.

Which was exactly what Gina had been afraid of.

The old man crossed the floor and peered through the glass. "They might crash through the window," he murmured. "But I don't think they will."

"What?" Gina blurted. "Why?"

"I shot one with silver. They don't like it much when one of their friends turns into a great ball of fire."

Gina had meant "Why would they crash through the window?" Wolves didn't *do* that. They also didn't turn into balls of fire when shot with—

"Silver?" Gina glanced at Jase, who shrugged. *The old man had finally snapped.* "Maybe we should call the police."

"They'll only die." At Gina's startled expression, Isaac lifted his rifle. "Their guns won't be filled with silver. They'd walk right into an ambush. Silver is the only way to kill a Tangwaci Cin-au'-ao."

"What, specifically, is a Tangwaci Cin-au'-ao?" Gina'd heard the word in Isaac's tales of the curse that lay at the end of Lonely Deer Trail. She'd thought it was merely what the Ute called their Angel of Death, but now she had her doubts.

"Man-wolf," Teo answered, then glanced at Isaac. "Right?"

Isaac merely shrugged and went back to watching the wolves.

"Man-wolf," Gina repeated, thinking of the glyph on the cavern wall. Things were beginning to connect. Strangely, the connections only brought more questions. "What the hell is a man-wolf?"

"Why do we suddenly have wolves where we never had wolves before?" Isaac's gaze remained fixed on the window.

Answering her question with a question wasn't even close to providing an answer. But then, with Isaac, sometimes the answer came in a roundabout way.

"Because they aren't wolves," he continued. "They're Tangwaci Cin-au'-ao."

"Man-wolves. I don't know what that means."

Isaac's dark, endless gaze met hers. "Werewolves, Gina."

"That's insane."

"Look at the eyes." Isaac swept his mottled hand forward to indicate the scene still spread before them. "Those ain't the eyes of a normal wolf."

Gina inched closer to the window. "Give me the binoculars."

Jase snatched Isaac's pair from the end table. The old man liked to scan the hills; he'd always said he was searching for deer, but Gina no longer believed him. She lifted the binoculars, focused on the nearest waiting wolf, and gasped.

The gaze that stared back was freakishly human.

Wolves' eyes were green or gray or brown, maybe yellow, but the color extended all the way to the lids; not a speck of white surrounded it. However, humans were a different story. Humans had eyes like . . .

That.

Gina lowered the binoculars, then handed them to Jase. "What's wrong with these wolves?"

"More than you can imagine," Isaac said softly.

"A virus? Rabies? What?"

"A virus, yes. One called lycanthropy. Why do you think there were no wolves round here till now?"

"There's gotta be a better explanation than lycanthropy," Gina muttered. Of course she was the one who'd been contemplating a sorcerer.

"Wolves avoid werewolves. They sense their otherness."

Gina glanced at Jase, but he still stared through the binoculars. Teo peered at Isaac as if he'd said something fascinating, instead of gibbering like a madman.

"I've never seen a wolf on this property. Not even one like that." Gina jabbed a finger at the semi-circle of freaks. "So what 'otherness' did they sense?"

"What lay beneath," Isaac intoned.

"The Tangwaci Cin-au'-ao," Teo said.

"We buried it. But animals know. From that point on no true wolf would come within fifty miles and the horses refused to walk there."

Gina was starting to get a headache.

"Jase," she said. "What do you know about this?"

He lowered the field glasses. His pupils were dilated so large she took a step backward. He almost looked like one of . . . them.

"Jase?" She reached for him, and he shoved the binoculars into her outstretched hand.

"Check the last one on the right." When she hesitated, he lifted his chin in a sharp, jerky movement. "Do it, Gina."

She did, tweaking the focus, moving a little closer, a little closer, waiting for the silvery-gray beast to turn his head her way.

When at last he did, Gina squeaked and dropped the binoculars on the floor.

Those were Mel's eyes.

The instant Gina gave a strangled cry and dropped the field glasses, both Matt and McCord started forward.

Matt reached her first, which only gave the other man an excuse to snarl, especially when Gina grasped Matt's outstretched hand and ignored his.

"That's— That's—" Her eyes were wide, exposing more of the whites than usual, which made Matt frown and glance at the wolves again.

What *was* it about their eyes?

"Impossible," she finished, her fingers clenching until his cracked in protest.

"What's impossible?" Matt asked, glancing at McCord, who continued to glare at him like a two-year-old denied his favorite toy.

Gina bent, picked up the binoculars, and handed them to Matt without a word.

One tug on his hand and she released him. Matt shoved his glasses on top of his head, then lifted the binoculars and zeroed in on the nearest wolf's eyes.

"Some kind of virus," he muttered, and Isaac snorted. "Which makes the sclera expand, while decreasing the amount of pigment." What other possible explanation could there be?

Not lycanthropy. He was with Gina on that one.

"What the hell is a sclera?" McCord muttered. "Speak English, Dr. Moldy."

"The white," Gina said, and Matt had to resist the urge to stick out his tongue at McCord. That would be a good way to get it ripped out of his head.

"You recognize any of them?" Isaac asked.

"Recognize?" Matt repeated. "The wolves?" Until yesterday there hadn't *been* any wolves.

"Look again," the old man urged.

Matt glanced at Gina, whose scleras seemed to have expanded, too. For an instant he worried that she'd caught the virus as well. But the transmission of viruses between species was very rare. Of course if these were werewolves and half-human, that could cause a prob—

Matt heard what his mind was saying and a choked laugh escaped. Talk about mass hysteria.

"Quit yucking it up," McCord grumbled, "and take another look."

"Look close," Gina urged, so Matt did.

One was black with gray eyes; another was sable with brown; the third from the left had a shiny, smooth coat, which was a lovely shade of gold, with blue eyes that stared into his and—

Matt yelped and dropped the binoculars.

Those were Ashleigh's eyes.

Gina set her hand on his arm. "You saw him?"

"Him?" He blinked several times, staring through the window at *her*. The Ashleigh-eyed wolf seemed to be staring back—and grinning.

"Mel." Gina pointed. "Over there."

"Mel's there, too?"

"Too?" Gina bent and retrieved the binoculars, peering through them until she saw—

"Ashleigh." Gina lowered the field glasses. McCord snatched them up, put them to his eyes, then cursed.

"And Juan." Isaac lifted a gnarled finger to indicate the second black wolf, this one with equally black eyes—except for the whites that blared freakishly against the dark fur.

Matt lowered his glasses back into place. He couldn't believe what he was thinking, what they were. There had to be another explanation, but he really couldn't fathom what it was. He needed more information. And Isaac appeared just the man to give it to him.

"What did you bury?" he asked.

Isaac's dark gaze cut from the wolves to Matt, then back again. "We better sit." He waved his wrinkled hand at the furniture. "Turn those round so we can keep our eyes . . ." He first pointed his forefinger and middle finger at his face, then jabbed them toward the window.

The younger men moved the couch, as well as two

wing chairs, while Gina retrieved Fanny and the two women went upstairs. In all the excitement, they'd forgotten about the "blond chick" sucking her thumb in the hall.

"All asleep," Gina said when she returned. "Except for the kid, who's playing some game on his phone and barely looked at me when I opened his door. Fanny will stay to make sure no one comes down and hears something they shouldn't. We can catch her up later."

"Fanny won't need catching up." Isaac sat on the couch. "The legend of the Tangwaci Cin-au'-ao has been known to my people since we confined him."

Gina glanced at McCord, who shrugged. "It's a legend." He made a mouth with his hand, opening and shutting his fingers and thumb while muttering, "Blah, blah, blah. We've got a million."

Isaac shot his grandson an irritated glare. "This legend became a legend on *this* land. The creature is—" His mouth twisted. "*Was.* Buried here."

Matt took the wing chair closest to Gina, ignoring McCord's inevitable snarl. "You call the buried creature the Tangwaci Cin-au'-ao, but you also call them," Matt pointed to the wolves, "Tangwaci Cin-au'-ao."

Isaac shrugged. "What do you want to call them?"

"Werewolves," Gina murmured.

"A different name don't make 'em somethin' they're not."

"You should probably start at the beginning," Matt said, and the old man inclined his head, then did.

"Centuries ago—at least four, maybe five—an army came from the south. There'd been rumors for years of this army, which swept over the land, leaving blood and death and destruction behind. Those they didn't kill they stole, and took them back to the place where

Tauaci, the sun, lives, never to be seen or heard from again."

Matt leaned forward. The people who lived with the sun *had* to be the Aztecs.

"However, the Nucio, the Ute people, were fierce, and they didn't die as easily as the others had. They killed more of the Sun People than anyone had before, and the invaders were forced to call forth their sorcerer."

Bingo, Matt thought; the two stories were beginning to mesh.

"This sorcerer could become a wolf, and he could make others into wolves, too."

Matt straightened as if he'd been jabbed in the butt with a stick. That wasn't how the story went. The Aztecs' sorcerer was a superwarrior—stronger, better, faster. He mowed through the opposition like a ravenous wolf.

Of course that was a translation, which was subject to interpretation. What if, instead, the sorcerer *was* a ravenous wolf?

Matt couldn't believe he was thinking this. He, who had broken his mother's heart, contributed to her death by sneering at her irrational belief in a sorcerer, was now considering a *werewolf* sorcerer.

Of course with all that had happened lately—howling black smoke, dead bodies getting up and walking away, wolves with the eyes of people he knew . . .

"Go on," Matt said.

"He replenished the Army of the Sun with the Tangwaci Cin-au'-ao, beings that couldn't be killed with anything other than pure silver."

"How'd the Ute know this?" Matt blurted. "Did they

just poke the creatures with every substance they had until one of them died?"

"Maybe." Isaac shrugged. "*How* they knew isn't part of the story."

"Okay," Matt said, though for him the how and the why and the what *were* the story.

"No matter how many of the Tangwaci Cin-au'-ao were killed," Isaac continued, "the sorcerer made more. He created an army, and the People had no choice but to call forth their own maker of magic."

"We had a sorcerer?" McCord murmured. "Cool."

"Shaman," Isaac corrected.

"Whatever." McCord ignored the narrow-eyed stare his grandfather shot his way. "What did he do?"

"He confined the Tangwaci Cin-au'-ao beneath," Isaac said, as if that explained everything.

"How?" Matt asked.

"A spell, which imprisoned the creature beyond the door. Then the Ute filled in the cavern and told everyone the area was cursed. It didn't take long before death made their lies the truth."

"What does that mean?" Gina asked.

"People died there."

"Voilà," Matt murmured. "It is cursed."

"But *why* did people die there?" Gina's voice wavered.

Matt laid his hand on hers. Outside, one of the wolves—he thought it might have been Ashleigh—yipped. He ignored them, along with McCord, who glared hard enough to put a hole in Matt's forehead.

"The Tangwaci Cin-au'-ao was buried, but his voice was never silenced. His calls are heard on the wind and in the mountains."

Beneath Matt's hand, Gina's jerked. He cast her a concerned glance, but she peered intently at Isaac.

"You're saying the howls of the unwolves were made by the Tangwaci Cin-au'-ao?" Matt asked.

"He called people to him. Because he was Nahua, every death made him stronger, keeping alive the whisper of his voice on the wind." Isaac shook his head. "That kind of power is damn hard to contain."

"So you spread the rumor that the place was cursed."

"It is," Isaac muttered. "But yeah. The less people who go there, the less chance their deaths will feed the beast."

"How'd the shaman confine him?"

"He learned their picture talk, then used it against them."

Understanding hit Matt like a flash of light. "The glyphs on the wall weren't drawn by the Aztecs but by the Ute shaman." Which explained why they were kind of off.

"The man-dog figure on the wall . . ." Gina tilted her head. "And the one in your mom's notebook. They both appeared overly vicious to represent loyalty. But what if they were meant to represent—" She turned her gaze to the window and lifted her chin to indicate the ever-patient circle of wolves.

What if the drawings of dogs weren't dogs at all but wolves? And the combination of the man with the dog didn't mean a loyal man but a man-wolf, which was exactly what the Ute had labeled him?

Why hadn't he seen it before? In his own defense, Matt had never heard the story until now.

"There were larger-than-life men," he murmured. "Both sorcerers. The size of the glyph indicated power, not actual size. One was a shape-shifter, the other—"

He closed his eyes and brought up the second glyph against the dark screen of his mind. "Magic." He opened his eyes and met Gina's gaze. "That's what the stars shooting from his hands meant. But—" Matt frowned as another puzzle presented itself. "What about the horses that looked like dogs, which had stars all around their feet?"

"Magic dogs," Isaac said. "It's what the Ute called horses."

Magic dogs. Matt liked that. The way people talked in times long past had always held a certain poetry for him.

"The Ute wrote what happened on the wall," Gina said. "How does that confine a monster?"

"Words have power," Isaac answered. "Words begin and end wars. They create and destroy families. They break hearts. They heal them. If you have the right words, there's nothin' on this earth you can't do."

As a professor, Matt had to agree. As a scientist, he needed more data.

"If words kept him in," Matt wondered, "how did he get out?"

"The story ends with the Tangwaci Cin-au'-ao being confined to the cavern. I never heard anything about his ever getting out."

Probably smart of the Ute in the long run. If there were no instructions on releasing the thing, then he would be pretty hard to release.

In theory.

Most experts would not have read the man-wolf glyph as *Nahual* and released the creature. Only Gina, who had known both too little and too much, could have done so.

The shaman had been very clever to draw things the

way he had. The glyphs could be deciphered, but only by a certain, and highly uncommon, few. The chances of the Nahual ever being freed had been slim. Of course *any* chance was still a chance. But it *had* taken nearly five centuries.

Unfortunately, that didn't help them now.

"How about confining him?" Matt asked. "You know the recipe for that?"

Isaac shook his head.

Swell.

"What happened to his werewolf army?" Gina asked.

"Without the Tangwaci Cin-au'-ao to replenish the numbers . . ." Isaac shrugged. "Eventually those he'd made were hunted down and eliminated."

"He made them," she murmured, "by killing them."

"The usual werewolf rules involve biting," McCord offered.

"I don't think the usual rules apply," Matt said.

"Well, it does explain what happened out there." Gina waved at the window. The gazes of the wolves followed her hand as if it were a dog treat.

"It does?" McCord asked. "Then explain it to me."

"The Tangwaci Cin-au'-ao killed Ashleigh. She, uh . . ." Gina glanced at Matt for help.

"Rose?" he suggested.

"She *rose* and ran off. Which clears up the single set of footprints leading away from the horse."

"By then Mel was dead," Matt added.

"So she joined him and together they . . ." She made the gesture of running with two fingers.

"Which also clarifies the two sets of footprints leading away from the . . ." Matt paused, glancing at Gina for help.

"Splotch?"

Matt let his head fall to the side and gave her a look that said: *Is that the best you could do?* Gina shrugged and spread her hands.

"What it doesn't *clarify*," McCord emphasized the word with a sarcastic twist of his lips, "is how he killed them."

"I'd . . . uh . . . hazard to guess that the torn throats were a pretty certain COD."

"Oh, you'd hazard, would you?" McCord mocked. "And what the hell does Cash On Delivery have to do with anything?"

"Cause Of Death," Gina translated, and when McCord turned his scowl on her she rolled her eyes. "Try watching some *CSI* instead of all-night TV poker."

"Still doesn't explain how a whoosh and howl could rip out someone's throat," McCord pointed out.

Everyone went silent, which caused McCord's frown to turn upside down.

"Just because Amberleigh and Melda didn't see them taken by someone," Gina swallowed thickly, "or something, doesn't mean they weren't."

"No tracks but the victim's," McCord said. "Human or wolf."

Matt had to give the guy credit. He was smarter than he appeared.

"There was nothing there," Gina said. "When we got to the open door, there was nothing behind it." She turned to Isaac. "What did they bury?"

The old man's mouth pulled down, causing the myriad creases in his face to deepen. "He was a man, at least part of the time."

"Could the sorcerer *be* killed?" This from McCord, who was eyeing the silver-filled rifle Isaac had placed next to himself on the couch.

"If he could be," the old man said reasonably, "there'd have been no need to confine him."

"A man, even one that was wolf, would have been dust by now," Matt said. Or at least a pile of bones.

"He was invincible," Isaac intoned. "Immortal. I'm sure he was more than dust."

"Black smoke swirled from the opening." Gina lifted one shoulder. "It could have been dust."

"That cavern was locked up for centuries," Matt said. "Maybe it was just dust."

Gina's gaze flicked to the window, then back again. She seemed to be hesitating, struggling, but at last she blurted, "Whatever it was swirled around me, whispered my name, then shot up and out of the hole."

Matt stared at her. "You didn't tell me this?"

"Would you have believed me before . . . ?" She waved at the wolves, then Isaac, then flipped her hands up in disgust.

"Pretty talented dust," McCord muttered.

"Which then snatched up two human beings and ripped out their throats. *Damn* talented dust," Matt agreed.

"The Tangwaci Cin-au'-ao is a sorcerer and a shapeshifter," Isaac said. "He may have been smoke at first, but by now . . ." The old man's dark gaze met each of theirs in turn. "He could be anything."

CHAPTER 19

"What the hell are we gonna do?" McCord asked.

Isaac continued to stare through the window, hand stroking his rifle as if he were just waiting for the wolves to give him an excuse. Any excuse.

"Why don't you just blast them, Granddad?" Mc-Cord sighted down his hand, which he'd contorted into the shape of a gun. "Bang, bang, bang. Like ducks in a pond."

Isaac didn't even glance his way. "They're not stupid. If I shoot one, the rest will scatter. I prefer 'em right where I can see 'em."

Matt understood the sentiment, although who knew how many more of them were out there in the dark that they couldn't see and didn't even know about?

Isaac's explanation that the beasts understood he had silver and was prepared to use it only indicated a human-level intelligence that freaked Matt out more than their human eyes.

"I'm gonna need to make a call." Isaac stood, passing the rifle to his grandson.

"Who?" Gina's voice sounded hopeful. Matt felt

kind of hopeful himself. *Calling someone is more productive than waiting to die.*

Matt turned his gaze back to the wolves. *Or become like them.*

Isaac shook his head and headed for the hall. He paused at the door and his dark gaze zeroed in on Matt. "You better come along," he ordered. "He may want to talk to you."

"He who?" Gina called, but Isaac's boots were already receding in the direction of her office.

Matt didn't like leaving Gina in a room with a sheer windowpane that seemed to be begging the wolves to crash through and add a few more to their army, even if Isaac didn't think they would.

"Go." Gina waved her hand. "We're good."

"Sure?"

"She's safer with me than with you, Moldy. Run along."

Gina narrowed her eyes. "I don't need anyone to take care of me."

McCord's only answer was a snort.

Gina glanced at Matt, shrugged, then tilted her head to indicate the back of the house. Matt went. As much as he disliked Jase McCord, Matt also believed the man would die before he allowed Gina to be hurt.

Isaac already had the phone pressed to his ear. As Matt stepped into the office, the call was answered on the other end of the line.

"Edward," Isaac said. "He escaped."

The room was so silent Gina heard Isaac speaking. She couldn't hear what he was saying, but she hoped whatever he learned from whomever he'd called would help.

"I'm going to check on Fanny and the others." Gina

couldn't sit there and watch those things watching them for another minute longer.

Jase merely lifted a hand as she left; he kept *his* gaze on the window and his hand on the gun.

Upstairs, she checked every room. Derek had nodded off, the TV flickering blue streaks across his slack face. He seemed even younger asleep. Like a scruffy Smurf in dirty sweats and bare feet.

Softly Gina shut his door. She had to get him out of here alive.

Fanny dozed in the rocking chair she'd dragged just outside of Amberleigh's room. A quick glance within revealed Amberleigh still sucking her thumb; the moon shining through the window and across her bed revealed a face tracked with tears. But she was asleep, along with all the others, and with luck they'd stay that way until morning. Then . . .

Who knew?

Would the werewolves remain in the yard, barring anyone from leaving the house? Except . . . didn't werewolves only troll around after dark? Gina hoped so. Being trapped in here with only one silver-filled rifle would be bad.

She paused outside her room. Where had Isaac gotten silver bullets? She doubted the local gunsmith sold them.

Maybe Isaac had made them. He was pretty good with his hands. Whenever anything broke in the tack room, Isaac was the one who fixed it. In which case . . .

Gina went into her room, not bothering to turn on the light. The moon had begun to fall and was now framed in the large windows set in the opposite wall. Everything looked cast in pewter.

Gina owned a lot of silver jewelry. This was the

Southwest after all. Sure, a lot of it was her mother's, but—

Gina lifted the lid of her jewelry box. She'd save those pieces for last.

Inside lay a jumble of stuff she didn't wear. Things that flitted around, caught the light, made a noise—like earrings, bracelets, even necklaces—could spook a horse.

Gina considered the pile. If Isaac melted it down he might get a few bullets out of it but . . . probably not enough to matter.

She shut the lid with a snap and turned toward the door.

Someone stood in the shadows, just past the reach of the moonlight, watching her.

"I dunno how he got out," Isaac said.

Whoever was on the other end spoke. Matt considered asking Isaac to put him on speakerphone, then saw the apparatus was so ancient it was one step above a rotary dial.

"I'm gonna let you talk to the guy who was there when it happened," Isaac continued. "He's some kind of Aztec expert." Isaac held out the receiver to Matt. "I wanna keep an eye on those wolves."

"Who'd you call?" Matt asked.

"Name's Edward Mandenauer. We met in the war."

Matt frowned. "War?"

"WW Two. Did a lot of scouting in Germany." His mouth twisted. "They always sent the Injuns scouting." Isaac lifted the phone higher. "Ran into this guy in the Black Forest. He was some sort of double agent."

"A spy?" Matt frowned. What good would that do them?

Isaac pressed the phone into Matt's hand. "Edward's spent a lifetime studying ancient, supernatural legends. Tell him what you saw, what you know. I gotta go back."

Matt put the phone to his ear, but before he could even introduce himself Edward Mandenauer, his accent still quite German despite the intervening years, snapped, "Tell me everything."

So Matt did—or almost everything. He left out the parts that were too crazy for words. The instant he said "Nahual," the old man interrupted. "Ah! This is a word that I know."

"An Aztec guardian angel in animal form. Kind of like the Native American spirit animal."

"Not quite. The stories of the Nahual that I have heard deal with a being referred to as '*lo que es mi vestidura o piel.*'"

"'Something that is my cloth or my skin,'" Matt translated. "I've only seen that translation for the Nahualli, protectors of Tezcatlipoca, the Aztec god of war and sacrifice."

Sacrifice. War. Changing of the skin like a cloth. All of these tales circled around to the same damn thing. Whether they called it Tangwaci Cin-au'-ao or a super-warrior or a Nahual, all the legends described what they had here.

"The two beings are as close as the words used to describe them," Mandenauer said. "The Nahualli a protector of the god, the Nahual a being very like a god."

"*Like* a god?" Matt echoed.

"What else would ancient peoples think when they saw a werewolf but that they had encountered a god?"

"Wait a second. Who said anything about werewolf?" Matt had been *thinking* it, but he hadn't *said* it.

"Did I get ahead of myself? I apologize, but I hate to

waste time. The only reason for Isaac to call me is for help. The kind of help only I can give."

"What kind of help is that?" Matt asked. "Isaac wasn't clear on what, exactly, you do."

"I kill monsters."

Silence settled over the line.

"Am I wrong in assuming you have werewolves?" Mandenauer at last broke the silence. "The glyphs you described—the man-wolf face, the larger-than-life being, the word *Nahual*—give that impression."

"I . . . uh . . . well . . ."

"Have dead people disappeared? Their bodies seeming to run off under their own power?"

"How did you know?" That had been one of the crazy parts Matt had left out.

"Once bitten, a human being will change within twenty-four hours. Moon, sun, rain, or shine, dead, or alive, the afflicted will become. Ever after they run beneath the moon only, but the first time is different— the first time they *must* kill. Later they need only imbibe fresh blood, although most kill anyway. Once the demon werewolf takes hold, they like it."

"What else do you know about the Nahual?" Matt asked.

"A sorcerer that grows stronger with every kill. Sacrifice increases his power. Blood and flesh are his sustenance."

"A cannibal."

"Of sorts," Mandenauer agreed.

"But how does smoke kill?"

"The Ute confined the creature with magic. The specifics of the spell might explain the Nahual's appearance, or lack of one. However, no record of the spell was kept, and the sorcerer who performed it was executed soon after."

"He saves their ass and they kill him for it?"

"The Ute understood that what they were dealing with was something that should never, ever get back out. The consequences could be catastrophic."

"In what way?"

"As far as my people have been able to determine, the Nahual is invincible."

Mandenauer had "people"? That was almost as disturbing as what his people had found out or, rather, not found out.

"No one's invincible," Matt said. "Every megalomaniac throughout history learned that."

"There's a first time for everything," Mandenauer muttered. "But I'd prefer it not happen on my watch."

"What's the Nahual going to do?" Matt asked.

"Create more of his kind, build an army, rule the world."

"Why?" Ruling the world had always seemed like a really shitty job to Matt.

"It's what megalomaniacs do."

"What about the others?" Matt asked. "There are werewolves in the yard, and some of them have the eyes of our friends."

"It is a horrible thing to view the eyes of a friend in the face of a beast. This I have seen many, many times. Right before I shoot them in the head."

Matt winced. Ashleigh might have been annoying, but he didn't want her dead. And Mel—Mel was fun.

"Isn't there another way?"

"To kill them?" Mandenauer sounded confused.

"*Than* killing them. Can't we cure them?"

"Of course."

Matt rubbed his face. Was the old man *trying* to make him insane?

"However, the cure is . . . singular. One-on-one. It takes time and must be applied physically, which can cause problems."

Like the one applying the cure getting his or her throat torn out? Matt could understand how that might be a problem.

"Sometimes it is best just to shoot them."

"How about if we try and cure them, and if there's a problem, then we shoot them?"

"Sounds like a plan," Mandenauer agreed; the modern phrase sounded very odd when spoken with his old-world accent.

"And the Nahual?" Matt continued. "Can he be cured?"

"No. The Nahual was not bitten; he was born. He is, for all intents and purposes, a god. He is evil on both sides of the moon. That cannot be cured."

Desperation tore at Matt, as sharp as the claws of those beasts outside. But he swallowed, striving for a calm he didn't feel. "Then what do we do?"

"Reconfine him."

"I thought no one knew how."

"No one alive," Mandenauer agreed.

Matt blinked. "What?"

"I will talk to my people. As the Nahual was imprisoned, seemingly for eternity, I have not pressed the issue. But now we must."

"How many people do you have?" Matt asked.

"Less than I need. They tend to die on me."

"I can imagine," Matt muttered. He had a feeling monster hunters died often and badly. If Mandenauer had lasted this long he must be the best of the best, which was exactly what they needed. "Can you come to Nahua Springs Ranch?"

"My boy, I am already on my way."

Quickly they exchanged cell-phone numbers. Matt thought the old man had hung up, but Edward had one last piece of advice: "Be careful. A sorcerer can do most anything."

Matt stood with the phone still in his hand as the implications of the conversation washed over him.

They not only had werewolves, but they also had a shape-shifting Aztec sorcerer intent on creating more of them. And the man Matt had just spoken to was a monster hunter. Which meant there were a lot more monsters than these in the world.

The phone began to squawk, and Matt replaced it in the cradle. But he didn't return to the living room. He needed to get his mind right.

How was he going to explain this to the others?

Pretty much the same way it was explained to him. Matter-of-factly. They'd already seen the evidence. It was standing out in the yard.

A creak from upstairs had him lifting his face to the ceiling. Strange. Everyone was supposed to be asleep. Sure, they could have awoken, headed for the bathroom or to get a drink of water, but the footsteps that followed that creak weren't the footsteps of a person moving purposely toward a place they had every business going to.

No, those footsteps had sounded like someone slowly creeping up on another someone who had no idea that they were there.

CHAPTER 20

Gina caught her breath. "Who's that?"

She didn't recognize the shape of whoever hovered in the hall, and she should. Why wouldn't she immediately recognize the outline of every person in the house? There weren't all that many.

She wanted to step away from the hovering shadow, but trapped in her room, she had nowhere to go. Instead, she made herself move forward, and as she did, the shadow solidified into—

"Jase." She let out her breath in a relieved rush, then immediately drew it in again. "Is something wrong?"

He stepped from the darkness and into the silvery light. "I don't know; is there?"

Gina frowned, annoyed. "I don't have time for games." She made to step past him, and he grabbed her elbow.

She glanced at his hand, then into his face. He appeared as annoyed as she. But why?

"What happened?" She tugged on her arm. He didn't let go; instead he urged her farther into the room.

A prickle of unease washed over Gina, which she

quickly quashed. This was Jase. She'd known him all her life. He would never hurt her, though right now . . . She shifted her shoulder; his grip wasn't exactly pleasant.

"What *did* happen?" he murmured, his dark eyes appearing even darker in the hazy gleam of the falling moon. "We were happy here."

"Happy?" she repeated. "I guess."

They'd been on the verge of bankruptcy. Working like mules. But, sure, they'd had some good times.

"Then he came and ruined it all."

"Teo?"

Jase's lip curled, and he let her go with a little shove. " 'Teo'?" he mocked. "You mean 'Dr. Moldy.' "

"I mean *Teo*. He saved us, Jase."

"Saved?" Jase laughed, but it wasn't his laugh, the one that made her laugh, too. This laugh was bitter and kind of mean. Not Jase's laugh at all. "How fast things changed once you let him fuck you."

"Bite me." She started for the door again. Jase stepped in her way.

"Did he bite you? Did you like it?"

Gina's hand curled into a fist. She very much wanted to sock Jase in the gut. Unfortunately, from previous experience she knew that his gut was rock hard and she'd only hurt her hand.

"Move your ass," she said quietly.

"Or what?"

"I'll call your mother. She's down the hall."

Fanny might appear mild mannered and sweet, but she could get downright nasty if Jase needed her to be. Right now, Gina thought he might need her to be.

Jase stepped back, but he didn't clear the path to the

door. "We were going to get married," he said, and his voice sounded broken.

"Who?" Gina blurted before her mind caught up to her mouth. "Us? Jase." She shook her head, took his hand. His was so cold she rubbed it between hers. "No. We weren't."

"If he'd never come—"

"It wouldn't have mattered. I don't love you that way."

"You would have eventually. We'd have gotten married, and raised our kids here, and everything would have been perfect."

Everything wouldn't have been perfect because the ranch would have been sold out from under them if not for Teo. But bringing that up again . . . probably not the best idea.

Teo had told her that Jase wanted to be more than a brother to her, that he'd warned other men away, and she hadn't believed him. Jase had always been her friend—her best friend, her only friend. But marrying him? Sleeping with him? Gina stifled a shudder.

"Jase." She squeezed his hand between hers until he looked into her face. "That was never going to happen."

His lips tightened; his eyes cooled. "It would have. You love me."

"Like a brother."

He yanked free. "I am *not* your brother!"

Before she could figure out what to do, what to say next, he grabbed her by the shoulders and he kissed her.

As kisses went, it was pretty bad. Too hard, too desperate. Way too much tongue.

She remained passive, hoping he'd catch a clue. But

when his hands began to wander below her neck she stomped on his foot.

"Hey!" At least he stopped kissing, and pawing, her. "What was that for?"

"Don't ever do that again," she said. "It was . . . ucky."

"Ucky? I thought it was hot."

Gina couldn't help it; she lowered her gaze to his jeans, then immediately yanked it back up. He *had* thought it was hot.

Now she was beyond grossed out.

"*Not* hot. Not *cool,* Jase. Get it through your head—I will never love you that way. I will never marry you. I will definitely never, *ever,* sleep with you. And if you keep pushing it, you're going to have to leave."

"We're partners."

"In name only. You don't own this place, and you don't own me."

His face darkened; his mouth twisted. "Is that what happened? Mecate bought you along with our ranch? There's a word for that, Gina."

Gina sighed. Jase was upset. He wasn't himself. She wasn't going to hold what he said now against him.

Much.

"We've got bigger problems than this, Jase. Don't tell me you left the window unguarded to come up here and—" Her lip curled; she couldn't help it. "Kiss me."

She wanted to wipe her hand across her lips; she wanted to jump in the shower and wash off the slurpy feeling his touch had left all over her skin. "You need to go downstairs."

"I don't take orders from you. I'm just an employee, so I guess I take orders from—"

"Me."

Both of them turned as Teo stepped into the room.

From the paleness of Gina's face, more had gone on here than an argument about who was the boss of whom. Which was all that Matt had heard upon arrival. But he hadn't liked the tone of McCord's voice, one he'd never heard the man direct at Gina before.

"Go downstairs," Matt ordered, but his gaze remained locked on Gina's. Physically she seemed all right, but her eyes . . . Matt didn't like the sadness that lurked there. A sadness that had been caused by her best friend in the world.

The best friend had to go. If necessary, Matt would make him. Matt thought he might enjoy it.

For an instant, McCord hesitated, and Matt thought, *Please take a swing at me. Just one.* Then the man cursed and stomped out the door. Matt reached over and shut it behind him, flicking the lock for good measure.

Gina stared at the closed door, confusion pushing the sadness from her eyes. "That was so unlike him."

Matt crossed the room, setting his hands on her shoulders, frowning when she tensed. "What did he do?"

She stepped out of Matt's reach, and his frown intensified. He didn't like this at all. "If he hurt you—"

"No," she said, but she rubbed at her arms as if she were freezing. "I think I hurt him."

"He looked fine to me."

Her lips curved, but she was still so sad. "All he wants is for me to love him, Teo, and I can't, because—" She broke off, biting her lip, then turning to stare through the window at the setting moon. "It'll be dawn soon."

"Why can't you love him, Gina?"

"I *do* love him," she insisted, and Matt's heart stuttered. He'd been hoping— "But not the way he needs me to. When he kissed me, I—"

"He kissed you?" Fury blasted through Matt, stronger and sharper than any he'd ever known. She was *his*. She always would be.

"Yeah," she said, and faced him. "It was awful."

"Really?" He lifted a brow. "Why's that?"

"Because he wasn't you."

This time when Matt reached for her, she came into his arms, burrowing against his chest with a sigh.

"I know we've got problems—big, toothy, deadly problems—and I want to hear what you found out from whoever Isaac called. But right now . . ." She leaned back. "Kiss me. Touch me. Make me forget that I probably just lost Jase forever."

Matt didn't think McCord would be so foolish as to throw away any part of Gina he could get—her friendship was better than nothing—but he also hadn't thought the man would be so stupid as to force a kiss on her.

Matt had to agree. That wasn't like McCord. Of course everyone snapped eventually. And if Matt had been in love with Gina and she hadn't loved him back . . .

Matt set his hand against her cheek. He *was* in love with Gina. The thought of her kissing McCord made him crazy. The sadness in her eyes made him want to move heaven and earth to erase it.

Matt framed her face with his palms and lowered his lips to hers.

Her taste was woman and warmth; her mouth opened, welcoming him in. She lifted her arms, tangling her fingers in his hair, pressing her unbound breasts to his chest. He went hard instantly.

Memories flickered. The two of them in the tent, their first time, which had been more about lust than love. However, those memories enhanced; they didn't distract. Because of them he knew that scraping his thumb just so, along the lip of her collarbone, would make her breath catch.

When he palmed her hips he remembered how he'd palmed them that night as he'd slid into her, filling her, stretching her, making her come. She'd been so tight, so hot.

Hell. If he didn't stop thinking about that night, her on her knees, her breasts swaying, her—

Matt cursed and lifted his mouth before he lost control and tossed her onto the bed, tore off her clothes, and did her exactly the same way all over again.

"Shh," she whispered, mouth searching for more, hands in his hair insistent, bringing his lips gradually, achingly, back to hers.

"Gina," he protested. "I want to be slow, gentle. I want you to know how I feel."

"I already know how you feel." She cupped him through his pants—when had one of her hands left his hair?—then ran a fingernail along his sac. He thought he might faint or, at the least, disgrace himself right then and there.

He grabbed her wrist, meaning to pull her away, but when she licked the line of his lips with just the tip of her tongue he had a change of heart. Instead, he laid his hand over hers and pulled it closer. There was something strangely erotic about using her hand to touch himself. From the curve of her mouth and the enthusiasm of the continued touching, she agreed.

His dreams of slow and gentle evaporated. He wasn't going to last that long.

As if she could read his mind, she removed her hand and stepped back. "They'll be looking for us soon."

She was right. Matt was surprised McCord hadn't started pounding on the door already, or at least sent his mother to do it. He ran a hand through his hair. "Yeah. We should stop."

"Stop?" Gina, whose fingers had just gone to the hem of her T-shirt, laughed. "I meant we should hurry."

Matt hesitated. Despite the call of his body to do just that, he didn't want to hurry. He wasn't going to. People could pound on the door all they wanted, but this time he was going to make love to Gina the way he'd never made love to anyone before.

As if he meant it. Because he loved her and he believed that she loved him. In this strange, uncertain world they'd tumbled into, love might be the one thing they had to hold on to.

He put his hands over hers. She glanced up, a question in her dark eyes. "Let me."

She smiled and lifted her arms.

He undressed her as if they had hours, touching and kissing, loving every inch as it was revealed. Within minutes, she'd forgotten about hurrying. He kind of thought she'd forgotten about everything.

Except them.

He herded her to the bed, and when her knees hit the mattress all it took was a little push for her to fall. Her laughter caused his belly to flutter. She *had* forgotten all that waited outside this room. Now he needed to. He doubted it would be much of a problem.

As Matt bent to tug the sweatpants from her hips, he paused. "Someday I'd like to see you in your boots." He lifted his gaze. "And nothing else."

"Someday," she agreed, then put a fuzzy stocking–

covered foot to the middle of his chest and shoved. "You're such a guy."

"Guilty." He tossed the sweatpants aside.

"I'm glad," she said.

"That I'm guilty?" He quickly divested her of her socks and panties, as well.

"That you're a guy." She dropped her now-bare foot to the part that made him a guy, and he gulped. "Lose the clothes, Professor."

With her leaning back on the bed, completely naked, her hair tumbling over her shoulders and caressing her breasts as he wanted to, he needed no further encouragement. He lost the clothes, set his glasses on the nightstand, then covered her body with his.

He spent a good long while just kissing her, enjoying the slide of skin along skin, thigh to thigh, chest to breast—even her feet felt good against his.

He could have gone on kissing her, learning the contours of her mouth with his tongue, for hours, except she began to squirm and the friction, the pressure, made him hiss in a breath and set his forehead to hers.

"Teo." She licked his collarbone, and he gritted his teeth. Was she *trying* to kill him?

"You smell like oranges, but you taste like . . ." She paused, and then she licked him again.

He was done for. He couldn't wait. He forgot all about gentle. Instead, he lifted his hips and he plunged.

Her breath caught; he was terrified he'd hurt her. He began to withdraw, but her nails dug into his shoulders even as her heels dug into his thighs.

He opened his eyes. Hers were right there—dark and fierce, stark with need.

"Don't. You. Dare," she said between her teeth.

He managed not to orgasm—barely. She was both

gloriously tight and unbelievably wet. He slid in with ease, but when he slid out she clenched around him, causing him to mutter expletives in three different languages. Her lips curved as if he'd whispered endearments.

He needed to concentrate if he wanted to keep from exploding, so he began to close his eyes. If he looked at her dark hair spread across the creamy sheets, her lips swollen from his, her eyes begging him to do her, do her hard, there was no way he'd last another minute.

Then she murmured, "No, Teo, don't," and he froze, uncertain.

"Don't close your eyes. Look at me. See me."

"Gina," he whispered. "All I ever see is you."

All I ever see is you.

The words hung between them, beautiful and infinitely sweet. Gina's throat closed; she wasn't sure she could speak.

She was poised on the rim of orgasm, and if the quiver in his arms, his belly, the part of him buried deep within, was any indication, so was he.

She rocked her hips, hoping to send them over the edge, and while the slow slip and slide was magnificent, they both seemed to be waiting for something more.

Gina touched his face. She reached up to kiss him, and the words tumbled out: "I love you."

He didn't answer, merely tilted his head and waited for her to come to terms with it—either take the statement back as a mistake, uttered in the heat of the strongest passion she'd ever known, or admit it was a truth she'd kept locked in her heart.

"I do love you," she repeated with some amazement. "I wasn't sure."

"I was." He thrust once. She couldn't breathe. "I am." A second time. His gaze bored into hers. "I always . . ." Three. "Always." Four. "Will be."

"Yes," she whispered. "Always."

Those declarations were what had been missing. The next instant they were coming together, falling apart, holding on as the storm washed over them and then away.

His head fell forward until it rested against hers, his hair shrouding them both from the dying rays of the moon. She ran her hand over his back, let her palm rest at the base of his spine, enjoying the sensation of his still being inside of her.

"Don't move," she whispered.

"I can't," he returned, and their laughter mingled along with their breath.

They had one more instant of peace, and then, somewhere in the house, someone screamed.

CHAPTER 21

Gina was never certain if she threw Teo off the bed or he rolled over so fast he fell. Either way, he landed on his ass on the floor.

The screams continued. The two of them dived for their clothes, shoving their bare feet through the legs of their sweatpants in such a hurry they didn't realize—

"Shit." Gina dropped the much too large garment to the ground, even as Teo cursed when her much too small pair got stuck at his knees. They tossed each other their respective pants as earsplitting shrieks threatened to puncture their eardrums.

Shoving her head and arms through her T-shirt, Gina followed him to the door, then rammed into his back when he tried to open it, forgot it was locked, and got nowhere.

As they ran down the stairs in the wake of everyone else, the screams suddenly stopped. Gina's ears continued to ring.

The guests all crowded into the kitchen, staring at a hysterical Amberleigh being soothed by Fanny as Isaac stood in the open doorway with his gun.

Gina pushed her way through the crowd. "What happened?"

Amberleigh took several gulping gasps, opened her mouth, and began to sob at nearly the same volume she'd shrieked.

"Sheesh," Derek muttered. "She's loud."

Melda scurried forward and folded the girl into her arms, urging her out of the room, away from the door that Amberleigh kept staring at as if it might sprout teeth and bite her, then into the dining room.

At least the old woman seemed more herself today. For that matter, so did Amberleigh. Loud really *was* her thing.

"Should that door be open?" Gina asked.

Isaac scowled and slammed it shut. "Sun's up. Wolves are gone."

"Gone where?"

"Back to being people. Shifted right there in the yard." He lowered his voice. "Mel's naked behind is somethin' I *never* wanna see again." Isaac fixed the group with a glare. "Just 'cause they look human now don't mean they are. Their selves died when they did. They'll do everything they can to lure us out, keep us there until they can make us like them. It's what they do."

"What set Amberleigh off?" Teo stepped into the room. His shirt was caught up on one side, revealing a slice of rippling abs. Gina swallowed the urge to lick him like an ice-cream cone. She settled for tugging down his shirt, then taking his hand.

When she glanced again at Isaac, his gaze was on those hands; then it went to Teo's chest and finally to her face. Though his dark eyes held no recrimination, she could tell that he knew where she'd been and whom she'd been doing.

Her fingers released Teo's, but he would not let hers go, and the next instant she was glad. Pretending they weren't together wouldn't work. Because they were and they were going to stay that way. Everyone needed to get used to it.

Isaac lowered his eyes. "She said Ashleigh wanted to see her."

"Ashleigh's a werewolf," Gina pointed out. "How would Amberleigh know what she wanted?"

"According to—" Isaac jerked his thumb toward the dining room, where Melda had gotten Amberleigh calmed down enough to emit only great, gulping, nearly silent sobs. *Go, Melda!* "She heard her name on the wind."

Gina stilled. *Uh-oh.*

Teo's fingers tightened on hers. Had she started? She wouldn't be surprised. "And then?" she urged.

"She snuck past Fanny, followed the sound downstairs, and found a wolf in the kitchen."

Now Gina started so violently she nearly yanked her hand from Teo's without even trying to. "Inside?"

"So she says."

"She's been sucking her thumb for two days," Tim pointed out. "Should we really believe anything she tells us?"

"I saw it!" Amberleigh shrieked, getting to her feet, ignoring Melda's attempts to stop her. "It was right there." She pointed a badly trembling finger at the floor next to Isaac. "The eyes," she moaned. "They were horrible." Then, strangely: "My ankle hurts."

"Let's go upstairs and . . ." Melda's voice trailed off. That seemed to happen a lot now that Mel was no longer around to finish her sentences. But Amberleigh allowed Melda to lead her away.

"She is one weird dude," Derek murmured.

"Not a dude," his father said. "But definitely weird."

"If one of them got inside, why would it leave?" Teo asked.

"If one of them got inside, *how* could it leave?" Gina countered. "Was the door open when you got here, Isaac?" He shook his head. "How would a wolf get out, or in?" She wiggled her free hand. "No thumbs."

"What if crazy chick let it in?" Derek asked. "What if it's *still* in?"

"If a werewolf got inside," Isaac said, "there would be more blood. If . . ." he lifted his brows, "crazy chick had opened the door, they'd all be in, not just one."

"*None* of them came in." Fanny, who had been sitting quietly at the kitchen table, now stood and moved to the window. She lifted a tiny sprig of dried purple flowers from the sill. "Wolfsbane," she said simply, then returned the plant to its place.

Gina glanced around, but no one, not even Isaac, seemed to know what in hell Fanny was talking about.

"What does that do?" Gina asked.

"Keeps them out." Fanny sat again at the table. "I placed a piece at every window and door. You don't think they sat out there all night because of one gun, do you?"

From Isaac's scowl, he had. "Where'd you learn that?"

"Mother."

"When did you—?"

"Nineteen-sixty-five." Isaac's scowl deepened, and Fanny shrugged. "Better safe than sorry."

"Why?" Isaac asked. "The Tangwaci Cin-au'-ao was confined. He was never supposed to get out."

"They're never *supposed* to get out," Fanny said. "You told the tale of the Tangwaci Cin-au'-ao at every campfire since I was old enough to understand words. It scared me. Once I put wolfsbane everywhere, I could sleep at night."

"So Amberleigh's crazy," Derek murmured. "Seeing things? Hearing them, too?"

"Not necessarily," Isaac said. "The Tangwaci Cin-au'-ao has been calling people to him since he was buried. Maybe he called Amberleigh."

"*Probably* he called Amberleigh," Gina said, and shrugged. "He called me."

Isaac's gaze narrowed. "When?"

"Since I fell in the cavern the first time."

"And you didn't mention this before now?" Isaac asked.

"Would you have believed me before now?"

"Yes," he said simply.

"Well, I didn't know that. I just thought I was imagining that the howls of the unwolves sounded like my name."

Or that I was nuts.

"I always wondered why you insisted on going out there even though I'd forbidden it. I guess if he was calling you—"

Gina shook her head. "I didn't hear it until we were rescued." Isaac frowned. "Or maybe I heard it down there first."

Which was why she'd always thought the voice part of her neurosis. After what had happened beneath the earth, why wouldn't she have issues? Didn't it make more sense that what she'd heard on the wind was nothing more than a guilt-induced echo of the last words she'd ever heard in her parents' voices, rather than the call of an invisible Aztec werewolf sorcerer that she hadn't even known about?

Teo squeezed her hand, and when Gina looked at him he smiled. "We may never figure all of this out. But since the sun's up and the werewolves are gone, we should probably all drive to town."

"I can't wait to get on a plane," Tim muttered.

"Excellent!" Derek announced, and gave his dad a high five.

"Everyone get dressed and packed," Gina said. The sooner she got the guests out of here, the better. "I'll have Jase—" She glanced around. "Where is Jase?"

No one answered. Gina got a prickling sensation along her back as her gaze rested on the door.

Jase wouldn't have done anything stupid.

Would he?

From the expression on Gina's face she thought Mc-Cord had walked out of the house and directly into the gaping wolf jaws of death.

Matt crossed to the window. Since there weren't pieces of McCord all over the place, he doubted it. Most likely the man was in the barn or one of the other rooms of the house, pouting.

Isaac went out the back door looking as worried as Matt had ever seen him. Though Matt would prefer never to lay eyes on Jase McCord again, he hoped they found him soon for everyone else's peace of mind.

The Gordons disappeared, no doubt to dress and pack at the speed of sound. Fanny had already pulled out a skillet, eggs, milk, and bacon. She pushed a button on the coffeepot and coffee began to stream into the carafe.

Gina jerked her head toward the hall. Matt followed her out of the kitchen and into her office.

"Shut the door," she said.

He lifted a brow, but he did as she ordered.

"You think Melda's going to leave Mel behind?" she asked.

Matt hadn't thought about it. He hoped so. The fewer warm bodies around here, the better.

"And Amberleigh," Gina continued. "We're gonna have to drop her at the local loony bin, then call her folks."

"Okay."

Gina nodded, chewing on her lower lip.

"You didn't call me in here to go over the plan, Gina."

She lifted her gaze. He wanted to cross the room and kiss the crease between her eyes. So he did.

She relaxed into his embrace. "I don't know what I'd do if you weren't here."

"Manage." He rubbed her back. "You always do."

"Not very well. I lost the ranch."

"It's yours now. I promise."

"Jase thinks I slept with you to get it back." She lifted her head. "Do you think that?"

"It never once crossed my mind." Her smile was worth a thousand sunrises, and when she laid her head back on his chest Matt ran a palm over her tangled brown hair. "You should have told me you heard that thing calling your name."

Her chest lifted and lowered against his, making him think of things other than the situation at hand, but he held her until she stepped away.

"Sorry. I can't think when you touch me." She sat behind her desk. "Or I can think, but not about any-thing but you."

Matt's chest went tight. He wondered if she'd agree to go to town and stay there until this was over. If he lost her, he didn't think he'd survive.

"Ten years ago I felt a . . . presence down there. I was out of it, scared, high from lack of oxygen maybe, but—" She lifted her gaze, and her pupils had dilated until her eyes appeared black. "When it's dark and I'm alone, I know that something evil played Duck, Duck, Goose with our lives."

"What does that mean, Gina?"

"Someone had to die. Then I didn't know why, but now I think sacrifice kept that thing alive, if alive is what he is. All the people who died on that piece of land fed him somehow, and when no one came, because of the curse, he called names until someone did."

As theories went, hers wasn't half-bad. Especially since she didn't know yet what Edward Mandenauer had told Matt.

"Maybe Amberleigh did hear what she said she heard," Gina continued. "Maybe she saw what she said she saw."

"She might have heard something, but I doubt she saw it. Fanny put wolfsbane at the entrances."

"Does that really work?"

"Hell if I know," Matt muttered. "But I think Isaac's right. If the werewolves could get in, they would have."

"And we'd all be dead. Or worse."

They remained silent, thinking about worse; then they both spoke at the same time.

"You should stay in town," Matt said.

"I want you to go back to Arizona," Gina blurted.

They stared at each other; then they both said, "I'm not leaving you."

"Well." Matt scrubbed a hand through his hair. "I'm glad that's settled."

"I can't leave my ranch, Teo. I won't."

"The cavern's still there waiting to be explored, and the wall with the glyphs could prove my mother's theory." Although if they'd been drawn by a Ute shaman Matt wasn't quite sure how. He still planned to study every last stick figure.

Eventually.

"You aren't going to be able to explore until we get rid of this thing, so you may as well—"

"No," he interrupted. "I want to be here when Edward comes."

"Edward?" She tilted her head. "*That's* who Isaac called?"

"You know him?"

"He's a friend of Isaac's from the war. Him and his granddaughter . . ." She paused, thinking. "Dr. Hanover. Elise. They came here to study the unwolves."

Matt lifted a brow. "I think they came to make sure the unwolves weren't werewolves." Quickly Matt told Gina what Edward had told him.

"The old German guy is a monster hunter," she said when Matt finished. "You're sure *he's* not nuts?"

"Yesterday I would have wondered that myself. Today . . ." Matt shrugged. "Let's hope he's not, because he's all we've got."

"Swell," Gina muttered, and let her forehead bang against the desk with a thud.

A half hour later everyone except Amberleigh, whom Melda had managed to get to sleep and they'd decided to leave asleep as long as they could, less noise that way, had eaten and assembled in the yard.

Jase walked out of the barn whistling. Gina experienced a wiggle of déjà vu. He used to do that every morning.

Until Teo showed up.

She glanced at Teo and shook her head, indicating he should stay where he was, then hurried to Jase. "Where have you been?"

She was half-afraid he would turn away without answering. Instead, he shot her a look as if she'd lost her mind. "In the barn. The horses needed feeding, watering, tending. You know, the usual?"

A slash of guilt tore through her. She hadn't thought of the horses once this morning. *Thank God for Jase.*

"I was worried," she said.

"The horses are fine."

Was he purposely misunderstanding her? Or was he giving her an out by pretending that nothing had happened between them to threaten what they'd always been to each other? Or at least what she'd *thought* they'd always been.

"Jase." Gina put her hand on his arm, and when he didn't pull away she continued. "I don't want to lose you."

"You won't lose me." He patted her hand and smiled his crooked smile. "It'll all work out."

Then he walked off, whistling again. Gina stared after him. He really seemed to have moved on, to have put the ugly scene between them earlier behind him. Or was he just that good at pretending? Gina never would have thought so until she'd discovered that he'd been pretending for years.

And what was she upset about? Did she want him to pine for her? *Hell no!* She should be thrilled that Jase was willing to fake a case of amnesia. She should try it.

Gina glanced toward the house. Teo stared at her, his concern evident. She tried a reassuring smile. But she obviously wasn't as good at feigning her feelings as Jase, because her smile caused Teo to frown.

"Jase," she called. "Can you get the van?"

He lifted a hand to indicate he'd heard, and changed his course from the barn to the garage.

Gina returned to the porch. "I'll get Amberleigh. Teo." She took his hand and gave it a reassuring squeeze, which seemed to work better than her smile, because his frown smoothed out as soon as she touched him. "Can you help with the bags?"

He nodded, and Gina went into the house, trotted up the stairs. She was so preoccupied with Jase's bizarre about-face, along with everything else, she'd opened the door to the As' room before she registered the strange sounds coming from the other side. Then she stood in the doorway and stared.

The place was trashed. Clothes strewn everywhere, most of them shredded. The curtains hung in tatters; the bedspread wasn't much better.

The strange sounds, which had morphed into gurgles, grunts, and growls, emanated from the bathroom along with the splash of running water.

"Amberleigh?" Gina called, crossing the floor and glancing inside.

The girl leaned over the rim of the bathtub, mouth directly under the gushing stream as she greedily guzzled. The smooth, golden perfection of her naked body was marred only by the seeping, bloody mess of one ankle.

No wonder it had hurt.

"Hey," Gina began.

Amberleigh's head whipped around, spraying water across the tile.

She didn't look like Amberleigh anymore.

Gina slammed the door. What had once been Amberleigh hit the other side with a thud that cracked the casing.

She should run, but she wasn't going to turn her back on that . . . thing. No way in hell.

A hand smashed through the wood. Those doors were pure oak. How had she done that? Perhaps the claws that had sprouted where her fingers had once been had helped.

Amberleigh's face appeared in the hole. Her hair hung in hanks; her eyes had gone feral. Were her teeth getting bigger? Or was her nose getting smaller?

"Shit," Gina muttered. Amberleigh was changing.

Gina no longer cared about turning her back; all she cared about was getting gone. She ran from the room, down the hall, trying not to scream, afraid to bring the others. Most of them would only be bait.

She tried to think. Where to go? What to do? How to keep Amberleigh in here until Gina could get to the gun out there?

The scritch of claws across the hall floor sounded like a dog trying to gain traction on hardwood. Gina reached the steps and glanced back.

Big mistake, because what she saw made her stiffen, lurch, and then she was falling, grasping at the railing, catching it just enough so that she didn't die, though by the time she reached the bottom she almost wished she had.

The wind was knocked out of her. She couldn't draw a breath. Couldn't move. Couldn't speak.

It got even worse when Amberleigh landed on her chest.

If the dirty-blond werewolf—guess Amberleigh

bleached her hair, big shock—with the big baby blues had gone right for Gina's throat, she'd have been done for. But apparently Amberleigh liked to play with her food.

Her lip pulled back in a snarl. Foam flecked her snout. If it hadn't been for the human eyes, Gina would believe a rabid wolf had crept into the house. But the eyes *were* human, and they *were* Amberleigh's.

The creature leaned slowly forward, waiting for Gina to panic, to squirm, to beg. Gina might have, if she'd yet been able to speak. However, the hundred-plus pounds of beast on her chest prevented her from doing anything but gasp.

Amberleigh quickly became bored—another thing the wolf and the girl had in common besides their eyes. She reared back to strike and—

Flames shot out the top of her head.

CHAPTER 22

Gina shoved the howling, fiery, dying mass of fur and fangs from her chest, then scooted away. Her back ran into something solid, and she gasped, whirled, then went into Teo's arms as he fell to his knees and caught her.

"Amberleigh," Gina managed, pressing her face into his chest, inhaling the sunshine and oranges scent of him—anything to make the odor of burning fur and flesh go away.

A movement had Gina jerking her head around. Would she ever be able to turn her back on anyone or anything again? The way the world was shaping up, she probably shouldn't.

The others stood in the entryway—Isaac with his blessed gun, the remaining guests all wide-eyed and pale, Fanny with Jase's arm around her. Everyone stared at the flaming werewolf, except Jase.

His gaze was on Gina and Teo, and he was no longer as nonchalant as he'd been outside. He was angry again, and she just didn't care.

"Why did she change?" Teo asked.

"She was bitten," Gina said. "On the ankle."

"Guess she wasn't nuts after all," Derek murmured, and when everyone glanced at him he shrugged. "She *said* there was a werewolf in the kitchen."

"No." Fanny left the circle of her son's arm. "They couldn't get in."

"Then how was she bitten?" Teo asked.

Fanny hurried to the kitchen, returning a minute later. "The wolfsbane is still there."

Though Gina would have preferred to remain in the circle of Teo's arms forever, she struggled to her feet, and he followed, steadying her when she swayed. She didn't want to be in charge, but this was her place, her people, her guests. She didn't have much choice.

"And Amberleigh is back to nuts," Gina said. "Although an imaginary werewolf didn't bite her ankle." Or at least Gina hoped not.

"Maybe she was bitten when Ashleigh was," Derek suggested.

"No," Teo said. "The first time a werewolf shifts it happens within twenty-four hours of the initial bite."

"How do you know?" Derek asked.

"Isaac . . . uh . . . called an expert."

Several sets of eyes widened, but no one seemed overly concerned that there even *was* a werewolf expert, let alone that Isaac had called one.

Gina glanced at the furry bonfire still crackling merrily in the front hall. How quickly the bizarre became commonplace when one was confronted with it over and over again.

"This means the wolfsbane doesn't work." Gina was proud that her voice didn't waver, even though her heart pounded so fast she was surprised she could talk at all.

"Maybe it does," Isaac murmured. "Like Fanny said, one gun wasn't going to keep all them wolves out, no matter how much I'd like to think it would."

"But one of them had to—" Teo began, and then, "Shit. The Nahual is smoke."

"So he could slip under the door?" Gina asked, and Teo shrugged. "Except . . . if he's smoke, how could he bite Amberleigh?"

"Same way he bit Ashleigh and Mel."

"Shit," Gina said. "We gotta get out of here."

Everyone turned toward the door, but Jase blocked their way. "We have a little problem with that." His gaze met Gina's over the crowd. "Can't take the van."

"Since when?"

"Since they used the tires for chew toys."

A chill went over Gina. "Truck? Car? Motorcycle?"

"They were obviously teething."

"Every vehicle we have is junk?"

"Pretty much."

"Call a tow truck," Teo said.

Jase turned a withering glare his way. "I would, if the phones weren't out."

"We used the phone last night."

"And then something ate the satellite dish."

"Frick," Gina muttered. That took care of the Internet, too.

Teo, Derek, and Tim pulled cell phones from their pockets. Gina held her breath. Together they frowned, shook the things, pressed buttons, then sighed and put them away.

"There's no way the werewolves could have eaten your cellular service," she said.

"No," Derek agreed. "It's not an eatable thing."

Gina glanced at Teo with lifted brows. How could

all the cell phones be out? He wiggled his fingers like a sorcerer.

Duh. The Nahual had enough juice to bite without teeth and begin a new werewolf army. Knocking out cell service had to be a cinch.

"We're stuck here?" Melda started to hyperventilate. "With those . . ."

Gina moved forward, but Jase crooked a finger, then jerked his head to indicate she should join him outside. She hoped he had a clue what to do, because she didn't.

Teo moved to follow, and she set her hand on his arm. "Would you help in here, please?"

Without a word, he went to the old woman, murmuring softly and herding her, along with the Gordons, away from both the door and the smoking wolf.

That was going to be a bitch to get out of the carpet.

As Gina left the house she marveled again at Teo. Anything she wanted or needed, anything she asked, and he was there. Was that kind of support what had held her parents together? What had kept Mel and Melda a pair for so long? Gina wasn't sure, but she thought so.

Being able to know with absolute certainty that there was someone on this earth who had your back, no matter what, went a long way toward fostering absolute trust and devotion.

"What are we going to do?" she asked when Jase paused just out of earshot of the others. "We can't walk to town. We'd never make it by sundown, which might just be what they're after."

"Gina," Jase said softly. "We have horses."

She blinked, then laughed, putting her hand over her mouth when she heard the slightly hysterical quiver beneath.

There was too much going on. She couldn't keep track of it all. She was becoming focused on one solution, and when it blew up in her face she wasn't able to see any of the others through the smoke.

Of *course* they had horses.

Gina dropped her hands. "What would I do without you, Jase?"

"I promise you'll never have to find out."

He sounded just like the old Jase, and then again he didn't. The old Jase would never have said anything so sappy. Of course the old Jase had always been her friend, with not a hint of anything more.

But the new Jase, the one who'd kissed her—still *uck* by the way—would not have said that, either, because she couldn't see him staying on and watching her and Teo together.

And they *would* be together. She could no longer imagine a life with the two of them apart.

What a mess. However, it was a mess she would deal with later.

If they survived.

However, things were looking up. On horses they'd reach town long before dusk, and in town there'd be plenty of guns, plenty of silver. She couldn't believe the Nahual had knocked out the phones, destroyed everything with a motor, and left the—

A series of small explosions—BB gun? Fireworks? Popcorn machine?—erupted in the barn. Then every last horse thundered out the open doors and disappeared over the ridge.

"That's not good," Jase murmured.

Gina ran after them. Why she had no idea. The cloud of dust on the horizon was still moving. She'd be lucky if the horses stopped running before they reached the ocean. She certainly had no prayer of catching them.

She crested the ridge just as the herd split, continuing on in half a dozen different directions. Bending, she clasped her knees and gasped for breath, then glanced over her shoulder.

Jase sat on the ground about twenty feet behind her, left boot off, rubbing his ankle.

Great.

Isaac stepped onto the porch, gun in hand. The others were visible in the hall behind him. Gina was surprised everyone hadn't spilled out of the house as soon as they heard the pops followed by the thunder of hooves.

Gina walked back to Jase.

"I stepped in a hole," he muttered, disgusted.

"Broke?" she asked.

"Nah." Jase shoved his foot into his boot and clambered to his feet, but when he crossed to the barn he limped. Could anything else go wrong?

Gina followed, keeping an eye peeled for holes. They stood shoulder to shoulder staring at the wide-open, empty stalls.

"When I was in here every horse was where it belonged; every stall was secure," Jase said. "I swear."

Gina cast him a quick glance. "I never thought otherwise."

"It's just . . ." He waved a hand at all the empty stalls. "How did that happen?"

"Same way the cell phones became crap, I imagine."

"Magic released the horses?"

"You got a better explanation?"

"I don't know if we need to explain it. But we do need to survive it."

"That's not going to be easy. We're stuck here with one rifle and a handful of silver bullets. And it appears that thing can get into the house."

"If he got inside, why didn't he make all of us furry at once?"

"Maybe he only has enough juice to do one person at a time." Teo *had* said that the Nahual gained power by killing.

"Maybe," Jase agreed.

They turned to stare at the distant puffs of dust that marked the stampeding horses.

"Any idea what set them off?" Gina asked.

"None," Jase answered. "I suppose we should look."

They searched the barn from top to bottom. Neither one of them found anything that could have caused the loud pops.

On any other day, the horses might drift back by nightfall. But with wolves all over the place—

Gina winced. She hoped the horses *had* kept running until they reached the ocean. That might be the only way *they'd* survive.

"What are we going to do, Jase?"

"Stay inside tonight. I'll jog into town after sunrise tomorrow."

"On that ankle?"

"Someone's gotta."

"Not you." In fact, not anyone. That idea had *trap* written all over it. She had the feeling the Nahual was just waiting for someone to get too far away from a silver bullet–filled gun.

"Besides," she said. "Edward is coming."

"That old friend of Granddad's from the war?" Jase snorted. "So what?"

"He's some sort of monster hunter."

"Really?" Jase glanced at Isaac, who still stood on the porch with his gun. "Interesting."

With a little help from Jack Daniel's, Matt managed to calm down Melda. The old woman fell asleep on the couch holding the bottle.

Now that the As were—Matt glanced at the smoldering pile of ashes in the hall—gone, the hysteria, as well as the noise, level had taken a good-sized hit.

Fanny moved about the house, checking for wolfsbane at every entrance with an attention to detail that Matt would have found reassuring if he didn't suspect that the biggest, baddest monster of all had the ability to slip through anyway.

Derek stood at the window staring at the place where the werewolves had been, murmuring, "Worgens need to be skinned."

When Matt lifted his brows in Tim's direction, the man said, "Cataclysm."

"I'd say so," Matt agreed.

"World of Warcraft," Tim clarified. "Video game."

"The Worgens are human and wolf," Derek explained. "They were cursed to shape-shift by night elves. But becoming horrible humanoid wolves destroyed their minds. They ran mad and were confined to prison in another dimension. But they were released."

"How?" Matt asked, intrigued.

"No one's really sure. I heard that in the newest version of WOW they show some of the background of the Worgens. They can be trapped by a circle of blood. Since those things fight to the death and they're pretty hard to kill—you gotta skin them—being able to trap them would be nice." Derek frowned. "Of course you're gonna have to collect enough blood to make that circle. Which means—"

Matt held up a hand. He didn't want to know how the kid, even in a game, would gather sufficient blood to encircle a Worgen.

"Nice *game*," Matt said.

"You should see some of the other ones," Tim muttered, earning a dirty look from his son.

Isaac turned up with a shovel and began to scoop Amberleigh into a big black garbage bag. It wasn't easy, considering the goopy texture of what was left.

Though Matt would have preferred to do pretty much anything else—well not *anything;* he didn't ever want to see Gina falling down the steps with a werewolf on her heels, and he could probably live without seeing a skinned Worgen—Matt left Melda on the couch and went to help.

Night fell. The wolves came back. There were a lot more of them now.

"Go to bed." Isaac stood in the doorway of the living room, where Jase, Gina, and Matt stared out at the werewolves that stared in. Isaac had been napping most of the afternoon and appeared as fresh and rested as an eighty-year-old man who'd spent a lifetime in the sun and wind could. He reached for the gun, and Jase handed it over. "No reason more than one of us should have to watch that all night."

"I'll stay," Matt said.

Isaac waved him off. "I've never slept more than four hours at a stretch in my life. Now that I've wasted the afternoon, I'm gonna be wide-eyed until tomorrow."

Matt glanced at Gina and saw that she was as uneasy about this as he was.

"I don't think anyone should be alone," Gina said. "What if the smoke comes?"

"If the smoke comes, girl, there ain't nothin' anyone's gonna be able to do about it."

He was right. Still—

"I'll stay," Jase muttered. "Just—" His gaze flicked first to Gina, then to Matt, and his eyes went cool and hard. "Go."

Matt understood the underlying text. Jase wanted him to go directly outside and walk straight into the jaws of the undeath waiting in the yard.

Right back atcha, pal, Matt thought.

"I'll come down in a few hours and spell you," Matt said, then left the room before anyone could argue.

Jase hadn't slept, and even though Matt didn't want to do the guy any favors, he didn't think an exhausted watchman was any kind of watchman. Matt also agreed that no one should be alone.

Earlier, Gina had coaxed Melda to rest in Fanny's room off the kitchen, which still sported twin beds from when Jase had lived with her there as a child. So the two women would pass the night together.

The Gordons had gone to their room at least an hour ago, though neither one of them had appeared tired. Nevertheless, staring at werewolves got old fast, especially when you were used to them attacking you with a sword.

Matt stopped at Gina's door to say good night, but she surprised him by clasping his hand and drawing him inside.

"I should—" He turned, and she slammed the door, spun the lock.

"Yes." She put her arms around his neck. "You definitely should."

"Gina, I was going to—"

She lifted a brow. "We aren't supposed to be alone, remember?" She pressed her body to his. "Everyone's paired up. You're the only one left to be my—" She leaned closer and licked his earlobe before whispering, "Buddy."

He'd planned to catch a few hours of sleep before going back downstairs—hadn't he just decided that an exhausted watchman was a useless watchman?—but the instant she touched him . . .

Matt was done for.

CHAPTER 25

CHAPTER 23

They needed to sleep—now before someone started to scream.

But Gina also needed Teo. How could she sleep without feeling his arms around her, without experiencing again the slide of his skin against hers?

She drew his mouth slowly downward until their lips brushed together. Just a hint, a wisp of a touch, before she flicked out her tongue and tasted.

His breath caught, the movement rubbing his chest against her breasts. The slight friction made her deepen the kiss welcoming him within.

Somehow her hands had gone beneath his shirt, her thumbs stroking his back, along his hips, and then across his belly, chasing the flutters of muscles beneath skin. She wanted to feel those flutters with her lips, trace them with her tongue.

So she did.

She tugged up his shirt as she slid to the floor, leaving a damp trail across his belly as she went. He got the message, tossing the garment aside, leaving plenty of skin for her to taste.

Her teeth grazed the spike of his hip; she ran her tongue just below his waistband. "Gina," he groaned.

"Shh," she whispered, and licked his tip.

He cursed, reaching down and yanking her up by the elbows, devouring her mouth, her neck, her breasts through the cotton of her shirt. The added friction of the cloth between his mouth and her flesh caused her to arch against him, pressing their lower bodies together.

Once again, any hopes they might have had about going slow disappeared as fast as the rest of their clothes. They fell onto the bed; Gina landed on top, mouth searching, hands seeking.

She grasped him in her palm, squeezing, kneading, running her thumb over and back, over and back, waiting for that catch in his breath, the slight swell against her hand before she guided him inside.

Only a few pumps of her hips and he came, then she did, whispering encouragements and endearments, nonsense that only they understood.

When it was over and their pulses had slowed, their skin had cooled, and they lay tangled together beneath the sheets, Gina took his hand. She'd have been content to fall asleep like that, nearly had, when the howl of a wolf, sharp, loud, and seemingly furious, jerked them awake.

Outside the moon shone down, silver and cool, as remote and uncaring as that wolf.

"Are we going to survive this?" Gina whispered.

Teo pressed his lips to her hair. "I don't know."

She leaned back. "You couldn't lie to me?"

His eyes, stark, honest, unfettered by his glasses, peered steadily into hers. "I won't ever lie to you again."

With that reassurance, along with the warm, solid

length of him, the sure, steady beat of his heart, Gina slept. She hoped she'd never have to sleep without him again.

But when she woke and reached for him the bed was empty, the space where Teo should have been gone cold. For an instant she wondered if everything had been a dream. Not only Teo Mecate but also the cavern, the werewolves, the Nahual, and the string of deaths.

She wasn't sure if she hoped it was or that it wasn't. Because even though Gina would prefer not to have an evil shape-shifting sorcerer roaming the ranch, she also didn't want to discover that the first man she'd ever loved was no more solid than the smoke that had started this mess.

Gina shoved her hair from her face, her feet already swinging to the floor when she remembered.

Teo had promised to take a turn on werewolf watch.

She should feel bad about keeping him up. Although really—her lips curved—he'd been "up" the instant she touched him.

She ran a palm over her hip, shivering at the memory of their lovemaking. Sex had never been a big thing for her. She could have taken it or left it, and most of the time she'd left it. But now . . .

She couldn't get enough. And it wasn't the sex; it was Teo. Being close to him gave her strength. Feeling one with someone else gave her courage. She had to believe they would both survive this, because the alternative was too horrific to contemplate.

A life without Teo Mecate was not a life she wanted to live.

Gina flicked a glance out the window. She was already turning away, preparing to climb back into bed, where the scent of Teo on the pillow would bring back the memory of his touch and the interlude they'd just shared, when what she'd seen registered.

There wasn't a single wolf in the yard.

Her bare skin prickled as gooseflesh raced from head to toe. She snatched up clothes, threw them on, hopped across the floor toward the door shoving her feet into her boots as she went, then flew down the stairs and burst into the living room.

"This is bad," she whispered as her gaze scanned empty space.

Isaac's rifle leaned against the chair he'd been sitting in. Gina checked the weapon. Plenty of ammo left, so she took it along while she searched the house.

The front door was closed; the back door, too. Not that a closed door seemed to do a damn bit of good. But there weren't any bodies lying about. No growls trailed from darkened corners. No rabid wolf with Teo's eyes burst from behind the couch.

But the night was young.

Gina glanced at the eastern horizon. *Make that old.* Though the sky was still navy blue, the clock indicated the sun would soon be up. Had the Nahual really left them alone all night? She didn't think so.

She was just about to check every room in the house—the men had to be somewhere close by—when a long, low howl rose from outside.

Giii-naaa!

At the very edge of the yard, where tamed became untamed, sat a single black wolf. The dying moon sparked off his eyes, making it impossible to tell if the beast was someone she knew, someone she loved. Her fingers tightened on the weapon. What if that was Teo? Could she kill him? She didn't know.

Come to me.

Gina's eyes widened. The wolf hadn't moved, hadn't even opened his mouth. So how had she heard those words?

Maybe she *was* dreaming. In all of the years she'd heard her name on the wind, she'd never heard anything but that.

Come to me now, and I will spare the rest.

Gina glanced over her shoulder, but no one was there. Did she want them to be? No. Because if anyone appeared, they'd talk her out of going. And she had to. If there was any chance to save the rest she would take it. But could she trust that thing?

No.

Did it matter?

Gina sighed. *No.*

Last chance.

The wolf rose to his feet, then disappeared into the scrub. The brush shivered as he moved inexorably onward. If she didn't hurry, the beast would soon be gone.

She couldn't; she shouldn't.

Gina crossed to the front door and did.

She brought the gun. The voice hadn't said she couldn't.

Which only meant the gun would be useless against the thing. But they'd already figured that out.

Bullets couldn't penetrate smoke.

Except the wolf in front of her wasn't smoke. From the way his body cut through the bushes and grass, he was as solid as she was.

So maybe this wolf was just the tour guide wolf. The Nahual was . . .

Gina glanced at the lighter blue sky where the clouds resembled smoke. Was he up there following them? She'd heard no more whispers. Then again, she was doing what he wanted. No reason to say anything else at all.

They moved through an unfamiliar area of the ranch. Several large rock formations were surrounded by low cacti, making it difficult for horses and people to navigate. Gina was tired and hot and scared. When her boot slipped on a rock and she nearly fell, Gina snapped, "Why me?"

The question had been rhetorical. A whiny thing people said. But the wolf whirled, lip lifted in a snarl as he started toward her. Startled, Gina brought up the gun and fired.

She was certain she'd hit the thing; she'd been too close not to. However instead of flames, howls, and death, the wolf snorted and rolled all-too-familiar eyes.

"Oh no," Gina whispered. "No."

The sun burst over the horizon, and the beast changed.

Bones crackled; joints popped; the fur seemed to be sucked within. The snout withdrew, separating into mouth and nose; the fangs became teeth, the claws nails. Several minutes later, Jase McCord rose from four legs to two. The bullet Gina had put into his chest tumbled to the ground.

"Why you?" he repeated. "Because all I've ever wanted is you."

He was naked, and she wasn't even freaked. Of course, watching someone you love turn from wolf to man makes dangling private parts the least of your worries.

"But you . . . it . . . he—" Gina took a breath. "What the hell, Jase? When were you bitten?"

"I wasn't."

"That's impossible."

Jase stretched, the muscles beneath the perfect, bronze skin rippling. They seemed bigger than before, not that she'd spent much time measuring his muscles. She'd never been interested.

"You just shot me with a silver bullet." He nudged it with his toe. Shouldn't he be howling, grabbing his foot, and hopping around as it smoked and burned? "Didn't even leave a mark. Impossible just ain't what it used to be."

He lifted his gaze, and the fury there, the barely contained violence, made Gina step back. Jase had been angry with her—pretty much non-stop since Teo had shown up—but he'd never looked as if he wanted to kill her before.

She turned to run, and he crossed the short distance between them too fast for a mere human to move, then grabbed her arm.

"No," he said softly, but beneath the voice she knew so well rumbled a growl that did not belong. He plucked the rifle from her hand and tossed it over his shoulder with an absent flick of his wrist. The weapon sailed a good hundred yards.

Gina was sorry to see it go, even though it hadn't done her a damn bit of good.

"You shot me." Jase shook her.

Her head snapped back, forward, once, twice; then he let her go to stalk across the ground, seemingly oblivious to the sharp rocks and cacti beneath his bare feet.

"It didn't hurt you," she said. *And why was that?*

"You thought it would kill me." He reached behind one of the six-foot-tall rock formations surrounding them. "Would you have shot him?"

Jase dragged a bound and gagged Mateo Mecate into view.

Matt was disgusted with himself. How had he let this happen?

To be fair, he hadn't *let* Jase tie him up. Matt had come downstairs as he'd promised, and the asshole had conked him on the head. Next thing Matt knew he was staring at stars and wishing he were dead.

But never more so than when he heard Gina's voice. *Why me?*

When McCord yanked him into view, Matt was still trying to piece together why Gina was here, what the gunshot had meant, and why the idiot was naked.

"Teo!" Gina ran to him and pulled the tape from his mouth—fast and sure, the best way, but it hurt. He sucked in a breath, and she murmured, "Sorry," as her hands searched for his bonds.

"Ah-ah-ah." McCord yanked her to her feet. "He stays like that."

She struggled. "Why bother? If a damn bullet didn't hurt you, he can't."

"A bullet didn't hurt him?" Matt pushed against the ground with his bound hands, managing to sit up, though he nearly wrenched his shoulder from its socket in the process.

"Silver right through the heart," she said, disgusted. "Not a mark on him."

"You shot McCord?" Matt asked. "Why? Not that I don't want to, but . . . he's your friend."

"That thing is not my friend." Her lip curled.

Strangely, McCord didn't seem bothered by her disgust. Another piece of information that made Matt very nervous. What did *he* know that they didn't?

It suddenly dawned on Matt why McCord was naked. In Matt's defense, he *had* been hit in the head. "He's a werewolf?"

"Yep."

"And you shot him, but nothing happened."

"I think you're right, Gina." McCord's lips curved. "Moldy isn't so moldy after all."

"You're the Nahual," Matt said.

Gina glanced back and forth between the two men. "That's impossible."

"You really need to stop saying that," Jase murmured, his gaze on Matt.

"The Nahual is smoke," Gina said, but her voice shook. She was starting to put the pieces together.

"Which gains strength and power from death," Matt continued. "From sacrifice. I figured he just became stronger, physically, mentally, magically. But it seems like he becomes more . . ." Matt searched for a word and settled on "solid."

"Less smoke," McCord said. "More me."

"That's not you," Gina snapped. "I mean you're not him."

McCord turned toward Gina so fast, Matt forgot he was bound, tried to get between them, and wound up tipping over and cracking his already-cracked head against the ground. He lay there in the dirt and the rocks, with a cactus poking his ass, and watched as McCord, who was not McCord, grabbed Gina by the collar of her shirt and pulled her close.

"When we were twelve," he said conversationally, "you convinced me to try your father's whiskey. We puked all night, swore to our parents we had the flu, refused to stray from the lie, and got away with it."

Gina paled. "I never told anyone that."

"Neither did I." He lifted a brow. "Still don't believe? When we were seventeen, my favorite horse died and you found me crying my heart out in its stall. You swore you'd never tell anyone."

"I didn't."

"You think I would?" He let her go. "Cowboys don't cry. Not even over a horse."

Gina had been leaning so hard in the opposite direction, she nearly fell. "Y-you. I mean h-he. J-Jase must have told." Her forehead creased. "You."

"I am Jase; Jase is me."

She spun toward Matt as he again gained his seat. "It's a shape-shifter. So it only looks like Jase, right?"

"I don't know, Gina. I'm sorry."

"Aw." McCord made an exaggerated sad face. "Too bad Moldy's not good for anything but the occasional fuck after all."

"Shut up," Gina said.

"If I'm not Jase, then how do I know all that I know?"

"You forced him to tell you. You hurt him." Her gaze flicked around the open area desperately. "Where *is* he?"

"He's me." McCord put his hand on his chest. "And soon there'll be no going back. He made a willing sacrifice." McCord's wide chest seemed to expand even more as he breathed in. "So much more power is gained from the giving of a life instead of the taking. My people knew that."

"The Ute did not practice sacrifice," Gina muttered, jaw tight.

"*My* people, not his."

The way McCord spoke of himself as if he were someone else, from a body that resembled his, using a voice that sounded like his yet wasn't, gave Matt the willies. Gina appeared ready to snap.

"The Aztecs could have cared less if their sacrifices were willing," Matt said. "In fact, they preferred they weren't, since that meant they were enemies, and the less of them the better."

"You know a lot, Doctor, but do you know this? Each year we chose one boy for a great honor. For twelve cycles of the moon, he impersonated the great god Tezcatlipoca, ruler of the night sky. He was given servants to attend his every wish, gifted with the best clothes and food. He was married to four virgins the month before he freely gave his life to the god of night so that Tezcatlipoca would allow the sun to take his place each day. Because that sacrifice was willing, Tezcatlipoca always agreed."

Gina glanced at Matt, who nodded. "He's right about the boy and the ritual. But the god of night didn't really allow the sun to rise because of a sacrifice."

"No?" McCord murmured. "Prove it."

Matt opened his mouth to argue, and Gina jumped in. "It doesn't matter. Jase would never have known any of that. That thing would never have known about the whiskey. Or his tears."

It was looking more and more like the Nahual not only was a shape-shifter but also could take over a consenting body. Edward *had* said a sorcerer could do most anything.

"Why would he let you in?" Gina whispered.

She was beginning to refer to the being in front of them as something other than McCord. Matt wasn't sure if that was good or bad.

"It was all thanks to you."

"Me?" Gina echoed.

"When he kissed you and you told him you'd never love him that way, he escaped into the night and there I was."

"All he ever wanted was me," she whispered.

The thing that was now Jase McCord smiled. "So I promised him just that."

CHAPTER 24

A sudden chill made Gina wrap her arms around herself and hold on. "You can't have me any more than he could."

"We'll see about that," the Nahual murmured, gaze on Teo.

Gina didn't like what she saw in that gaze at all.

"You think I'll let you touch me? You've been buried in the ground for centuries. You were bones, dust, smoke. You aren't really alive now. You're a parasite. You're living off his body."

Jase's shoulders shrugged. "Doesn't matter. I've *got* a body now, thanks to you."

"Stop saying that!"

The Nahual laughed, and the chill deepened. That wasn't Jase's laugh anymore. It was the laughter she'd heard on the wind, in the trees, and echoing through the mountains for nearly half her life.

"You're right," he said. "*Alive* isn't the right word, since I'll never die. But without sacrifice, without blood, I lose form."

"He becomes smoke," Teo murmured.

"Only death can bring me back."

"Which is why the werewolves watched but didn't kill us," Teo continued. "Until he'd gained form, stolen a body, recovered his magic," Teo kept his gaze on the monster that inhabited Jase's skin, "he needed all the murder juice he could get."

"Like I said, Moldy's not so moldy," the Nahual repeated. "The more willing the death, the more *murder juice* I get." He switched his attention to Gina. "How do you think I had enough *oomph* to call your name all these years?"

Gina swallowed thickly. "You killed my parents."

"I was confined. I was smoke," he mocked. "I didn't even have a body."

"That didn't stop you from killing Mel and Ashleigh."

"It didn't, did it?"

He was maddening. "What did you do to my family?"

"I gave them a choice."

Gina's chill increased along with her understanding. "Me or them."

"A sacrifice freely given." He breathed in and out again. "It was wonderful."

"And all the other deaths that happened on that land?"

"Guilty." He spread his hands. "I needed some form of sustenance."

"I didn't think you could die."

"There's death and there's a strange realm in between. I went there sometimes. Years, decades, maybe a century would pass. But eventually, someone always wandered near my tomb and died."

"Why did you call me?" Gina asked.

"Why not?" The Nahual shrugged. "Your parents

gave up their lives for you. Both of them without the slightest hesitation. I was curious. Then, when you came at last, you released me, and I knew I had been right to call. Once I inhabited this body, I understood how I could get everything that I wanted."

He tapped Jase's finger against Jase's temple. "There's all sorts of great information in here. Took me a while to understand—the phones, the satellites, computers, the technology—but now I see . . . I'll have no trouble gaining the trust of thousands, turning them into my army, then taking over the world."

"What are you going to do with the world?"

"Whatever I want."

Gina rubbed her forehead. "Fine. Whatever." She couldn't be bothered with saving the world right now. Let Edward deal with it if he ever showed up. Right now she had to save Teo and the others. That was the only reason she'd come out here.

"You said you'd spare them if I came with you."

"Them," the Nahual agreed. "Not him."

Gina didn't like the sound of that, but then she hadn't liked the sound of much in years.

"Which him are you talking about?"

The grin was back, less like Jase than ever before. "You choose."

Gina was starting to get a very bad feeling. "No. Uh-uh."

The Nahual ignored her protests as if she hadn't even made them. "Willing sacrifice gives me strength."

"Got that."

"I want to rule the world."

"Heard you the first time."

"With you."

"Huh?" Gina gasped.

"He's me; I'm him." The Nahual rubbed his bare chest. "He wants you. I want the world. If I make you like me, I'll be your maker. You'll never leave me. Him. Us."

"No, thanks."

"Come to me freely and your lover lives."

Gina shot a glance at Teo. "No, Gina," he said. "Don't."

She yanked her gaze back to the Nahual. "Where does the choice come in?"

He tilted his head, the movement more like a dog than a human, and she saw again those beloved eyes in a vicious lupine face. Would she ever be able to look at that without feeling ill?

Maybe. If her own eyes were set in an equally furry face.

"You become like me," the Nahual explained, "and lover boy lives. Best buddy . . ." He stroked his own chest again. *Ick.* "And I become one forever. No going back. To separate us would kill him."

"What if I choose best buddy? You gonna let Jase go?"

The Nahual shrugged. "Sure. There's another body right here, and I'm certain he'll be happy to accommodate me to save you."

"Great idea," Teo piped up. "All for it."

"Shut up, Teo," Gina said.

He didn't. "I'm a better choice. You think there's a lot of info in that head, you oughta see mine."

"No." Gina kept her gaze on the Nahual's face. "He isn't going to let me or Jase go just because he takes you."

The monster's lips curved. "You know me too well."

"I'm starting to. Even if he jumps ship," Gina waved

between Jase and Matt, "he'll still need me, or someone else, to sacrifice themselves so he can bond, or
whatever the hell he needs to do, with a body."

The Nahual spread Jase's hands. "You got me."

"The sacrifice has to be willing, Gina. Don't be."

"If you won't give willingly," the Nahual said, "I'll
just take. You'll still grow a tail beneath the moon forever. Then I'll mow through everyone at the house
until I find someone who'll give in. I'm sure the kid, or
maybe his dad, even the woman who birthed this body
would be happy to give his or her life for someone they
love."

Derek. Tim. Fanny. Isaac. Melda. People Gina loved
and people who trusted and depended on her. She
couldn't let them die and/or become a werewolf because she didn't have the guts to give in.

However . . .

Gina glanced at the sky where the sun blazed only
halfway up the eastern horizon. There was still a good
long time until dusk. Maybe Edward would arrive, find
them, free Jase, then kill that thing and they'd all live
happily ever after.

Hey, it could happen. There were werewolves running around, and an Aztec sorcerer had possessed her
best friend. In Gina's opinion, reality was up for grabs.

"I need to think," Gina murmured.

"And here I figured that the instant I threatened
lover boy you'd be signing right up."

"You can't turn me until nightfall anyway. What's
the rush?"

The Nahual lifted Jase's face to the sun. "I crave the
moon," he agreed. "Only beneath it can I increase my
army."

"Bummer for you," Teo said. "You'd think an

unkillable sorcerer would have more control over the environment."

"But I do," the Nahual whispered.

His gaze swept the ground; then he snatched up a sharp-edged rock and grabbed Gina's arm.

"Hey!" She tried to pull away, but he slashed her palm, then clapped his own to the blood that flowed.

When he released her, she held her stinging hand to her chest. However, the wound was the least of her worries as the Nahual smeared her blood over his palms, then lifted them in glistening supplication to the heavens.

He shouted in gibberish as the earth began to shake. The sun dimmed, swirled, then shifted from yellow to white.

Gina glanced at Teo. "Nice one," she said.

And the cerulean sky went black.

Gina recalled the man-wolf figure on the wall of the cavern lifting its arms to a sky that contained two circles—one gold, one silver—and understood.

The bastard could bring the moon.

Okay, new plan. The Nahual was going to make her a werewolf, and there was nothing she could do about it but agree.

Fine. To save Teo she would do anything. Maybe once she was one of them she could figure out how to end the creature. She didn't believe there wasn't a way. The world didn't work like that. Nothing was unkillable. Everything died eventually. Besides, what choice did she have?

Gina peered at the moon. Right now? Absolutely none.

"No." Teo attempted to get to his feet, but they were bound as tightly as his hands. One shove of the Nahual's bare heel against his chest and Teo landed on his rump, then banged his head against the ground as the momentum carried him backward.

"Untie him," Gina ordered, and when the Nahual hesitated, she snapped, "You said you'd spare him, so untie him, and let him go."

"And if I don't?"

"As soon as I'm furry, I'll kick your ass."

Jase laughed the Nahual's horrible laugh. "You can try," he said, but he untied Teo.

Teo lunged, and the sorcerer backhanded him. One quick flick of the wrist that didn't even appear to have much heat behind it and Teo was lifted off his feet, then thrown into a rock. His head cracked against the stone, and he landed in a heap at the base.

Gina cried out, starting toward him. The Nahual stepped in her way. "Time's up. I brought the moon, but I can't hold it there forever."

"You said you wouldn't hurt him." Gina tried to scoot around.

The Nahual grabbed her elbow. "I said I wouldn't *kill* him." His eyes began to glow. "I never said anything about you."

"Wh-what?"

"The first thing you'll need to do after you change is . . ." His smile was terrible, all teeth becoming fangs, changing a face she knew and loved into something almost unrecognizable. "Kill."

"I won't," she insisted. "Not him."

Now the Nahual really laughed. "You think you'll care? He's meat. Running meat if he wakes up." The brow that had begun to recede creased. "I probably shouldn't have knocked him out. It's better when they run."

"I love him," Gina said. She'd meant for the words to come out strong and sure; instead her voice wavered.

"Love means nothing to a monster."

The thing that lived in Jase's body threw back his head and howled.

"Teo!" Gina screamed. "Wake up!"

The Nahual released her. Kind of hard to hold on to someone's arm when your hands are paws.

He dropped to the ground on all fours as dark hair sprouted from every pore. Fingers and toes became claws; his nose and mouth melded into snout. The crinkling and crackling, the popping of bones sharp as firecrackers in the still, silver air.

Gina was unable to do anything but watch. Why run? This beast would catch her, and she wasn't going to leave Teo alone and unconscious.

No matter what the Nahual said, she had to hold on to the belief that her love would survive the coming change. That belief, that love, might be all she had left of herself.

Man had nearly become beast, except for the tail, which unfurled last, like a treacherous snake from the glistening black wolf that had once resembled Jase McCord.

Gina shrieked as the creature's fangs sank into her thigh. It shouldn't hurt that much. She'd been bitten by horses. They had a helluva lot bigger teeth. However, the werewolf's seemed red-poker hot; she imagined poison rushing through her veins already.

He withdrew, resting on his haunches to watch, mouth open, tongue lolling, as if grinning. Gina wanted to kick the beast in the head, but she couldn't lift a finger, let alone her leg. Everything was so heavy.

She fell to the ground like a sack of bones. The sky

above was a kaleidoscope of stars, so much brighter than they should be. The moon called; she craved its sheen. The silvery light soothed her burning skin.

Her teeth itched. She managed to drag her hand up to touch them. They were definitely longer, sharper; as she lowered her arm, she caught sight of her nails. They were longer and sharper, too.

Suddenly this world disappeared, and she was running through a forest of trees not common anywhere near here, thick and cool, with a carpet of moss beneath her paws. She chased something big and tasty, something that smelled like . . .

Ted.

Gina jerked free of the . . . What the hell had that been?

A delusion? A hallucination? Perhaps a fever dream? Because right now her skin was so on fire she thought she might explode.

It had certainly *not* been a memory. No matter how much it might have felt like one.

And who the hell was Ted?

Her senses heightened. She heard the dirt sifting beneath her as she moved, smelled her own blood on the breath of the Nahual that continued to watch, eyes so bright they hurt her head.

Gina looked away and became distracted by hair the shade of mahogany, which had sprouted all the way up her arm.

Slam.

She left her body again. This time she flew across familiar terrain, past the crooked tree and the place where her parents had died. Ahead two blond girls giggled and sang as they walked toward a tent.

Her body was a wolf's, yet she was smoke. She

called out, a howl of triumph and hunger, then swooped low and carried one of the girls off. The shrieks of the other were music to Gina's invisible ears.

And the blood. The texture, the scent, the *flavor*—glorious. It had been so damn long.

The smoke that was also a wolf lifted his head and howled to the moon, the sound echoing across the plain. He was weak; he needed sustenance to fuel both his body and his magic. The creature swirled lower, gaze touching on a boy, an old woman, an old man.

Duck. Duck. Goose.

Gina crashed into her own body once more, the memories of the Nahual when he had taken first Ashleigh and then Mel alight, and very real, in her mind.

Her spine arched, bones reshaping, realigning. She didn't fight; instead she gave in to the change. She welcomed it; she'd begun to crave it as she craved the moon. Those thoughts that had been like memories had brought an understanding of what the Nahual had meant.

Monsters don't love; they lust—for the kill, the blood, and that blessed, silver moon. Beneath it they became something nearly indestructible. Once Gina was a wolf very little could hurt her. If someone tried to take away her ranch, she'd eat them.

Problem solved.

She sniffed at the air, recognized the scent—oranges and sunlight—and her stomach contracted with need. There was still enough of her left to fight that need, but that part was shrinking fast. Once she was a wolf, all she would care about was the blood.

"Gina?"

Gina lifted her head. Her eyes met Teo's, and the

voice that came from her moving, changing mouth hovered between woman and wolf.

"Run."

The Nahual made a hacking, snorting, wheezing noise that sounded like laughter—or as close to laughter as a wolf could get. Matt didn't wait around to see what was so funny; he already knew. The Nahual was riding Mc-Cord's brain, and Matt had no doubt McCord would find it hysterical when Gina killed him.

He wasn't going to get away. A human couldn't out-run a regular wolf, let alone a werewolf, and Matt wasn't at his best. His head felt like it might crack open and spill agony down the front of his face.

But Matt ran anyway. He couldn't help himself.

The moon shone like a beacon, lighting his way, re-vealing the dips and rolls of the rocky ground. He began to duck behind one rock, then scoot to another. Staying out of sight might keep him alive a few seconds longer, though he was certain Gina could follow his scent with-out too much trouble.

He had little memory of how he'd gotten here, which meant he had no idea how to get back to the ranch. Not that he'd ever make it that far.

No, he was stuck here to face—

A triumphant howl lifted to the moon.

Her.

Would Gina remember him if he spoke of his love? Of hers? He doubted it. When she'd lifted her face, when she'd told him to run, that had been the last bit of Gina left.

A low, rumbling growl rippled across the night, bringing to mind a stalking lion instead of a wolf. The click of claws against half-buried rocks announced her arrival an instant before a shaggy reddish-brown head appeared around the edge of the stone formation to Matt's left.

"Gina," he began, but further words stuck in his throat. He couldn't speak of love when her eyes followed him as if he were a choice piece of steak.

Her mouth open in a canine grin, she stalked him. As a cloud danced over the moon, throwing that horrible human Gina gaze into shadow, she reminded him of a dog ready to play fetch a bone.

Then the cloud went away, and that gaze very clearly said the bone was him.

Matt had planned to face his death like a big boy, stare Gina straight in the eye; maybe that would reach her. But while the eyes were hers, the being behind them was not, and so he decided . . .

There was something to be said for turning away.

He spun around just as a tall, dark figure stepped from behind the nearest rock. Matt was so dumbfounded, he just stood there, staring into the barrel of a gun.

CHAPTER 25

"Get down!"

Considering the gun in Matt's face, that sounded like a good idea. But as he hit the deck he realized what the newcomer intended, and Matt's arm shot up, smacking the barrel of the rifle skyward before it could blow off Gina's head.

"*Dummer Arsch*," the man muttered, in a voice Matt recognized. "What have you done?"

Matt glanced over his shoulder in time to see Gina's tail disappear into the gloom. "You can't kill her!"

"I assure you, my boy, that I can." Edward Mandenauer stepped over Matt and went in pursuit.

Matt scrambled to his feet and followed. He caught up just in time to see Mandenauer take aim again, but Matt was too far away to stop him.

The gun went off. No yelp. No flames. But the silvery light of the moon began to turn gold, and the sky went from midnight to dawn.

"Did you see that?" Mandenauer murmured. "I shot that *Arschloch* right between the eyes, and it turned to smoke and disappeared. I *hate* it when that happens."

"That happens to you a lot?"

"You have no idea." Mandenauer peered at the moon, which now seemed a lot like the sun.

His hair had once been blond but had faded nearly to white. His blue eyes had faded, too, though their expression remained sharp. Edward was tall and achingly thin, but he didn't stoop and he must still be fairly strong to be able to cart around the load of guns and ammo positioned at various points on his body.

Mandenauer turned his gaze to Matt. "Mecate?"

Matt nodded. "How did you find me?"

"Your cell phone."

"Doesn't work."

"I discovered that when I tried to call. However, I was still able to track it by satellite."

That seemed beyond the capabilities of NASA, let alone an ancient German man who liked guns. But Edward was here. How else could the man have found him?

"What went on here?"

"The *Arschloch* . . ." Matt paused. "What does that mean?" Matt was thinking maybe "brave one" or "strong beast," even "wolf-man."

"Asshole." Mandenauer sniffed.

Matt decided not to ask what *Dummer Arsch* meant. He could figure it out.

"The Nahual brought the moon," Matt said.

"Interesting. You will tell me exactly how later. Now, we should move on."

"I'm not leaving Gina behind."

"The owner?" Edward peered around. "Where have you hidden her?"

"In a wolf suit," Matt muttered.

"Ah." The old man nodded. "That explains your misbehavior with the gun. But she has become a demon werewolf. There is nothing you can do."

Panic fluttered in Matt's chest, nearly choking him. "You said there was a cure."

"I did. However, it is nothing *you* can do. I have sent for my granddaughter. Unfortunately, she is busy elsewhere at the moment. She will arrive as soon as she can. Let us hope that in the meantime your Gina does not force me to put a silver bullet through her brain."

"I doubt anyone could force you to do anything you didn't want to do."

"If I again discover her inches from killing you, I will very much *want* to do it." Mandenauer stared out over the now-sunny terrain. "Gina is no longer Gina but werewolf. The virus strangles her humanity; the demon burns within. She will kill. She will not be able to help herself. Even now—" He waved a battered, emaciated hand in the direction she had disappeared. "She is stalking her first victim."

"She wouldn't—"

"She *has* to. The bloodlust is maddening. All that pounds in her lupine brain is hunger. Until she satisfies it with a kill, she exists for nothing else."

Matt rubbed his face. "She did it for me."

Mandenauer set a hand on Matt's shoulder. "Tell me everything."

The wolf that had once been Gina O'Neil followed the men. She made certain not to let them know it.

The tall one with the long stick that smelled like death and fire was dangerous. He would have killed her if the other one—

She tilted her head. There was something about the other one that made her more uneasy than the dangerous man with the silver-filled weapons. She'd wanted to kill him, needed to with a desperation that had left little room for anything else. Yet still she'd hesitated and nearly lost her life. That maddening scent of fruit and warmth and her—

Gina growled. She didn't like it that he smelled of her. It was confusing.

The slowly spreading madness hadn't yet obliterated all sense. She understood that the other one had saved her life. What she didn't understand was why.

Hunger roared in both belly and brain, the pulse red-hot, excruciating. If she didn't appease it, she would split in two from the pain. Or maybe it was the being split in two—woman and wolf—that was causing the pain in the first place.

Along with the hunger and the flashes of memories that were not hers alone came knowledge—bite and make others like you, devour, and kill.

Giii-naaa!

On the horizon stood a man, naked, bronzed, and gleaming in the newly born sun. Her maker. He had gifted her with a whole new world. One where she was stronger, faster, better. She would never again think herself less than. From now on she would always be more.

Gina loped in his direction. In moments she stood on the hill at his side. He laid one hand on her head, then lifted the other to point back in the direction she'd come. In the distance two familiar figures trudged across the land.

"Take your pick," he said in a voice that no longer held even a hint of Jase McCord.

* * *

"Let us talk as we walk," Mandenauer said.

"Walk where?" Matt asked, though they were already doing just that.

"You must show me the cavern that contained this beast."

"Why?"

"We will get to that when we get there."

"It's pretty far," Matt said. If he was right about where they were and where they had to go, it might take days. Considering there was now a pack of werewolves out there . . . "We should probably head to the ranch and—"

"No need." Mandenauer pointed to the horizon.

Matt squinted. "Is that a car?"

"How do you think I got here?"

Matt hadn't thought. He'd had a few other items on his mind.

"We won't be able to make it all the way to the site in that."

The old man shrugged. "We can get much closer."

They reached the vehicle, a boxy old Mercedes. An SUV, a Hummer, perhaps a tank, would have been better, but wheels were wheels. Once inside, Matt gave Mandenauer directions and sat back. Matt could use a nap, but before he could even take a breath, Edward spoke.

"Tell me what happened since our last conversation."

It took a lot longer than Matt would have thought. By the time he finished, they'd reached the end of the road. Literally.

"Does wolfsbane keep werewolves out?" Matt asked.

"Sometimes." Mandenauer's bony fingers turned off

the motor. "Depends on the werewolf. Once the Nahual inhabited Jase McCord, I doubt wolfsbane would
have bothered him at all. Possession is strange. The
two become one, yet still there are two. The wolfsbane
might only affect the Nahual in wolf form, or perhaps
not affect it at all. Or the creature's magic may have
been stronger than the magic of the charm."

"Sorcerers are a pain in the ass," Matt muttered.

"I should put that on a bumper sticker." Mandenauer
got out of the car. He began to sling rifles and bullet
bandoliers over his skinny shoulders before shoving a
few pistols into his belt.

"You want me to help with that?" Matt asked.

The old man stopped just long enough to hand Matt
one of the pistols before he started walking. Matt let
out a surprised snort-cough and followed, shaking his
head.

Matt kept a wary eye on every bush, tree, and crevice.
If Gina came charging out, fangs bared, Mandenauer
would kill her. Matt needed to be prepared to—

What? Throw himself in front of a silver bullet?

In a word—yes. He was not going to let Gina die if
there was any chance of putting her back the way she'd
been. If it meant *he* had to die or even become like her,
Matt would. He could perform sacrifice as well as the
next Aztec.

The tree of life inched slowly out of the horizon.
Matt glanced at Mandenauer, but he seemed to be doing fine despite the weight of the guns and ammo.
Were Matt to analyze who was breathing harder, he'd
have to say *he* was. If the old guy wasn't careful, someone might shoot *him* with silver one day just to see if he
died.

Matt expected Mandenauer to return the favor and

tell Matt all that he knew, but he didn't. Finally, Matt couldn't wait any longer. "Did you find a way to kill the Nahual?"

"No."

"But—" Matt stopped walking as sick, slick dread washed over him. "There has to be a way to end that thing."

"If there was," Mandenauer didn't stop, and Matt had to hurry to catch up so he didn't miss a word of what the old man said, "then why did the Ute confine him?"

"What do you plan to do?"

Mandenauer didn't answer and the sick, slick dread deepened.

"I won't let you hurt her," Matt said quietly.

"It may come down to her or you."

"I choose her."

Mandenauer peered down his nose. "You do not get to choose."

"She can be cured," Matt insisted. "You said so yourself."

The old man stared straight ahead. "Sometimes those we cure run mad. There have been days where I wonder if it would not be better to put them out of their misery like the rabid dogs I often tell witnesses that they are."

"No," Matt said. "Just . . . no."

The old man shrugged, not an agreement but probably the best Matt was going to get from him.

"If the Nahual can't be killed, then what's your plan?"

"As I told you on the phone, we will simply confine the creature again."

"And as I told you, everyone alive when the deed

was done is dead, and no one bothered to leave an instruction booklet. We're screwed."

"Not any longer. I spoke with the man who confined him."

"Are you high?" Matt asked. "The guy's dust."

"So was the Nahual once."

Matt's eyes narrowed. "What did you do?"

"Raised the dead."

Matt laughed. Mandenauer did not.

"I—uh—how?"

"Voodoo can be very useful in my line of work."

"You practice voodoo?"

"My boy, I'd dance the hoochie-coochie on the Empire State Building if it got me what I wanted."

"How in hell did you learn voodoo?"

"I have a priestess on staff."

Matt stifled a repeated urge to laugh.

"Okay," he allowed. He'd really like to know more, but . . . Matt peered ahead. Their destination loomed a few hundred yards away. "What did the shaman tell you?"

"Words have power," Mandenauer said. "What occurs in a being's life is what makes them who they are."

Matt thought about the wall that had told the Nahual's story, or at least what the Ute who had created it had known of the story, and understood why those glyphs were there.

"He also said sacrifice was needed to . . ." Mandenauer's thin lips pursed. "Set the spell."

"What kind of sacrifice?"

"Blood."

That figured.

"What do we do?"

"This incarnation of that ancient being has a new

tale. To confine the creature, we write *that* tale on his tomb."

"And then the Nahual just strolls in and holds still while we bury him?"

Mandenauer shot Matt a glance that reminded him very much of his mother when he'd annoyed her. "Hardly."

"Then how do we get him in there?"

"You let me worry about that."

Not long afterward, Matt rappelled into the cavern. He reached the bottom and waited, expecting Mandenauer to follow. Instead, the old man waved him off. "I will stay here and keep watch."

"It's daytime."

"For Gina," Mandenauer said, "that does not matter. Until she has killed, she will remain in wolf form."

"You think she'll come after us again?"

"I know she will."

"Do *not* kill her," Matt reminded him.

"Make sure I do not have to. The sooner you are finished, the better off we all will be."

Matt moved past the glyph-covered wall, past the stone doorway, and around the corner, where he started on a fresh canvas, so to speak.

With the paints and brushes he'd discovered in the knapsack Mandenauer had handed him—one Matt had thought held clips, ammo, maybe a few grenades—he worked fast. Matt wasn't an artist, and he didn't care how the glyphs looked. All he cared was that they were legible enough to hold meaning. That appeared to be the key.

He drew the man-wolf figure, adding the *la* glyph as the Ute had before. The ingeniousness of that little quirk in meaning added a kind of "lock" to the spell that only blind, dumb luck had managed to "unlock."

Matt sketched a woman standing before a scribbled-upon wall, black smoke whooshing out an open doorway, and the magic dogs—because he liked them. In the distance he drew the ranch, surrounded by wolves. Stepping back, he examined his handiwork. Something was missing.

Matt picked up the lantern he and Gina had left behind, then crossed the short space until he stood in front of the original panorama. He immediately saw the difference between this wall and the new one. A thin, wobbly line encircled the entire tableau.

"Words have power," he murmured. "What occurs in a being's life is what makes them who they are. Willing sacrifice is the ultimate power." Then he thought of Derek's game, the spell that could imprison a Worgen. It had seemed silly then—really violent and kind of disgusting—but silly. Now . . . ?

Matt traced a finger along the reddish-brown line and knew without a doubt how the Aztecs had "set" the spell and confined the Nahual.

He headed for the opening. But as he approached he heard a whoosh, a howl, a thud.

Then nothing.

CHAPTER 26

Gray light filtered through the opening. When had the sun gone down?

Matt hurried back in the direction he'd come. Even if Mandenauer was still alive, they had no time left for discussion. Matt would have to move forward with his theory without confirmation. Right now, he didn't have much choice.

Setting the lantern down, Matt tore through the knapsack. But where the old man kept every type of weaponry on his person, in his knapsack not so much. The sharpest thing Matt found was the broken end of a paintbrush. How had Mandenauer planned on making a blood sacrifice with nothing but that?

Matt scanned the ground. Snatching up a likely rock, he dragged the jagged edge across his arm. Blood welled; he dabbed a finger, then began to paint.

"Not enough," he muttered. He was going to need a bigger hole.

A soft thud, followed by the pitter-patter of wolf feet, had him grasping at the first idea that flitted through his head. Matt ducked behind the stone door, then pulled it as close to his body as he could. He was trapped in the small space, but at least the Nahual couldn't rip out his throat.

A snarl erupted, and something slammed into the door on the other side, driving the stone into Matt's chest and his chest seemingly through his shoulder blades and into the wall at his back.

Matt fought for breath as he gathered his thoughts. He needed blood—a lot of it and fast. He didn't have a knife, but he did have fangs. Or at least the Nahual did. According to Mandenauer there was a cure for lycanthropy. He'd take the man up on it.

If they survived.

Before he could think any more about it, Matt offered his leg, and an instant later the creature's teeth sank into his calf.

Matt cried out, his fingers clenching around the edge of the door. The Nahual tore free a bite-sized chunk of flesh and blood sprayed. Matt yanked his leg back where it belonged.

Then he saw the gap in his plan that loomed as large as the one in his calf. How was he going to paint a circle around the tableau if he was holding on to the door to keep the Nahual from latching onto his throat?

"I never said it was a foolproof plan," Matt murmured.

Burning pain shot through his veins. His vision flickered. For an instant he was somewhere else, running across the range, chasing a herd of—

Bam. Matt was back in his body, still clinging to the door as the Nahual paced and snarled on the other side.

Had those been teenagers?

Matt shook his head. "I never chased any kids. I never ran on four paws."

Yet.

"Mandenauer!" Matt shouted.

He hadn't heard any shots or any screams. Just a thud. Maybe the old man had merely dropped his gun.

As if that would ever happen.

Another muffled thump in the distance had Matt's spirits lifting. The old man wasn't dead. He was—

A second snarl reverberated down the stone hall. Matt risked a peek just as the reddish-brown wolf with Gina's eyes emerged from the gloom.

Gina smelled blood and she wanted it, needed it, craved it like she craved the moon. She was half-mad with the pulse of hunger. When she caught the scent of the man who smelled like oranges what was left of Gina's control snapped.

How dare anyone take what was hers?

She charged, crashing into her maker, who stood between her and the kill. She relished the battle. The crunch of bodies, the snap of teeth, the rip of flesh, then the splatter of blood against the dirt like rain. Fighting kept her from remembering the siren call of insanity, which made her want to howl at the moon, scrape at the ground, and whine until the voices shrieking in her head went away. They were loud, those voices, and they hurt her ears, even as the agonizing hunger pierced her stomach with razor-sharp claws.

Beneath those screams something whispered that she couldn't kill her maker—literally—that this was foolish, suicidal, wrong. But the hunger, the smell of oranges and blood, and that flicker of memory—a man's laughter, his kiss, his touch, the way he made her feel. Every time she thought she knew who she was, another memory would surface and confuse her, increasing the lure of that madness.

However, violence, blood, pain—they grounded her in this body, solidifying her as the wolf she knew herself to be. Her maker would never die? Fine with her. That only meant she could hurt him again and again and again. He was the perfect toy.

She didn't even notice when her prey stopped hiding and began to move.

This was his chance.

Matt let go of the door, swiped his fingers through the bleeding mess that was his leg, and got back to work. It was the race of a lifetime.

Would he finish the job before one of the werewolves won the battle over who got to kill him?

Would he complete the circle of blood around the drawings before he passed out?

Or would he become a werewolf first and have no fingers for painting, let alone enough humanity left to care?

Would what he was doing even work?

It didn't matter, because this was all that he had.

Matt's hand trembled. Precious droplets of blood ran down his arm, fell to the floor. But there was more pouring from his leg—so much that the dirt beneath his feet had gone dark and muddy.

"Shouldn't have made the damn vista so big," he muttered.

His teeth were beginning to chatter or perhaps just to change. They seemed too big for his mouth. They kept clacking together, distracting him.

Snarls, growls, the rending of flesh, the thud of bodies, continued behind him. Matt ignored it all. It was when the sounds stopped that he needed to worry.

Then, suddenly, they did.

Matt risked a glance. Gina lay on the ground, broken, bleeding, breathing, but barely. He had to force himself not to run to her. There was nothing he could do, and she wouldn't know him anyway.

A rumble trilled across the damp air. Matt lifted his gaze from Gina's inert form to the Nahual's eyes. They were still Jase McCord's eyes, and they hated Matt.

The creature stalked forward, tongue lolling, fangs dripping. He made sure Matt had time to see his coming bloody, painful death—and to be afraid.

Instead, Matt brushed his fingers over his leg one last time and sealed the circle.

The sleek black wolf's ruff lifted. He turned his head, tilted it in confusion; then, an instant too late, he knew.

A single yelp escaped, and then an unseen force drew him backward, claws digging into the dirt, making furrows all the way into the crypt. The door slammed shut, cutting off his desperate howl. The silence that followed was both eerie and welcome. Then a low growl rumbled through the gloom as Gina rolled to her feet, ravenous eyes fixed on Matt.

Matt didn't move. He had nowhere to go, even if he could take a step without falling. However, she lifted her nose, sniffed once, snarled, and turned away.

He was like her now, or near enough, and she needed human blood.

Gina had taken a single step toward the opening when a figure staggered from the shadows.

She leaped; a gun fired. She fell.

Matt lifted his gaze to Edward Mandenauer, and the old man shot him, too.

CHAPTER 27

Gina awoke in her own bed. She hurt all over, especially her head. When she tried to remember what had happened, the headache bloomed toward migraine.

"Shit," she muttered, and pulled the covers over her face.

However, with the darkness came flickering images of blood and death and mayhem. They scared her so much she yanked the covers back down.

A gorgeous blond woman stood at the foot of Gina's bed.

"You remember me?" the woman asked.

"Dr. Hanover."

"Elise."

"What kind of doctor are you?" Some kind of "olo-gist," but Gina didn't think it was *psych*ologist. Which, considering what was in her head, was the only kind of doctor she needed.

"Virologist." Elise sat on the side of the bed. She didn't appear afraid that Gina might grow fangs and tear out her throat.

Maybe those thoughts, which had seemed like memories, were only dreams after all.

"I cured you," Elise continued.

"Of what?"

"Lycanthropy."

Or not.

Gina sighed and closed her eyes.

"Don't worry," Elise continued. "Moon comes up, you'll still be you. I promise. How are you feeling?"

Gina's eyes snapped open. "How do you think I'm feeling? My best friend is . . ." She paused. "*What* is he?"

Dead? Trapped?

Screaming?

"Gone," Elise said. "He was gone the instant he agreed to let the Nahual in."

"How did I get home?"

"Edward's got all kinds of connections. He called in a helicopter. Got both you and Matt out of there and back here so I could—"

"Teo!" Gina sat up so fast the whole world spun, and Elise reached out to touch her shoulder with a hand that had a pentagram on the palm. Odd place for a tattoo.

"Whoa," Elise said. "You're still a little shaky."

"Where is he? Is Teo okay?"

"He's fine," Elise assured her. "I cured him, too."

Gina frowned. Teo had been bitten? Had she—?

No. He'd been bleeding when she arrived. She'd wanted that blood so badly. But then . . .

Images flickered. The fight. The Nahual howling. The door slamming. She'd gotten up, stomach rumbling, planning to make it stop with him, but by then he'd been more werewolf than human.

Hell.

"He hasn't woken yet," Elise continued. "He lost a lot of blood."

Blood. Gina could smell it, almost taste it, and that memory brought back the hunger. The desire to rip into Teo's flesh and—

"God!" Gina smacked herself in the forehead with the heel of her hand. Elise took that hand and pulled it back down.

"That wasn't you," Elise said. "It was the demon."

"It was more me than you think," Gina returned.

Even now what she'd felt bubbled within her—the thrill of the hunt, the excitement of the kill, the ecstasy that lay in the blood.

"I know what it's like," Elise said.

Gina peered into the other woman's clear, blue eyes and saw the memories there. Elise *did* know; she would always know.

"You have to be strong. If you let yourself give in to the . . ." Elise searched for a word.

"Sadness?" Gina offered. "Madness?"

"Gladness?" whispered a voice that gave her a start. Had that been the Nahual?

No. That voice had been hers. Which almost made Gina want the Nahual's voice back.

"Darkness," Elise said. "If you let yourself dwell on that swirl of guilt and memories, you'll never move on, and the demon wins."

"I wanted people to die screaming because of me," Gina whispered.

"But they didn't, Gina. You never killed anyone. Edward got to you in time."

That was good. That should make her feel better. Except—

"Will I always remember that I wanted to?"

Elise looked away. "Yes."

"Teo," Gina continued. "I didn't . . . hurt him, did I?"

"You saved me."

Gina glanced up and he was there, pale, shaky, on crutches—but alive.

Elise stood. "I'll leave you two alone."

She went out of the room and closed the door.

Teo crutched across the floor as if he'd been using the things for years. However, when he got to the side of the bed, he let them clatter to the ground and kind of collapsed where Elise had just been. He took Gina's hands, and he didn't let go when she tried to pull away.

"Don't," he said, his voice even rougher than usual. "I love you."

"The woman you loved died."

"No. The woman I loved saved me. Twice."

At first she was confused—once maybe; what was he talking about? Then she remembered the cavern and she laughed, scaring herself with how un*her* that laugh sounded. "I wanted to be the one to kill you, Teo. I wasn't trying to save you *from* him, but win you for myself."

"Doesn't matter."

"It does to me."

His hands tightened on hers. "I felt it, too, Gina. The lust for blood, the passion for the kill, the craving for the rise of the moon that gives you power over life and death. That pounding hunger, which makes you want to do anything if only it will stop. But we'll get past this. Together. You'll see."

Gina swallowed. "Jase is dead."

"The Jase you knew, yeah. The thing he became . . ." Teo shook his head. "The Nahual's still there. We're going to have to make sure he never gets out."

"What if I start hearing him again?"

"Have you?"

"No." She tilted her head, listened. "Or at least not yet."

"If we can keep people away from there, the creature's voice will die."

"The Nahual's voice will never die," Gina said. "And neither will he."

"He'll be silenced." Teo's eyes had gone the shade of gray-green smoke. "It's the best we can do."

"Jase—" Her voice broke. "It's my fault."

"McCord chose to give that thing access to his body and his mind so that he could hurt us, hurt you. How is that your fault?"

"When I chose you, I doomed him."

"When he chose the Nahual, he doomed himself."

Which was exactly what Elise had said. When the words were repeated in Teo's reasonable tone, the truth of them began to unfold.

"Sacrifices have been made," Teo continued. "If you don't want those sacrifices to be in vain you need to live the life you were meant to live. In the sun. With a smile." He touched her face. "With me."

Though the memories still hovered, shadows at the edges of her mind, hope, which glowed like the sun, began to push them back. She'd no doubt have terrible dreams for a long time, perhaps forever. But Elise was right; she couldn't let the demon win.

Gina leaned her cheek into Teo's hand. She would never again crave the moon, but she would always, always crave him.

EPILOGUE

Matt sat on the porch, watching the sun set with Edward. Several of the horses—though not all—had found their way home and milled in the paddock. Matt had been thrilled to discover that Spike was one of them.

The ranch was fairly quiet. The remaining guests had been hustled off in the same helicopter that had delivered Gina and Matt. According to Mandenauer, they were being "debriefed."

Matt figured that was a nice word for being told what to say and do and think in regard to all that had happened to them on Nahua Springs Ranch. He also figured that in about five years there was going to be a brand-new and very popular video game that dealt with Aztec mythology. Sorcerers, werewolves, sacrifice— how could Derek resist? Matt wondered if Edward would take a cut.

Mandenauer had sent his very best engineers with state-of-the art equipment to the tree of life. They would make certain the tomb of the Nahual remained a tomb.

Matt had his doubts. No amount of earth was going to keep that thing buried forever.

Isaac and Fanny seemed to be coming to terms with the loss of Jase. That he'd chosen to become one with the Nahual, would have cheerfully killed or turned anyone, including his own family, in order to further his nefarious plan, seemed to go a long way toward convincing them that even though Jase wasn't truly dead, he wasn't exactly alive, either.

Monsters were something in between.

That Jase had tied up his own grandfather and stuffed him into the pantry in order to kidnap Matt and turn Gina into a werewolf had helped them see the truth. The Jase McCord they'd known was gone.

Edward was still furious that he'd allowed the Nahual to take him by surprise. He'd *known* the thing was smoke, yet when smoke appeared he'd been distracted. The creature had used magic to render him unconscious, no doubt planning to return and finish him off later, once he'd dealt with Matt, or even let Gina do it when she arrived, but she'd been lured below by the smell of blood.

"You will never be able to prove your mother's theory now," Edward murmured, drawing Matt's attention back to the present.

The two men had spent a lot of time talking. Mandenauer had wanted to learn all he could about the Nahual, and it had felt good for Matt to discuss Nora's theory, which had turned out to be more fact than fiction. He still felt bad about not believing in her, and he wished that he could tell the world how right she had been. But he couldn't.

Matt shrugged. "Oh well."

What had been so important when he'd come here meant nothing any longer. All Matt cared about was Gina, this place, and their life together. He'd already called George Enright and resigned. With Matt's money and Gina's skill, they'd turn Nahua Springs back into the most respected quarter-horse breeding facility in the country.

"The cavern must remain buried," Edward continued. "No one can ever know. We cannot have academics swarming the area, digging, searching, perhaps finding."

"I own this place," Matt said. "No one's digging. Ever."

And he'd be around to make certain of that. Though once he couldn't imagine a life other than the one he had had—that of teaching, seeking, learning—now he couldn't imagine a life anywhere but here. Because here was where Gina was and always would be.

Matt had tried to hand the ranch over to Gina. She'd refused. "Fifty-fifty," she said. "For the rest of our lives."

She was doing pretty well, considering. Sometimes Matt caught her listening to the wind, staring at the mountains, and waiting for un–wolf howls that were no longer there. But the more time that passed without them, the less she would listen.

"When is the wedding?" Mandenauer asked.

"As soon as we can arrange it." Gina and Matt had learned well the concept that every day could be their last. They weren't going to waste a single instant of the rest of their lives. "You . . . uh . . . wanna be a witness?"

"My boy, I would like nothing better."

"Elise is going to stand up for Gina."

Elise had rented a room in the ranch house. She would be there until she hunted down and cured all the wolves that now howled in the once-wolfless hills.

Matt wasn't exactly sure what the cure involved. Something to do with that pentagram on her palm and the vials and syringes in her black doctor's bag. As long as it worked—he cast a glance at Edward, whose sharp gaze remained on the distant mountains—Matt didn't care if the cure involved Elise doing the hoochie-coochie on the Empire State Building.

"He will be released again," the old man said softly.

"Maybe not for another five hundred years."

Edward remained silent for a few seconds, then shrugged. "I should be dead by then."

And deep in the soon-to-be-buried cavern,
the Nahual began to again crave the moon.

Don't miss the previous two Nightcreature novels from
New York Times bestselling author

LORI HANDELAND

MARKED BY THE MOON
ISBN: 978-0-312-38934-5

"Sly, sultry...sizzling hot desire."
—*Fallen Angel Reviews* (5 Angels)

MOON CURSED
ISBN: 978-0-312-38935-2

"Riveting!"
—*RT Book Reviews*

*Both novels—and all the others in this sensational series!—
are available from St. Martin's Paperbacks.*